PENGUIN BOOKS

On the Island

Tracey Garvis Graves lives in a suburb of Des Moines, Iowa, with her husband and two children. This is her first novel. She blogs at www.traceygarvisgraves.com, using colourful language and a snarky sense of humour to write about pop culture, silly television shows and her suburban neighbourhood. She is hard at work on her next novel.

Reviews from online readers

'I chose this book at random while looking for something to start reading before bed. I wound up staying up into the early morning, finishing it in one sitting . . . A four-star book for me is one that I can't put down. A five star is when I put it down and I can't stop thinking about it for days afterward.' *****

Kate

'This was such a great book! I LOVED this story and look forward to more books from this author. I could not put this book down!' *****

Debbie K. Quatraro

'A MUST-READ!! Amazing, touching, heartfelt love story. I laughed, I cried and I finished it in one day, and longed for more. Enough said. READ IT!!!' *****

Aimeelein

'I loved this book! I'm very picky and a book has to catch me right away. This one definitely did. I had trouble putting it down, staying up way too late reading it. Couldn't wait to find out what would happen next. Can't wait for the next book by this author! I highly recommend!' *****

Kathy

'Loved it. Bought this book based on the positive reviews and it did not disappoint. Read it in a little less than two days. Loved the back and forth of both Anna's and T.J.'s points of view – in fact, I did not want it to end. Will ABSOLUTELY buy more from this author.' *****

C. Witter

'Wonderful, did not want to put it down. What a delight! Beautifully written, the author did everything right. The story is woven so delicately, nothing is rushed nor does she drag out the details.

The story is told from both of the main characters' perspectives, allowing the reader to form a deep bond with both of them. This technique also creates richly developed characters. This was one of those books where work was a hindrance to my reading time, actually pretty much everything got in the way. Highly recommended.' *****

Lisa LLF

'I loved this book. It was a major page turner for me. I simply could not put it down and finished in one sitting.' *****

MotherofFour

'Amazing! I'm so glad that I took a chance on this book. I am coming off the *Fifty Shades of Grey* trilogy and was looking for something a little lighter . . . This book exceeded my expectations . . . If you are looking for a love story that conquers all, this is the book for you.' *****

Julie

'I love this book, from the beginning to the end. I read this book in one day, for me that's a record! Tracey Garvis Graves knows how to captivate readers. I loved the fact that it is the point of view of each character: Anna and T.J., they live in a world apart, and during those few hours of reading, I lived with them.' *****

Kiwi

'Beautifully and sensitively written from both a male and female perspective, this was an engrossing and hard to put down novel; I am amazed that this is a first novel. A very enjoyable book, was sad to turn the last page!' *****

Kaz

'SIMPLY AMAZING! Wow, I am completely speechless over this book! I have only just finished reading it and had to write a review now so that I won't forget just how I am feeling at this moment. I've loved some books over the years but I have to say this is one of the most amazing I've ever read . . . For two days I was on that island with Anna and T.J. going through every hardship and triumph with them . . . Amazing characters, amazing story, amazing author! If a book should ever be made into a movie . . . this is it!' *****

Bristol

'I could not put this down. The relationship in this book is spell-binding. I rooted for this couple from the beginning.' *****

Kelkeligan

'What a great read! Couldn't put it down. In fact, I really haven't. I keep going back to it. The author does a great job of really putting you in their situation. At times it feels like you are spying on them. For a first book, this one is good. I can't wait to read her next one! . . . If you are looking for something to fill the gap after reading *Fifty Shades* . . . here it is!' *****

Danielle

'This story will grip you from the start and not let you go. I laugh and cried right along with Anna and T.J. This is one for my keeper shelf.' *****

Jody Duffy

'If a book doesn't pique my interest from the very beginning, I won't read past the first few pages. This book had me hooked from the first paragraph!! The writing is so good, you feel as if you're on the island with them. I highly recommend this book.' *****

Irene Georgedakis

'I started this book thinking I'd just read a few chapters but then couldn't put it down until I finished. Wow.' *****

Rachel

'I loved, loved, loved this. It was a perfect way to spend a cold Friday night stuck at home.' *****

Kelly

On the Island

TRACEY GARVIS GRAVES

PENGUIN BOOKS

PENGUIN BOOKS

Published by the Penguin Group
Penguin Books Ltd, 80 Strand, London WC2R ORL, England
Penguin Group (USA) Inc., 375 Hudson Street, New York, New York 10014, USA
Penguin Group (Canada), 90 Eglinton Avenue East, Suite 700, Toronto, Ontario, Canada M4P 2Y3
(a division of Pearson Penguin Canada Inc.)
Penguin Ireland, 25 St Stephen's Green, Dublin 2, Ireland (a division of Penguin Books Ltd)
Penguin Group (Australia), 250 Camberwell Road, Camberwell, Victoria 3124, Australia
(a division of Pearson Australia Group Pty Ltd)
Penguin Books India Pvt Ltd, 11 Community Centre, Panchsheel Park, New Delhi – 110 017, India
Penguin Group (NZ), 67 Apollo Drive, Rosedale, Auckland 0632, New Zealand
(a division of Pearson New Zealand Ltd)
Penguin Books (South Africa) (Pty) Ltd, Block D, Rosebank Office Park,
181 Jan Smuts Avenue, Parktown North, Gauteng 2193, South Africa

Penguin Books Ltd, Registered Offices: 80 Strand, London WC2R ORL, England

www.penguin.com

First published in the United States of America by CreateSpace 2011
First published in Great Britain in Penguin Books 2012
002

Copyright © Tracey Garvis Graves, 2011
All rights reserved

The moral right of the author has been asserted

Set in 12.5/14.75 pt Garamond MT Std
Typeset by Jouve (UK), Milton Keynes
Printed in England by Clays Ltd, St Ives plc

ISBN: 978-1-405-91021-7

www.greenpenguin.co.uk

MIX
Paper from
responsible sources
FSC
www.fsc.org   FSC™ C018179

Penguin Books is committed to a sustainable
future for our business, our readers and our planet.
This book is made from Forest Stewardship
Council™ certified paper.

ALWAYS LEARNING   **PEARSON**

For Meira

Chapter 1
Anna

June 2001

I was thirty years old when the seaplane T.J. Callahan and I were traveling on crash-landed in the Indian Ocean. T.J. was sixteen, and three months into remission from Hodgkin's lymphoma. The pilot's name was Mick, but he died before we hit the water.

My boyfriend, John, drove me to the airport even though he was third on my list, below my mom and my sister Sarah, of the people I wanted to take me. We fought the crowd, each of us pulling a large, wheeled suitcase, and I wondered if everyone in Chicago had decided to fly somewhere that day. When we finally reached the US Airways counter, the ticket agent smiled, tagged my luggage, and handed me a boarding pass.

'Thank you, Miss Emerson. I've checked you all the way through to Malé. Have a safe trip.'

I slipped the boarding pass into my purse and turned to say goodbye to John. 'Thanks for driving me.'

'I'll walk with you, Anna.'

'You don't have to,' I said, shaking my head.

He flinched. 'I want to.'

We shuffled along in silence, following the throng of slow-moving passengers. At the gate John asked, 'What's he look like?'

'Skinny and bald.'

I scanned the crowd and smiled when I spotted T.J. because short brown hair now covered his head. I waved, and he acknowledged me with a nod while the boy sitting next to him elbowed him in the ribs.

'Who's the other kid?' John asked.

'I think it's his friend, Ben.'

Slouched in their seats, they were dressed in the style favored by most sixteen-year-old boys: long, baggy athletic shorts, T-shirts, and untied tennis shoes. A navy blue backpack sat on the floor at T.J.'s feet.

'Are you sure this is what you want to do?' John asked. He shoved his hands in his back pockets and stared down at the worn airport carpeting.

Well, one of us has to do something. 'Yes.'

'Please don't make any final decisions until you get back.'

I didn't point out the irony in his request. 'I said I wouldn't.'

There was really only one option, though. I just chose to postpone it until the end of the summer.

John put his arms around my waist and kissed me, several seconds longer than he should have in such a public place. Embarrassed, I pulled away. Out of the corner of my eye, I noticed T.J. and Ben watching it all.

'I love you,' he said.

I nodded. 'I know.'

Resigned, he picked up my carry-on bag and placed the strap on my shoulder. 'Have a safe flight. Call me when you get there.'

'Okay.'

John left and I watched until the crowd enveloped him, then smoothed the front of my skirt and walked over to the boys. They looked down as I approached.

'Hi, T.J. You look great. Are you ready to go?'

His brown eyes briefly met mine. 'Yeah, sure.' He had gained weight and his face wasn't as pale. He had braces on his teeth, which I hadn't noticed before, and a small scar on his chin.

'Hi. I'm Anna,' I said to the boy sitting next to T.J. 'You must be Ben. How was your party?'

He glanced at T.J., confused. 'Uh, it was okay.'

I pulled out my cell phone and looked at the time. 'I'll be right back, T.J. I want to check on our flight.'

As I walked away I heard Ben say, 'Dude, your babysitter is smokin' hot.'

'She's my tutor, asshole.'

The words rolled off me. I taught at a high school and considered occasional comments from hormone-riddled boys a fairly benign occupational hazard.

After confirming we were still on schedule, I returned and sat in the empty chair next to T.J. 'Did Ben leave?'

'Yeah. His mom got tired of circling the airport. He wouldn't let her come in with us.'

'Do you want to get something to eat?'

He shook his head. 'I'm not hungry.'

We sat in awkward silence until it was time to board the plane. T.J. followed me down the narrow aisle to our first class seats. 'Do you want the window?' I asked.

T.J. shrugged. 'Sure. Thanks.'

I stepped to the side and waited until he sat down, then buckled in next to him. He took a portable CD player out

3

of his backpack and put the headphones on, his subtle way of letting me know he wasn't interested in having a conversation. I pulled a book out of my carry-on bag, the pilot lifted off, and we left Chicago behind.

Things started to go wrong in Germany. It should have taken a little over eighteen hours to fly from Chicago to Malé – the capital city of the Maldives – but we'd fallen behind schedule after spending the entire day and half the night at the Frankfurt International Airport waiting for the airline to re-route us after mechanical problems and weather delays rendered our original itinerary obsolete. T.J. and I sat on hard plastic chairs at 3:00 a.m. after finally being confirmed on the next flight out. He rubbed his eyes.

I pointed to a row of empty seats. 'Lie down if you want.'

'I'm okay,' he said, stifling a yawn.

'We aren't leaving for several hours. You should try to sleep.'

'Aren't you tired?'

I was exhausted, but T.J. probably needed the rest more than I did. 'I'm fine. You go ahead.'

'Are you sure?'

'Absolutely.'

'Okay.' He smiled faintly. 'Thanks.' He stretched out on the chairs and fell asleep immediately.

I stared out the window and watched the planes land and take off again, their red lights blinking in the night sky. The frigid air conditioning raised goose bumps on my arms, and I shivered in my skirt and sleeveless blouse.

4

In a nearby restroom, I changed into the jeans and long-sleeved T-shirt I'd packed in my carry-on bag, then bought a cup of coffee. When I sat back down next to T.J., I opened my book and read, waking him three hours later when they called our flight.

There were more delays after we arrived in Sri Lanka – this time due to a shortage of flight crew – and by the time we landed at Malé International Airport in the Maldives, the Callahan's summer rental still two hours away by seaplane, I had been awake for thirty hours. My temples throbbed and my eyes, gritty and aching, burned. When they said they had no reservation for us, I blinked back tears.

'But I have the confirmation number,' I said to the ticket agent, sliding the scrap of paper across the counter. 'I updated our reservation before we left Sri Lanka. Two seats. T.J. Callahan and Anna Emerson. Will you please look again?'

The ticket agent checked the computer. 'I'm sorry,' he said. 'Your names are not on the list. The seaplane is full.'

'What about the next flight?'

'It will be dark soon. Seaplanes don't fly after sunset.' Noticing my stricken expression, he gave me a sympathetic look, tapped his keyboard, and picked up the phone. 'I'll see what I can do.'

'Thank you.'

T.J. and I walked to a small gift shop, and I bought two bottles of water. 'Do you want one?'

'No thanks.'

'Why don't you put it in your backpack,' I said, handing it to him. 'You might want it later.'

I dug a bottle of Tylenol out of my purse, shook two into my hand, and swallowed them with some water. We sat down on a bench, and I called T.J.'s mom, Jane, and told her not to expect us until morning.

'There's a chance they'll find us a flight, but I don't think we'll get out tonight. The seaplanes don't fly after dark so we may have to spend the night at the airport.'

'I'm sorry, Anna. You must be exhausted,' she said.

'It's okay, really. We'll be there tomorrow for sure.' I covered the phone with my hand. 'Do you want to talk to your mom?' T.J. made a face and shook his head.

I noticed the ticket agent waving at me. He was smiling. 'Jane, listen I think we might –' and then my cell phone dropped the call. I put the phone back in my purse and approached the counter, holding my breath.

'One of the charter pilots can fly you to the island,' the ticket agent said. 'The passengers he was supposed to take are delayed in Sri Lanka and won't get here until tomorrow morning.'

I exhaled and smiled. 'That's wonderful. Thank you for finding us a flight. I really appreciate it.' I tried to call T.J.'s parents again, but my cell phone roamed without connecting. Hopefully I'd get a signal when we arrived on the island. 'Ready, T.J.?'

'Yeah,' he said, grabbing his backpack.

A mini-bus dropped us off at the air taxi terminal. The agent checked us in at the counter, and we walked outside.

The Maldives' climate reminded me of the steam room at my gym. Immediately, beads of sweat broke out on my forehead and the back of my neck. My jeans and

6

long-sleeved T-shirt trapped the hot, humid air against my skin, and I wished I had changed back into something cooler.

Is it this sweltering all the time?

An airport employee stood on the dock next to a seaplane that bobbed gently on the water's surface. He beckoned us. When T.J. and I reached him, he opened the door and we ducked our heads and boarded the plane. The pilot was sitting in his seat, and he smiled at us around a mouthful of cheeseburger.

'Hi, I'm Mick.' He finished chewing and swallowed. 'Hope you don't mind if I finish my dinner.' He appeared to be in his late fifties and was so overweight he barely fit in the pilot's seat. He wore cargo shorts and the largest tie-dye T-shirt I had ever seen. His feet were bare. Sweat dotted his upper lip and forehead. He ate the last bite of his cheeseburger and wiped his face with a napkin.

'I'm Anna and this is T.J.,' I said, smiling and reaching out to shake his hand. 'Of course we don't mind.'

The Twin Otter DHC-6 seated ten and smelled like airplane fuel and mildew. T.J. buckled himself in and stared out the window. I sat down across the aisle from him, shoved my purse and carry-on under the seat, and rubbed my eyes. Mick started the engines. The noise drowned out his voice, but when he turned his head to the side his lips moved as he communicated with someone on his radio headset. He motored away from the dock, picked up speed, and we were airborne.

I cursed my inability to sleep on airplanes. I'd always envied those who passed out the minute the plane took off and didn't wake until the wheels touched down on the runway. I tried to doze, but the sunlight streaming through the seaplane's windows, and my confused body clock, made drifting off impossible. When I gave up and opened my eyes, I caught T.J. staring at me. If the look on his face and the heat on mine was any indication, it embarrassed us both. He turned away, shoved his backpack under his head and fell asleep a few minutes later.

Restless, I unbuckled my seat belt and went to ask Mick how long it would be until we landed.

'Maybe another hour or so.' He motioned toward the co-pilot's seat. 'Sit down if you want.'

I sat down and buckled my seat belt. Shielding my eyes against the sun, I took in the breathtaking view. The sky, cloudless and cobalt above. The Indian Ocean, a swirl of mint green and turquoise blue below.

Mick rubbed the center of his chest with his fist and reached for a roll of antacids. He put one in his mouth. 'Heartburn. That's what I get for eating cheeseburgers. But they taste so much better than a damn salad, you know?' He laughed, and I nodded my head in agreement.

'So, where are you two from?'

'Chicago.'

'What do you do there in Chicago?' He popped another antacid into his mouth.

'I teach tenth-grade English.'

'Ah, summers off.'

'Well, not for me. I usually tutor students in the summer.' I motioned toward T.J. 'His parents hired me to help him catch up with his class. He had Hodgkin's lymphoma and he missed a lot of school.'

'I thought you looked way too young to be his mom.'

8

I smiled. 'His parents and sisters flew down a few days ago.'

I wasn't able to leave as early as the Callahan's because the public high school where I taught let out for summer break a few days later than the private high school T.J. attended. When T.J. found out, he convinced his parents to let him stay behind in Chicago for the weekend and fly down with me instead. Jane Callahan had called to see if it was all right.

'His friend Ben is having a party. He really wants to go. Are you sure you don't mind?' she asked.

'Not at all,' I said. 'It will give us a chance to get to know each other.'

I'd only met T.J. once, when I interviewed with his parents. It would take a while for him to warm up to me; it always did when I worked with a new student, especially a teenage boy.

Mick's voice interrupted my thoughts. 'How long are you staying?'

'For the summer. They rented a house on the island.'

'So he's okay now?'

'Yes. His parents said he was pretty sick for a while, but he's been in remission for a few months.'

'Nice location for a summer job.'

I grinned. 'It beats the library.'

We flew in silence for a while. 'Are there really twelve hundred islands down there?' I asked. I'd only counted three or four, scattered across the water like giant puzzle pieces. I waited for his answer. 'Mick?'

'What? Oh, yes, give or take a few. Only about two hundred are inhabited, but I expect that to change with all the development going on. There's a new hotel or resort opening every month.' He chuckled. 'Everybody wants a piece of paradise.'

Mick rubbed his chest again and took his left arm off the control yoke, stretching it out in front of him. I noticed his pained expression and the light sheen of sweat on his forehead. 'Are you okay?'

'I'm fine. I've just never had heartburn this bad before.' He put two more antacids in his mouth and crumpled the empty wrapper.

An uneasy feeling washed over me. 'Do you want to call someone? If you show me how to use the radio I can call for you.'

'No, I'll be fine once these antacids start working.' He took a deep breath and smiled at me. 'Thank you, though.'

He seemed okay for a while, but ten minutes later he took his right hand off the yoke and rubbed his left shoulder. Sweat trickled down the side of his face. His breathing sounded shallow, and he shifted in his seat as if he couldn't find a comfortable position. My uneasy feeling blossomed into sheer panic.

T.J. woke up. 'Anna,' he said, loud enough for me to hear him over the engines. I turned around. 'Are we almost there?'

I unbuckled and went back to sit beside T.J. Not wanting to shout, I pulled him closer and said, 'Listen, I'm pretty sure Mick's having a heart attack. He has chest pains and he looks awful, but he's blaming it on heartburn.'

'What! Are you serious?'

I nodded. 'My dad survived a major heart attack last

year, so I know what to watch for. I think he's scared to admit there's something wrong.'

'What about us? Can he still fly the plane?'

'I don't know.'

T.J. and I approached the cockpit. Mick had both fists pressed against his chest and his eyes were closed. His headset sat askew and his face had taken on a grayish cast.

I crouched down next to his seat, fear rippling through me. 'Mick.' My tone was urgent. 'We need to call for help.'

He nodded. 'I'm going to put us down on the water first and then one of you will have to get on the radio,' he gasped, trying to get the words out. 'Put on life jackets. They're in the storage compartment by the door. Then get in your seats and buckle in.' He grimaced in pain. 'Go!'

My heart thundered in my chest and adrenaline flooded my body. We rushed to the storage compartment and rifled through it.

'Why do we have to put on life jackets, Anna? The plane has floats, right?'

Because he's afraid he might not get us out of the air in time.

'I don't know, maybe it's standard operating procedure. We're landing in the middle of the ocean.' I found the life jackets wedged between a cylinder-shaped container that said LIFE RAFT and several blankets. 'Here,' I said, handing one to T.J. and putting mine on. We sat down and fastened our seatbelts, my hands shaking so badly it took me two tries.

'If he loses consciousness I'll need to start CPR immediately. You'll have to figure out the radio, T.J., okay?'

He nodded, his eyes wide. 'I can do that.'

I gripped the armrests of my seat and watched out the

window, the rolling surface of the ocean growing closer. But then instead of slowing we picked up speed, descending at a steep angle. I glanced toward the front of the plane. Mick was slumped over the yoke, not moving. I unbuckled my seat belt and lunged into the aisle.

'Anna,' T.J. yelled. The hem of my T-shirt slipped through his grasp.

Before I could reach the cockpit, Mick jerked backward in his seat, his hands still on the yoke, as a massive spasm racked his chest. The nose of the plane pulled up sharply and we hit the water tail-first, skipping erratically across the waves. The tip of a wing caught the surface and the plane cartwheeled out of control.

The impact knocked me off my feet, as if someone had tied a rope around my ankles and yanked it hard. The sound of shattering glass filled my ears, and I had the sensation of flying followed by searing pain as the plane broke apart.

I plunged into the ocean, seawater pouring down my throat. Completely disoriented, the buoyancy of my life jacket lifted me slowly upward. My head broke the surface, and I coughed uncontrollably, trying to get the air in and the water out.

T.J.! Oh God, where is T.J.?

I pictured him trapped in his seat, unable to get his seatbelt unbuckled, and I scanned the water frantically, squinting in the sun and screaming his name. Just when I thought he had certainly drowned, he surfaced, choking and sputtering.

I swam toward him, tasting blood, my head throbbing so hard I thought it might explode. When I reached T.J.,

I grabbed his hand and tried to tell him how happy I was that he made it, but my words wouldn't come out right and I drifted in and out in a hazy fog.

T.J. yelled at me to wake up. I remembered high waves and swallowing more water and then I remembered nothing at all.

Chapter 2
T.J.

Seawater churned all around me, up my nose, down my throat, in my eyes. I couldn't breathe without choking. Anna swam toward me, crying and bleeding and screaming. She grabbed my hand and tried to talk, but her words came out all fucked up, and I couldn't understand anything she said. Her head wobbled, and she splashed face-down in the water. I pulled her up by her hair. 'Wake up, Anna, wake up!' The waves were so high, and I was afraid we'd get separated, so I shoved my right arm under the strap of her life jacket and held onto her. I lifted her face up. 'Anna. Anna!' *Oh God.* Her eyes stayed shut and she didn't respond, so I shoved my left arm under the other strap of her life jacket and leaned back with her lying on my chest.

The current pulled us away from the wreckage. The pieces of the plane disappeared below the surface, and it didn't take long before there was nothing left. I tried not to think about Mick strapped in his seat.

I floated, stunned, my heart pounding in my chest. Surrounded by nothing but rolling waves, I tried to keep our heads above water and forced myself not to panic.

Will they know we crashed? Were they tracking us on radar?

Maybe not, because no one came.

The sky darkened and the sun went down. Anna mumbled. I thought she might be waking up, but her body shook and she puked on me. The waves washed it away, but she trembled and I pulled her closer, trying to share body heat. I was cold, too, even though the water had felt warm right after the crash. There wasn't any moonlight, and I could barely see the surface of the water around us, black now, not blue.

I worried about sharks. I freed one of my arms and put my hand under Anna's chin, lifting her head off my chest. I'd felt something warm just below my neck where her head rested. Was she still bleeding? I tried to get her to wake up, but she'd only respond if I shook her face. She wouldn't talk, but she'd moan. I didn't want to hurt her, but I wanted to know if she was alive. She didn't move for a long time, which freaked me out, but then she puked again and shivered in my arms.

I tried to stay calm, breathing slowly in and out. Handling the waves was easier floating on my back, and Anna and I rode them as the current carried us. The seaplanes wouldn't fly in the dark, but I was sure they'd send one when the sun came up. Someone would have to know we'd crashed by then.

My parents don't even know we were on that plane.

Hours passed, and I didn't see any sharks. Maybe they were there, and I didn't know it. Exhausted, I dozed for a while, letting my legs hang down instead of fighting to keep them near the surface. I tried not to think of the sharks that might be circling below.

When I shook Anna again, she didn't respond. I thought I could feel her chest rising and falling, but I wasn't sure. There was a loud splash, and I jerked upright. Anna's head fell loosely to the side, and I pulled it back toward me. The splashing continued, almost like a rhythm. Picturing not just one shark but five, ten, maybe more, I spun around. Something jutted out of the water, and it took me a second to figure out what it was. The splashing was the waves hitting the reef surrounding an island.

I'd never felt such massive relief in my whole life, not even when the doctor told us my cancer was gone and the treatment had finally worked.

The current pulled us closer to the island but we weren't heading straight at it. If I didn't do something, we'd pass it by.

I couldn't use my arms because they were still under the straps of Anna's life jacket, so I stayed on my back and kicked my feet. My shoes fell off, but I didn't care; I should have taken them off hours ago.

Land was still fifty yards away. Farther off-course than before, I had no choice but to use one of my arms, and I sidestroked, dragging Anna's face through the water.

I lifted my head. We were close. Kicking frantically, my lungs on fire, I swam as hard I could.

We reached the calm water of the lagoon inside the reef, but I didn't stop swimming until my feet touched the sandy bottom of the ocean floor. I had only enough energy to drag Anna out of the water and onto the shore before I collapsed next to her and passed out.

The blazing sun woke me. Stiff and sore, I could only see out of one of my eyes. I sat up and took off my life jacket, then looked over at Anna. Her face was swollen and bruised, and cuts crisscrossed her cheeks and forehead. She lay still.

My heart hammered in my chest, but I made myself reach over and touch her neck. Her skin felt warm and relief washed over me a second time when I felt her pulse beating under my fingers. She was alive but the only thing I knew about head injuries was that she probably had one. What if she never woke up?

I shook her carefully. 'Anna, can you hear me?' She didn't respond so I shook her again.

I waited for her to open her eyes. They were amazing, big and dark grayish-blue. They were the first thing I noticed when I met her. She had come to our apartment to interview with my parents, and I was embarrassed because she was beautiful and I was skinny and bald and looked like shit.

Come on Anna, let me see your eyes.

I shook her harder and it was only when she finally opened them that I slowly let out the breath I'd been holding.

Chapter 3
Anna

Two blurry images of T.J. hovered above me, and I blinked until they merged into one. He had cuts on his face and his left eye was swollen shut.

'Where are we?' I asked. My voice sounded scratchy and my mouth tasted like salt.

'I don't know. Some island.'

'What about Mick?' I asked.

T.J. shook his head. 'What was left of the plane sank fast.'

'I can't remember anything.'

'You passed out in the water, and when I couldn't wake you up I thought you were dead.'

My head throbbed. I touched my forehead and winced when my fingers grazed a large bump. Something sticky coated the side of my face. 'Am I bleeding?'

T.J. leaned toward me and combed through my hair with his fingers, looking for the source of the blood. I cried out when he found it.

'Sorry,' he said. 'It's a deep cut. It's not bleeding as much now. It bled a lot more when we were in the water.'

Fear gripped me, traveling through my body like a wave. 'Were there sharks?'

'I don't know. I didn't see any, but I was worried about it.'

I took a deep breath and sat up. The beach spun. Placing my hands flat on the sand, I braced myself until the worst of the dizziness passed. 'How did we get here?' I asked.

'I looped my arms through the straps of your life jacket, and we drifted with the current until I saw the shore. Then I dragged you up on the sand.'

The realization of what he'd done sank in. I looked out at the water and didn't say anything for a minute. I thought about what might have happened if he'd let go of me or if the sharks had come or if there hadn't been an island. 'Thank you, T.J.'

'Sure,' he said, only meeting my gaze for a few seconds before looking away.

'Are you hurt?' I asked.

'I'm okay. I think I hit my face on the seat in front of me.'

I tried to stand and failed, overcome by dizziness. T.J. helped me back up and this time I stayed on my feet. I unbuckled my life jacket and let it drop on the sand.

I turned away from the shore and looked inland. The island looked just like the pictures I'd seen on the Internet except it didn't have a luxury hotel or any vacation homes sitting on it. Barefoot, the pristine white sand felt like sugar under my feet; I had no idea what had happened to my shoes. The beach gave way to flowering shrubs and tropical vegetation and then finally a forested area where trees grew close together, their leaves forming a green canopy. The sun, high in the sky, burned with an intense heat. The ocean breeze failed to lower my rising body temperature, and sweat trickled down my face. My clothes clung to my damp skin.

'I have to sit back down.' My stomach churned, and

I thought I might throw up. T.J. sat down next to me and when the nausea finally passed I said, 'Don't worry. They have to know we crashed and they'll send a search plane.'

'Do you have any idea where we are?' he asked.

'Not really.'

I used my finger to draw in the sand. 'The islands are grouped in a chain of twenty-six atolls running north to south. This is where we were headed.' I pointed to one of the marks I made. I dragged my finger through the sand and pointed at another. 'This is Malé, where we started. We're somewhere in between, I guess, unless the current took us east or west. I don't know if Mick stayed on course, and I don't know if seaplanes file a flight plan or if they're tracked on radar.'

'My mom and dad have got to be freaking out.'

'Yes.' T.J.'s parents had undoubtedly tried to call my cell phone, but it was probably at the bottom of the ocean by now.

Should we build a signal fire? Isn't that what you're supposed to do when you're lost? Build a fire so they know where you are?

I had no idea how to build one. My survival skills were limited to what I had seen on T.V. or read in books. Neither of us wore glasses, otherwise we could have angled a lens toward the sun. We didn't have any flint or steel either. That left friction, but did rubbing sticks together actually work? Maybe we didn't need to worry about a fire, at least not yet. They'd see us if they were flying low and we stayed near the beach.

We tried to spell out SOS. First we used our feet to flatten the sand, but we didn't think it would be visible from the air. Next, we tried to use leaves but the breeze scattered

20

them before we could form letters. There weren't any large rocks to hold the leaves down, only pebbles and fragments of what I thought were coral. Moving around made us hotter and the pain in my head worse. We gave up and sat down.

My face burned in the sun and T.J.'s arms and legs turned red. Soon we had no choice but to move away from the shore and take shelter under a coconut tree. Coconuts covered the ground, and I knew they contained water. We banged them against the trunk of the tree, but we couldn't get them open.

Sweat ran down my face. I gathered my hair into a pile and held it on top of my head. My swollen tongue and dry mouth made it hard to swallow.

'I'm gonna take a look around,' T.J. said. 'Maybe there's water here somewhere.' He hadn't been gone long when he came back to the coconut tree holding something in his hand.

'I didn't see any water but I found this.'

It was the size of a grapefruit and green, spiny lumps covered its surface.

'What is it?' I asked.

'I don't know, but maybe it's got water inside, like the coconuts.'

T.J. peeled it, using his fingernails. Whatever it was, the bugs had gotten there first and he dropped it on the ground, kicking it away with his foot.

'I found it under a tree,' he said. 'There were lots of them hanging but they were up too high for me to reach. If you get on my shoulders, you might be able to knock one down. Do you think you can walk?'

I nodded. 'If we go slow.'

When we arrived at the tree, T.J. clasped my hand and helped me climb onto his shoulders. I stood five-six and weighed a hundred and twenty pounds. T.J. had at least four inches and probably thirty pounds on me, but he wobbled a bit trying to hold me steady. I reached up as high as I could, my fingers stretching toward the fruit. I couldn't get a grip on it, so I hit it with my fist instead. The first two times it didn't budge, but I hit it a little harder and it went flying. T.J. lowered me to the ground, and I picked it up.

'I still don't know what this is,' he said, after I handed it to him.

'It might be breadfruit.'

'What's that?'

'It's a fruit that's supposed to taste like bread.'

T.J. peeled it, and the fragrant smell reminded me of guava. We divided it in half and sucked on the fruit, the juice flooding our dry mouths. We chewed and swallowed the pieces. The rubbery texture probably meant the breadfruit needed to ripen longer, but we ate it anyway.

'This doesn't taste like bread to me,' T.J. said.

'Maybe it would if it was cooked.'

After we finished it, I climbed back on T.J.'s shoulders and knocked down two more, which we consumed immediately. Then we walked back to the coconut tree, sat down, and waited again.

Late in the afternoon, with no warning, the sky opened up and a torrential rain poured down on us. We got out from under the tree, turned our faces to the sky, and opened our mouths, but the rain ended ten minutes later.

'It's the rainy season,' I said. 'It should rain every day,

probably more than once.' We didn't have anything to collect the water in, and the drops I managed to catch on my tongue only made me want more.

'Where are they?' T.J. asked when the sun went down. The desperation in his voice matched my own emotional state.

'I don't know.' For reasons I couldn't fathom, the plane hadn't come. 'They'll find us tomorrow.'

We moved back to the beach and stretched out on the sand, resting our heads on our life jackets. The air cooled and the wind blowing off the water made me shiver. I wrapped my arms around myself and curled into a ball, listening to the rhythmic crashing of the waves hitting the reef.

We heard them before we figured out what they were. A flapping sound filled the air followed by the silhouettes of hundreds, maybe thousands, of bats. They blocked out the sliver of moonlight, and I wondered if they'd been hanging above us somewhere when we walked to the breadfruit tree.

T.J. sat up. 'I've never seen so many bats.'

We watched them for a while and eventually they scattered, off to hunt elsewhere. A few minutes later, T.J. fell asleep. I stared up at the sky, knowing that no one was searching for us in the dark. Any rescue mission undertaken during the daylight hours wouldn't resume until morning. I pictured T.J.'s distraught parents, waiting for the sun to rise. The possibility of my family getting a call brought tears to my eyes.

I thought about my sister, Sarah, and a conversation I'd had with her a couple months ago. We'd met for dinner at a Mexican restaurant and when the waiter brought our drinks I took a sip of my margarita and said, 'I accepted that tutoring job I told you about. With the kid who had cancer.' I set my drink down, scooped some salsa onto a tortilla chip, and popped it in my mouth.

'The one where you have to go on vacation with them?' she asked.

'Yes.'

'You'll be gone so long. What does John think about this?'

'John and I had the marriage talk again. But this time I told him I also wanted a baby.' I shrugged. 'I figured, why not go for broke?'

'Oh, Anna,' Sarah said.

Until recently, I hadn't really given much thought to having a baby. I was perfectly content being an aunt to Sarah's kids – two-year-old Chloe and five-year-old Joe. But then everyone I knew started thrusting blanket-wrapped bundles at me to hold, and I realized I wanted one of my own. The intensity of my baby fever, and the subsequent ticking of my biological clock, surprised me. I always thought the desire to have a child was something that happened slowly, but one day it was just there.

'I can't do this anymore, Sarah,' I continued. 'How could he handle a baby when he can't even commit to marriage?' I shook my head. 'Other women make this look so easy. They meet someone, fall in love, and they get married. Maybe in a year or two they start a family. Simple, right? When John and I discuss our future, it's about as romantic as a real estate transaction, with almost as much countering.' I grabbed my cocktail napkin and wiped my eyes.

'I'm sorry, Anna. Frankly, I don't know how you've waited this long. Seven years seems like enough time for John to figure out what he wants.'

'Eight, Sarah. It's been eight.' I picked up my drink and finished it in two big gulps.

'Oh. I missed a year in there somewhere.' Our waiter stopped by and asked if we wanted another round.

'You should probably just keep them coming,' Sarah told him. 'So, how did the conversation end?'

'I told him I was leaving for the summer, that I needed to get away for a while to think about what I wanted.'

'What did he say?'

'The same thing he always says. That he loves me, but he's just not ready. He's always been honest, but I think for the first time he realized that maybe it's not just his decision to make.'

'Did you talk to Mom about it?' Sarah asked.

'Yes. She told me to ask myself if my life was better with him or without him.'

Sarah and I were lucky. Our mother had perfected the art of giving simple, yet practical, advice. She stayed neutral, and she never judged. A parental anomaly, according to many of our girlfriends.

'Well, what's your answer?'

'I'm not sure, Sarah. I love him, but I don't think that's going to be enough for me.' I needed time to think, to be sure, and Tom and Jane Callahan had given me the perfect opportunity to get some distance. Literal space to make my decision.

'He'll see this as an ultimatum,' Sarah said.

'Of course he will.' I took another drink of my margarita.

'You're handling it pretty well.'

'That's because I haven't actually broken up with him yet.'

'Maybe it is a good idea for you to be alone for a while, Anna. Sort things out and decide what you want for the rest of your life.'

'I don't have to sit and wait for him, Sarah. I have plenty of time to find someone who wants the same things I do.'

'You do.' She finished her margarita and smiled at me. 'And look at you, jetting off to exotic locations just because you can.' She sighed. 'I wish I could go with you. The closest thing I've had to a vacation in the last year was when David and I took the kids to see the tropical fish at Shedd Aquarium.'

Sarah juggled marriage, parenting, and a full-time job. Flying solo to a tropical paradise probably sounded like nirvana to her.

We paid our bill and as we walked to the train I thought that maybe, just this once, my grass was a little greener. That if my situation had an upside, it was the freedom to spend the summer on a beautiful island if I felt like it.

So far, that plan hadn't worked out very well.

My head ached, my stomach growled, and I'd never been so thirsty in my life. Shivering, my head resting on my life jacket, I tried not to think about how long it might take them to find us.

Chapter 4
T.J.

Day 2

I woke up as soon as it got light. Anna was already awake, sitting on the sand beside me looking up at the sky. My stomach growled, and I didn't have any spit.

I sat up. 'Hey. How's your head?'

'Still pretty sore,' she said.

Her face was kind of a mess, too. Purple bruises covered her swollen cheeks and there was crusty, dried blood near her hairline.

We walked to the breadfruit tree and Anna climbed on my shoulders and knocked down two. I felt weak, unsteady, and it was hard to hold her. She got off and while we were standing there, a breadfruit fell off a branch and landed at our feet. We looked at each other.

'That will make things easier,' she said.

We cleared away the rotten breadfruit under the tree so if we came back and found any on the ground, we'd know we could eat them. I picked up the one that fell and peeled it. The juice tasted sweeter and the fruit wasn't so hard to chew.

We desperately needed something to collect water in, and we walked along the shoreline looking for empty cans, bottles, containers – anything that was watertight and would hold the rain. We spotted debris, which I thought might be wreckage from the plane, but nothing else. The lack of any human garbage made me wonder just where the hell we were.

We went inland. The trees blocked the light from the sun and mosquitoes swarmed us. I slapped at them and wiped the sweat off my forehead with my arm. We saw the pond when we came to a small clearing. More like a large puddle, it was full of murky water, and my thirst kicked into overdrive.

'Can we drink that?' I asked.

Anna knelt down and stuck her hand in. She swirled the water around and wrinkled her nose at the smell. 'No, it's stagnant. It's probably not safe to drink.'

We kept walking but we couldn't find anything that would hold water so we went back to the coconut tree. I picked up one of the coconuts from the ground and smashed it against the trunk of the tree, then threw it when I couldn't get it to crack. I kicked the tree, which hurt my foot. 'Goddamn it!'

If I could get one coconut open, we could drink the coconut water, eat the meat, and collect rain in the empty shell.

Anna didn't seem to notice my tantrum. She shook her head back and forth and said, 'I just don't understand why we haven't seen a plane yet. Where are they?'

I sat down next to her, breathing hard and sweating. 'I don't know.' We didn't say anything for a while, lost in our own thoughts. Finally, I said, 'Do you think we should build a fire?'

'Do you know how?' she asked.

'No.' I'd lived in the city all my life, and I could count on one hand the number of times I'd been camping and still have fingers left over. And we'd lit our campfires with a lighter. 'Do you?'

'No.'

'We could try to make one,' I said. 'We seem to have the time.'

She smiled at my lame attempt at a joke. 'Okay.'

We rubbed two sticks together for the next hour. Anna managed to get hers hot enough to burn her finger before she quit. I did a little better – I thought I saw some smoke – but no fire. My arms ached.

'I give up,' I said, dropping my sticks and using the bottom of my T-shirt to wipe the sweat before it dripped into my eyes.

It started raining. I concentrated on trying to catch the drops on my tongue, grateful for the small amount of water I swallowed. The rain ended after a few minutes.

Still sweating, I walked down to the shore, stripped off my T-shirt, and waded in wearing just my shorts. The temperature of the lagoon reminded me of bathwater, but I ducked my head under and felt a little cooler. Anna followed me, stopping before she reached the water. She sat down on the sand, holding her long hair off her neck with one hand. She had to be roasting in her long-sleeved shirt and jeans. A few minutes later she stood up, hesitated, and then pulled her T-shirt over her head. She unbuttoned and unzipped her jeans, stepped out of them, and walked toward me, wearing nothing but a black bra and matching underwear.

'Just pretend I'm in my swimsuit, okay?' she said when she joined me in the water. Her face was red, and she could hardly look at me.

'Sure.' I was so stunned I barely got the word out.

She had an awesome body. Long legs, flat stomach. Really nice rack. Checking her out should have been the last thing on my mind, but it wasn't. You wouldn't think I'd be able to get hard either, considering how thirsty and hungry I was and how seriously fucked up our situation had become, but you'd be wrong. I swam away from her until I got myself under control.

We stayed in the water for a long time and when we got out she turned her back to me and put her clothes on. We checked the breadfruit tree but there weren't any on the ground. Anna climbed up on my shoulders and when I steadied her by pressing down on her thighs, the image of her bare legs flashed into my mind.

She knocked down two breadfruits. I wasn't very hungry, which was weird since I should have been starving. Anna must not have been hungry either because she didn't eat the fruit after she sucked out all the juice.

When the sun went down, we stretched out near the shore and watched the bats fill the sky.

'My heart is beating really fast,' I said.

'It's a sign of dehydration,' Anna said.

'What are the other signs?'

'Loss of appetite. Not having to pee. Dry mouth.'

'I have all those.'

'Me, too.'

'How long we can go without water?'

'Three days. Maybe less.'

I tried to remember the last time I drank anything. Maybe at the Sri Lanka airport? We were getting a little in our mouths when it rained but it wouldn't be enough to keep us alive. The realization that we were running out of time scared the shit out of me.

'What about the pond?'

'It's a bad idea,' she said.

Neither of us said what we were thinking. If it came down to the pond water or no water, we might have to drink it anyway.

'They'll come tomorrow,' she said, but she didn't sound like she believed it.

'I hope so.'

'I'm scared,' she whispered.

'So am I.' I rolled over on my side, but it was a long time before I fell asleep.

Chapter 5
Anna

Day 3

When T.J. and I woke up, we both had a headache and felt nauseous. We ate some breadfruit, and I thought I might throw mine up, but I didn't. Even though we had very little energy, we returned to the beach and decided to try building a fire again. I was convinced a plane would fly over that day, and I knew a fire was our best chance to make sure they spotted us.

'We did it all wrong yesterday,' T.J. said. 'I was thinking about it last night, before I fell asleep, and I remember watching a show on TV where the guy had to make a fire. He spun the stick instead of rubbing two of them together. I have an idea. I'm going to see if I can find what I need.'

While he was gone, I gathered anything that would burn if we actually managed to produce a flame. The air was so humid, and the only thing on the island that was dry was the inside of my mouth. Everything I picked up felt damp, but I finally found some dry leaves on the underside of a flowering plant. I also pulled the pockets of my jeans inside out and found a bit of lint which I added to the pile in my hand.

T.J. returned with a stick and a smaller chunk of wood. 'Do you have any lint in your pockets?' I asked him. He turned his pockets inside out, found some, and handed it to me.

'Thanks.' I formed the lint and leaves into a little nest. I also gathered small sticks and collected a mound of damp, green leaves we could add to make plenty of smoke.

T.J. sat down and held the stick upright, perpendicular to the chunk of wood it rested on.

'What are you doing?' I asked him.

'I'm trying to figure out a way to spin the stick.' He studied it for a minute. 'I think the guy used a string. I wish I hadn't kicked off my shoes; I could have used the laces.'

He twisted the stick back and forth with one hand but he couldn't spin it fast enough to get any friction. Sweat ran down his face.

'This is fucking impossible,' he said, resting for a few minutes.

With renewed determination, he used both hands and rubbed them together, with the stick in between them. It spun much faster, and he quickly found a rhythm. After twenty minutes, the spinning stick produced a little pile of black dust in the notch he'd worn in the chunk of wood.

'Look at that,' T.J. said, when a wisp of smoke drifted up.

Shortly after that, there was a lot more smoke. Sweat ran into his eyes but T.J. didn't stop spinning the stick.

'I need the nest.'

I set it down next to him and held my breath, watching as he blew gently on the notch in the wood. He used the stick to carefully dig out the glowing red ember and transfer it to the pile of dry leaves and lint. He picked the nest up and held it in front of his mouth, blowing softly, and it burst into flames in his hands. He dropped it on the ground.

'Oh my God,' I said. 'You did it.'

We piled small pieces of tinder on top of it. It grew fast and we quickly used up the sticks I'd collected. We hurried to find more, and we were both running toward the fire with an armful when the sky opened up and poured. In seconds, the fire turned into a soggy pile of charred wood

We stared at what was left of it. I wanted to cry. T.J. sunk to his knees on the sand. I sat down next to him, and we lifted our heads to catch the raindrops in our mouths. It rained for a long time and at least some of it went down my throat, but all I could think about was the water soaking into the sand around us.

I didn't know what to say to him. When it stopped raining, we lay down under the coconut tree, not talking. We couldn't make another fire right away, because everything was too wet, so we dozed, lethargic and despondent.

When we woke up in the late afternoon, neither of us wanted breadfruit. T.J. didn't have enough energy to make another fire and without some kind of shelter, we wouldn't be able to keep it lit anyway. My heart pounded in my chest, and my limbs tingled. I'd stopped sweating.

When T.J. stood up and walked away, I followed. I knew where he was going, but I couldn't make myself tell him to stop. I wanted to go there, too.

When we reached the pond, I knelt at the water's edge, scooped some into my hand, and raised it to my mouth. It tasted horrible, hot and slightly brackish, but I immediately wanted more. T.J. knelt beside me and drank straight from the pond. Once we started, neither of us could stop.

After drinking all we could, we collapsed on the ground, and I thought I might throw it all back up, but I held it down. The mosquitoes swarmed, and I slapped them away from my face.

We wandered back to the beach. It was almost dark by then so we stretched out next to each other on the sand, laying our heads on our life jackets. I thought everything would be okay. We'd bought a little time. They'd come tomorrow for sure.

'I'm sorry about the fire, T.J. You worked so hard, and you did a great job. I would never have been able to figure that out.'

'Thanks, Anna.'

We fell asleep, but I woke up a while later. The sky was black, and I thought it was probably the middle of the night. My stomach cramped. I ignored it and rolled onto my side. Another cramp hit me, this one more intense. I sat up and moaned. Sweat broke out on my forehead.

T.J. woke up. 'What's wrong?'

'My stomach hurts.' I prayed the cramping would stop but it only got worse, and I knew what was about to happen. 'Don't follow me,' I said. I stumbled into the woods, and I barely got my jeans and underwear down before my body purged everything in it. When there was nothing left, I writhed on the ground, the cramps continuing in waves, one after the other. Drenched in sweat, the pain radiated from my stomach down each leg. For a long time I lay still, afraid the slightest movement would cause more misery. The mosquitoes buzzed around my face.

Then the rats came.

Everywhere I looked, pairs of glowing eyes lurked in

the darkness. One ran over my foot, and I screamed. I staggered to my feet and yanked my jeans and underwear back up, but the movement brought intense pain, and I collapsed again. I thought I might be dying, that whatever had contaminated the pond water wasn't something you could survive. I stayed still after that. Exhausted and weak, with no idea where T.J. was, I passed out.

A buzzing noise woke me. *Mosquitoes.* But the sun was up and most of the bugs, and the rats, were gone. I struggled to lift my head while lying on my side with my knees pulled up to my chest.

It was the sound of a plane.

I pushed myself up on all fours and crawled toward the beach, screaming for T.J. Rising to my feet, I stumbled toward the shore, trying with the last of my strength to lift my arms above my head and wave them back and forth. I couldn't see the plane, but I could hear it, the sound moving farther and farther away.

They're looking for us. They'll turn around any minute.

The sound of the plane grew fainter until I could no longer hear it. My legs buckled, and I fell onto the sand and cried until I hyperventilated. I lay on my side, my sobs tapering off, staring out at the water in a daze.

I had no idea how much time had passed, but when I looked over, T.J. was lying next to me.

'There was a plane,' I said.

'I heard it. I couldn't move.'

'They'll come back.'

But they didn't.

I cried a lot that day. T.J. was silent. He kept his eyes closed, and I wasn't sure if he was sleeping or just too weak to talk. We didn't make another fire or eat any bread-fruit. Neither of us moved out from underneath the coconut tree, except when it rained.

I didn't want to be near the woods when it got dark so we moved back to the beach. As I lay on the sand next to T.J., there was only thing I knew for sure. If another plane didn't come, or we couldn't figure out a way to collect water, T.J. and I would die.

I dozed fitfully throughout the night and when I finally fell into a deeper sleep, I woke up screaming because I dreamed a rat was chewing on my foot.

Chapter 6
T.J.

Day 4

When the sun came up, I could barely lift my head off the sand. Two seat cushions from the plane had washed up overnight, and something blue next to them caught my eye. I rolled toward Anna and shook her to wake her up. She looked at me with sunken eyes, her lips cracked and bleeding.

'What is that?' I pointed to the blue thing but the effort required to hold my hand up was too much, and I let my arm drop back onto the sand.

'Where?'

'Over there. By the seat cushions.'

'I don't know,' she said.

I lifted my head up and shielded my eyes from the sun. It looked familiar and suddenly I realized what it was. 'That's my backpack. *Anna, that's my backpack.*'

I stood up on wobbly legs, walked to the shore, and grabbed it. When I came back, I knelt down next to Anna, opened the backpack, and pulled out the bottle of water she'd given me at Malé Airport.

She sat up. 'Oh my God.'

I twisted the cap off and we passed the bottle back and forth, being careful not to drink it too fast. It held thirty-two ounces, and we drank it all, but it barely took the edge off my thirst.

Anna held up the empty bottle. 'If we use a leaf for a funnel, we can collect rainwater in this.'

Shaky and weak, we walked to the breadfruit tree and plucked a large leaf from one of the lower branches. Anna tore it until it was the right size and stuffed it into the mouth of the empty water bottle, making the opening as wide as possible. There were four breadfruits on the ground, and we carried them back to the shore and ate them all.

I dumped everything out of my backpack. My Chicago Cubs baseball cap was soaking wet, but I put it on anyway. There was also a gray hooded sweatshirt, two T-shirts, two pairs of shorts, jeans, underwear and socks, a tooth-brush and toothpaste, and my CD player. I picked up my toothbrush and toothpaste. The inside of my mouth tasted like something I couldn't even begin to describe. I unscrewed the cap on the toothpaste, squeezed some onto my toothbrush, and held it out to Anna. 'You can share my toothbrush if you don't mind.'

She smiled. 'I don't mind, T.J. But you go first. It's yours.'

I brushed my teeth and then rinsed the toothbrush in the ocean and handed it to her. She squeezed more tooth-paste onto it and brushed her teeth. When she was done, she rinsed it and handed it back to me. 'Thanks.'

We waited for it to rain and when it did, in the early afternoon, we watched the bottle fill with water. I handed it to Anna; she drank half of it and handed it back to me. After I finished it, we put the leaf back in, and the rain filled it up again. Anna and I drank that, too. We needed more, a lot more probably, but I started to think that maybe we wouldn't die after all.

We had a way to collect water, we had breadfruit, and we knew we could make a fire. Now we needed shelter because without it, our fire would never stay lit.

Anna wanted to build the shelter on the beach because the rats freaked her out. We broke off two Y-shaped branches and drove them down into the sand, placing the longest stick we could find between them. We made a crappy lean-to by propping more branches up against each side. Breadfruit leaves lined the floor except for a small circle where we could build our fire. Anna collected pebbles to place in a ring around it. It would be smoky inside, but that might help keep the mosquitoes away.

We decided to wait until morning to make another fire. Now that we had shelter, we could collect wood and store it inside the lean-to so it could dry.

It rained again and filled our water bottle three times; I had never tasted anything so good in my entire life.

When the sun went down, we took the seat cushions, life jackets, and my backpack into the lean-to.

'Good night, T.J.' Anna said, laying her head on one of the seat cushions, the fire pit between us.

'Good night, Anna.'

Chapter 7
Anna

Day 5

I opened my eyes. Sunlight filtered between the cracks of the lean-to. The pressure on my bladder – something I hadn't felt in a while – confused me for a second, and then I smiled.

I need to go to the bathroom.

I left the lean-to without waking T.J. and walked into the woods. I squatted behind a tree, wrinkling my nose at the strong smell of ammonia coming from my pee. When I pulled my pants back up, I cringed at the dampness between my legs.

T.J. was awake and standing next to the lean-to when I returned.

'Where were you?' he asked.

I grinned and said, 'Peeing.'

He high-fived me. 'I need to go, too.'

When he came back, we went to the breadfruit tree and scooped up three lying on the ground. We sat down and ate our breakfast.

'Let me see your head,' T.J. said.

I leaned over and T.J. combed through my hair with his fingers until he found the cut.

'It's better. You probably should have had stitches,

though. I can't see any dried blood, but your hair is so dark it's hard to tell.' He pointed to my cheek. 'The bruises are fading. That one is turning yellow.'

T.J.'s appearance had improved, too. His eye was no longer swollen shut, and his cuts were healing well. He'd fared better than me thanks to his seatbelt. His face – very handsome, though still quite boyish – would bear no permanent scars from the plane crash. I didn't know if I could say the same, but I wasn't concerned about that at the moment.

After breakfast, T.J. made another fire.

'Pretty amazing, city boy,' I said, squeezing his shoulder.

He smiled, adding small pieces of firewood and coaxing the flames higher, clearly proud of himself. He wiped the sweat out of his eyes and said, 'Thanks.'

'Let me see your hands.'

He held them out to me, palms up. Blisters covered the raw, calloused skin, and he winced when I touched them.

'That has to hurt.'

'It does,' he admitted.

The fire filled our shelter with smoke, but it wouldn't go out when it rained. If we heard a plane, we could knock it down and throw green leaves on the fire to create smoke.

I had never gone so long without a shower, and I smelled horrible. 'I'm going to try and clean up,' I said. 'You have to stay here, okay?'

He nodded and handed me a short-sleeved T-shirt from his backpack. 'Do you want to wear this instead of your long-sleeved shirt?'

'Yes. Thanks.' The T-shirt would fit me like a dress, but I didn't care.

'I'd give you some shorts, but I know they're too big.'

'That's okay,' I said. 'The shirt will really help.'

I walked along the shore, stopping to take off all my clothes only when I could no longer see T.J. or the lean-to. I scanned the blue, cloudless sky.

Now would be an excellent time for a plane to fly overhead. Surely, someone would notice the naked woman on the beach.

I waded into the lagoon, and the fish scattered. The sunburn on my hands and feet had faded into a dark tan, which contrasted with my white arms and legs. My hair hung to my shoulder blades in a rat's nest of tangles.

I washed my body with my hands, and then retrieved my clothes from the shore, rinsing them out in the ocean. I finger combed my hair and wished for a ponytail holder.

Slightly cleaner when I came out of the water, I put my wet underwear and bra on, and pulled T.J.'s T-shirt over my head. It hung down to mid-thigh so I didn't bother with my jeans.

'I know I'm not wearing pants,' I explained when I returned to the lean-to. 'But I'm hot, and I want to let them dry.'

'No big deal, Anna.'

'I wish we had something to catch fish with. There are tons of them in the lagoon.' My mouth watered and my stomach growled.

'We could try and spear them. After I get cleaned up, we can look for some long sticks. Our firewood supply is low, too.'

T.J. came back to the lean-to five minutes later, with wet hair, wearing clean clothes. His arms were wrapped around something large and bulky.

'Look what I found in the water.'

'What is it?'

He set the object down and spun it around so I could read the writing on the side.

'That's the life raft from the plane.' I knelt down next to it. 'I remember seeing it when I was looking for the life jackets.'

We opened the container and pulled the raft out. I ripped open the attached waterproof bag and took out a sheet of paper that listed the contents. I read it aloud:

'*Raft canopy, located inside accessories case, features two roll-down doors and a rain water collector in the top of the roof panel. Custom packs available including radio beacons and emergency locators.*'

My hopes soared. 'T.J., where's the accessories case?'

T.J. looked in the container and pulled out another waterproof bag. My hands shook as I tore into the plastic, and as soon as I made a big enough hole, I turned it upside down and dumped everything onto the sand. We rifled through it, our hands bumping into each other as we examined each item.

We found nothing that would lead to rescue.

No emergency locator. No radio beacon, satellite phone, or transmitter.

My hopes plummeted. 'I guess they figured the custom pack was an unnecessary upgrade.'

T.J. shook his head slowly.

I thought about what might have happened if we'd found an emergency locator.

Do you just turn it on and wait for them to come get you?

Tears filled my eyes. Blinking them back, I began inventorying the contents of the accessories case: knife, first-aid kit, tarp, two blankets, rope, and two collapsible sixty-four ounce plastic containers.

I opened the first-aid kit: Tylenol, Benadryl, antibiotic ointment, cortisone cream, band-aids, alcohol wipes, and Imodium.

'Let me see your hands,' I said to T.J.

He held them out, and I put antibiotic ointment and band-aids on his blisters.

'Thanks.'

I picked up the bottle of Benadryl. 'This can save your life.'

'How?'

'It'll stop an allergic reaction.'

'What about that one?' T.J. asked, pointing at a white bottle.

I glanced at him and looked away. 'That's Imodium. It's an anti-diarrheal.'

He snorted when he heard that.

The life raft inflated with a carbon dioxide canister. When we pushed the button, it filled with gas so quickly we had to jump out of the way.

We attached the roof canopy and rainwater collector. The life raft resembled one of those bounce houses my niece and nephew loved to jump around in, though not nearly as tall.

'This should hold about three gallons of water,' I said, pointing at the water collector. Thirsty again, I hoped the afternoon rain came early.

45

Nylon flaps hung down on the sides and attached to the life raft with Velcro. Leaving them up during the day would allow light and air inside. The roll-down mesh doors provided a small opening.

We pushed the life raft next to the lean-to and put more wood on the fire before walking to the coconut tree. T.J. cut the husk off a coconut. He split it open by sticking the blade of the knife into the coconut, and hitting the handle with his fist. I caught the water that spilled out in one of the plastic containers.

'I thought it would be sweeter,' T.J. said, after he took a drink.

'Me too.' It tasted slightly bitter, but it wasn't bad.

T.J. scraped out the meat with the knife. Starving, I wanted to eat every coconut on the ground. We shared five before my aching hunger dissipated. T.J. had one more, and I wondered how much food it took to fill up a sixteen-year-old boy.

The rain came an hour later. T.J. and I got soaked, smiling and cheering, watching the various containers fill to the top. Grateful for the sheer abundance, I drank until I couldn't hold any more, the water sloshing around in my stomach when I moved.

Within an hour, we both peed again. We celebrated by eating another coconut and two breadfruits.

'I like coconut better than breadfruit,' I said.

'Me, too. Although now that we have a fire, maybe we can roast it and see if it tastes better.'

We gathered more firewood and found long sticks for spearing fish. We threw the tarp over the top of the lean-to and tied it on with the rope for added protection from the rain.

T.J. carved five tally marks on the trunk of a tree. Neither of us mentioned another plane.

At bedtime, we built the fire up as high as we could without burning down the lean-to. T.J. crawled into the life raft. I went in after him, wearing the shirt he'd given me for a nightgown. I closed the roll-down door behind me; at least we'd have some protection from the mosquitoes.

We lowered the nylon flaps and attached them with the Velcro fasteners. I spread the blankets out and put the seat cushions down for pillows. The blankets were scratchy but they'd keep us warm when the sun went down and the temperature dropped. The seat cushions were thin and smelled of mildew, but it was luxuriously comfortable compared to sleeping on the ground.

'This is awesome,' T.J. said.

'I know.'

A bit smaller than a double bed, sharing the life raft with T.J. would leave only a few inches between us. I was too tired to care.

'Good night, T.J.'

'Good night, Anna.' He sounded drowsy already, and he rolled onto his side and passed out.

Seconds later, I did too.

I woke up in the middle of the night to check the fire. Only glowing embers remained, so I added more wood and poked it with a stick, sending sparks into the air. When the fire burned strong again, I went back to bed.

T.J. woke up when I lay down beside him.

'What's wrong?' he asked.

'Nothing. I put more wood on the fire. Go back to sleep.'

I closed my eyes, and we slept until the sun came up.

Chapter 8
T.J.

I woke up with a hard-on.

I usually did, and it wasn't like I had any control over it. Now that we weren't almost dead, my body must have decided all systems were a go. Sleeping so close to a girl, especially one that looked like Anna, pretty much guaranteed I'd wake up with a boner.

She lay on her side facing me, still asleep. The cuts on her face were healing and lucky for her, none of them looked deep enough to leave a scar. She'd kicked off her blanket sometime during the night, and I checked out her legs which was the wrong thing to do considering what was going on in my shorts. If she opened her eyes, she'd catch me staring so I crawled out of the life raft and thought about geometry until my hard-on went away.

Anna woke up ten minutes later. We ate coconut and breadfruit for breakfast, and I brushed my teeth afterward, rinsing with rainwater.

'Here,' I said, handing the toothbrush and toothpaste to her.

'Thanks.' She squeezed some toothpaste on it and brushed her teeth.

'Maybe there will be another plane today,' I said.

'Maybe,' Anna said. But she didn't look at me when she said it.

'I want to look around some more. See what else is on this island.'

'We'll have to be careful,' she said. 'We don't have shoes.'

I gave her a pair of my socks so her feet wouldn't be completely bare. I ducked behind the lean-to and changed into my jeans, to protect my legs from the mosquitoes, and we walked into the woods.

The humid air settled on my skin. I passed through a swarm of gnats, keeping my mouth closed and swatting them away with my hands. We walked farther inland and the smell of rotting plants grew stronger. The leaves overhead blocked almost all the sunlight and the only sound was the snapping of branches and our breathing as we inhaled the heavy air. Sweat drenched my clothes. We continued in silence, and I wondered how long it would take us to clear the trees and come out on the other side.

We came upon it fifteen minutes later. Anna trailed slightly behind me, so I spotted it first. Stopping short, I turned around and motioned for her to hurry up.

She caught up to me and whispered, 'What is that?'

'I don't know.'

A wooden shack, roughly the size of a single-wide mobile home, stood fifty feet ahead. Maybe someone else lived on the island. Someone who hadn't bothered with an introduction. We walked toward it cautiously. The front door hung open on rusty hinges, and we peered inside.

'Hello?' Anna said.

No one answered, so we stepped over the threshold onto the wooden floor. There was another door on the far side of the windowless room, but it was closed. There wasn't any furniture. I nudged a pile of blankets in the corner, and we jumped back when the bugs scattered.

When my eyes adjusted to the dim light, I noticed a large, metal toolbox on the floor. I bent down and opened it. It held a hammer, several packages of nails and screws, a tape measure, pliers, and a hand saw. Anna found some clothes. She picked up a shirt and the sleeve fell off.

'I thought maybe we could use that, but never mind,' she said, making a face.

I opened the door to a second room, and we crept in slowly. Empty potato chip bags and candy bar wrappers littered the floor. There was a wide-mouthed plastic container lying next to them. I picked it up and peered inside. Empty. Whoever lived here probably used it to collect water. Maybe if we'd explored the island a little more, walked farther and found the shack earlier, we wouldn't have been forced to drink the pond water. Maybe we would have been on the beach when the plane flew overhead.

Anna looked at the container in my hand. She must have made the same connection because she said, 'What's done is done, T.J. There's nothing we can do about it now.'

A moldy sleeping bag lay crumpled on the floor. In the corner, propped up against the wall, stood a black case. I flipped open the clasps and lifted the lid. Inside was an acoustic guitar in good condition.

'That's random,' Anna said.

'Do you think someone lived here?'

'It sort of looks that way.'

'What were they doing?'

'Besides channeling Jimmy Buffet?' Anna shook her

head. 'I have no idea. But whoever it was, they haven't been home for a while.'

'This isn't scrap wood,' I said. 'It's been cut at a lumber yard. I don't know how he got it here, boat or plane I guess, but this guy was serious. So where did he go?'

'T.J.,' Anna said, her eyes growing wide. 'Maybe he'll come back.'

'I hope so.'

I put the guitar in the case and handed it to her. I picked up the toolbox, and we retraced our steps back to the beach.

At lunchtime, Anna roasted breadfruit on a flat rock next to the fire while I cracked coconuts. We ate it all – the breadfruit still didn't taste like bread to me – and washed it down with coconut water. The heat from the fire, plus a temperature that had to be near ninety, made it hard to sit inside the lean-to for very long. Sweat trickled down Anna's red face, and her hair stuck to her neck.

'Do you want to get in the water?' I regretted the words as soon as they came out of my mouth. She'd probably think I just wanted her to strip in front of me again.

She hesitated, but she said, 'Yes. I'm burning up.'

We walked down to the shore. I hadn't changed back into my shorts, so I took off my socks and T-shirt, and stepped out of my jeans. I wore gray boxer briefs.

'Pretend they're my swim trunks,' I said to Anna.

She glanced at my underwear and cracked a smile. 'Okay.'

I waited for her in the lagoon, trying not to stare while she took her clothes off. If she had the balls to undress in front of me, I wasn't going to be a jackass about it.

I got hard again, though, and hoped she didn't notice.

We swam for a while and when we got out of the water, we dressed and sat on the sand. Anna stared up at the sky.

'I thought for sure that plane would make another pass,' she said.

When we got back to the lean-to, I threw some wood on the fire. Anna took one of the blankets from the life raft, spread it on the ground, and sat down. I grabbed the guitar and sat down beside her.

'Do you play?' she asked.

'No. Well, one of my friends taught me part of a song.' I plucked at the strings and then played the opening notes of 'Wish You Were Here.'

Anna smiled. 'Pink Floyd.'

'You like Pink Floyd?'

She nodded. 'I love that song.'

'Really? That's awesome. I wouldn't have thought that.'

'Why, what kind of music do you think I listen to?'

'I don't know, like, Mariah Carey?'

'No, I like the older stuff.' She shrugged. 'What can I say? I was born in '71.'

I calculated her age. 'You're thirty?'

'Yes.'

'I thought you were twenty-four or twenty-five.'

'No.'

'You don't act thirty.'

She shook her head and laughed softly. 'I don't know if that's good or bad.'

'I just meant that you're easy to talk to.'

She smiled at me. I strummed some more, playing the same Pink Floyd riff, but I had to stop because my hands ached from making the fire.

'If we had something to use for a hook, I could turn this into a fishing pole,' I said. 'The guitar string would probably make a decent line.' I thought about using a nail from the tool box, but the fish weren't very big, and I needed something smaller and lighter.

Later, when we went to bed, she said, 'I hope that party you stayed behind for was worth it.'

'It wasn't a party. I just told my parents that.'

'What was it?'

'Ben's parents were out of town. His cousin just got back from college for the summer, and he was supposed to come over with his girlfriend. She was going to bring two of her friends. Ben convinced himself he could score with one of them. I bet him twenty bucks that he couldn't.' I didn't tell Anna I had planned to try, too.

'Did he?'

'They never showed. We sat around all night, drinking beer and playing video games instead. Two days later I got on the plane with you.'

'Wow, T.J. I'm sorry,' she said.

'Yeah.' I waited a minute and then I asked, 'Who was that guy at the airport?'

'My boyfriend, John.'

I remembered the kiss he'd given her. It looked like he was trying to jam his tongue down her throat. 'You must miss him.'

She didn't answer right away, but then she finally said, 'Not as much as I probably should.'

'What's that mean?'

'Nothing. It's complicated.'

I turned on my side and shoved my seat cushion under

my head. 'Why do you think that plane didn't come back, Anna?'

'I don't know,' she said. But I thought she did.

'They think we're dead, don't they?'

'I hope not,' she said. 'Because then they'll stop looking.'

Chapter 9
Anna

The next morning, T.J. used the knife to whittle the ends of two long sticks into sharp points.

'Ready to spear some fish?' he asked.

'Definitely.'

When we reached the shore, T.J. knelt down and picked something up.

'This must be yours,' he said, handing me a dark blue ballet flat.

'It is.' I looked out at the water. 'Maybe the other one will wash up.'

We waded into the lagoon, hip deep. The heat wasn't as intolerable in the morning, so I wore T.J.'s T-shirt, instead of just my bra and underwear. The hem soaked up water like a sponge and clung to my thighs. We tried unsuccessfully for over an hour to spear a fish. Small and quick, they scattered as soon as we made any kind of movement.

'Do you think we'd have better luck a little farther out?' I asked.

'I don't know. The fish are probably bigger, but it might be harder to use the spear.'

I noticed something then, bobbing in the water. 'What is that, T.J.?' I shielded my eyes with my hand.

'Where?'

'Straight ahead. Do you see it bobbing up and down?' I pointed at it.

T.J. squinted into the distance. 'Oh, fuck. Anna, don't look.'

Too late.

Right before he told me not to look, I figured it out. I dropped my spear and threw up in the water.

'He's going to wash up, so let's go back to the shore,' T.J. said.

I followed him out of the water. When we reached the sand I threw up again.

'Is he here yet?' I asked, wiping my mouth with the back of my hand.

'Almost.'

'What are we going to do?'

T.J.'s voice sounded shaky and unsure. 'We're going to have to bury him somewhere. We could use one of our blankets, unless you don't want to.'

As much as I hated giving up one of our few possessions, wrapping him in a blanket seemed like the respectful thing to do. And if I was being honest with myself, I knew there was no way I could touch his body with my bare hands.

'I'll go get it,' I said, grateful for an excuse not to be there when he washed up.

When I returned with the blanket, I handed it to T.J., and we rolled the body up in it by pushing it with our feet. The smell of decomposing, waterlogged flesh filled my nose, and I gagged and buried my face in the crook of my elbow.

'We can't bury him on the beach,' I said.

T.J. shook his head. 'No.'

We picked a spot under a tree, far away from the lean-to, and started digging in the soft dirt with our hands.

'Is that big enough?' T.J. asked, looking down into the hole.

'I think so.'

We didn't need a large grave because the sharks had eaten Mick's legs and part of his torso. And an arm. Something else had been working on his bloated, white face. Scraps of the tie-dye T-shirt he'd been wearing hung from his neck.

T.J. waited while I dry-heaved, and then I grabbed one edge of the blanket and helped him drag Mick to the grave and lower him into the hole. We covered him with dirt and stood up.

Silent tears rolled down my face. 'He was already dead when we hit the water.' I said it firmly, like a statement.

'Yes,' T.J. agreed.

It started to rain so we went back to the life raft and crawled inside. The canopy kept us dry, but I shivered. I pulled the blanket over us – the one we'd now be sharing – and we slept.

When we woke up, T.J. and I gathered breadfruit and coconut. Neither of us said much.

'Here.' T.J. handed me a piece of coconut.

I pushed his hand away. 'No, I can't. You eat it.' My stomach churned. I'd never get the image of Mick out of my head.

'Is your stomach still upset?'

'Yes.'

'Try some of the coconut water,' he said, passing it to me.

I lifted the plastic container to my lips and took a drink.

'Did that go down okay?'

I nodded. 'Maybe I'll just stick to this for a while.'

'I'm going to get some firewood.'

'Okay.'

He had only been gone a few minutes when I felt the trickle.

Oh God, no.

Hoping for a false alarm, I walked in the opposite direction from where T.J. had gone and yanked my jeans down. There, on the white cotton crotch of my underwear was the proof that I'd just gotten my period.

I hurried to the lean-to and grabbed my long-sleeved T-shirt. Back in the woods, I tore off a strip, balled it up, and shoved it in my underwear.

I need this miserable day to be over.

When the sun went down, the mosquitoes feasted on my arms.

'You must have decided being cooler was worth a few bites,' T.J. said, when he noticed me slapping at them. He had put on his sweatshirt and jeans as soon as the bugs came out.

I thought of my long-sleeved shirt, hidden under a bush I only hoped I'd be able to find again.

'Yeah, something like that.'

Chapter 10
T.J.

We ate nothing but coconut and breadfruit for the next eighteen days and our clothes hung on us. Anna's stomach growled in her sleep, and I had a constant ache in mine. I doubted the rescuers were still looking for us, and a hollow, empty feeling that had nothing to do with hunger joined the pain in my gut whenever I thought of my family and friends.

I thought it would impress Anna if I could spear a fish. I managed to stab myself in the foot instead, which hurt like hell, not that I let her know.

'I want to put antibiotic ointment on it,' Anna said. She dabbed it on the gash and covered it with a band-aid. She said the island humidity was perfect for germs and the thought of one of us getting an infection scared the crap out of her. 'You'll have to stay out of the water until that heals, T.J. I want to keep it dry.'

Great. No fishing and no swimming.

The days passed slowly. Anna got quiet. She slept more, and I caught her wiping her eyes when I came back from collecting firewood or exploring the island. I found her sitting on the beach one day, staring up at the sky.

'It's easier if you quit thinking they're coming back,' I told her.

She looked up at me. 'So I should just wait for a plane to randomly fly overhead someday?'

'I don't know, Anna.'

I sat down beside her. 'We could leave on the life raft,' I said. 'Load it with food and use the plastic containers to collect rainwater. Just start paddling.'

'What if we ran out of food or something happened to the raft? It'd be suicide, T.J. We're obviously not in the flight path for any of the inhabited islands, and there's no guarantee a plane would fly over. These islands are spread over thousands of miles of water. I can't be out there. Not after seeing Mick. I feel safer here, on land. And I know they're not coming back, but saying it out loud seems like giving up.'

'I used to feel that way, but I don't anymore.'

Anna studied me. 'You're very adaptable.'

I nodded. 'We live here now.'

Chapter 11
Anna

T.J. yelled my name. I was sitting next to the lean-to, staring off into space. He ran toward me, dragging a suitcase behind him.

'Anna, is it yours?'

I stood up and raced to meet him halfway. 'Yes!'

Please let it be the right one.

I threw myself down on the sand in front of the suitcase and yanked on the zipper, then flipped open the lid and smiled.

I pushed my wet clothes aside and searched for my jewelry. I found the Ziploc bag, opened it, and poured everything out. Sifting through it, my fingers closed around a chandelier earring, and I held it up triumphantly for T.J. to see.

He smiled, studying the curved wire the earring hung on. 'That will make an excellent fish hook, Anna.'

I took everything out of the suitcase: Toothbrush and two tubes of regular toothpaste, plus a tube of tooth-whitening Crest, four bars of soap, two bottles of body wash, shampoo and conditioner, lotion, shaving cream, and my razor and two packages of replacement blade cartridges. Three deodorants – two solids and one gel – baby oil and cotton balls for taking off my makeup, cherry Chap-Stick, and – *thank you Jesus* – two boxes of tampons. Nail polish and polish remover, tweezers, Q-tips, Kleenex, a bottle of Woolite for hand washing my swimsuits, and two tubes of Coppertone with an SPF of 30. T.J. and I were already so dark I didn't think the sunscreen would make a difference.

'Wow,' T.J. said when I finished sorting all the toiletries.

'The island we're supposed to be on didn't have a drugstore,' I explained. 'I checked.'

I'd also packed a comb and brush, hair clips and ponytail holders, a deck of cards, my datebook and a pen, two pairs of sunglasses – Ray-Ban aviators and a pair with big black frames – and a straw cowboy hat I always wore to the pool.

I picked up each item of clothing, wringing the water out and spreading it on the sand to dry. Four swimsuits, cotton lounge pants, shorts, tank tops, T-shirts, and a sundress. My tennis shoes and several pairs of socks. A blue REO Speedwagon concert T-shirt, and a gray Nike one with a red swoosh that said *Just Do It* on the front. They were size large, and I wore them to sleep in.

I threw my underwear and bras back in the suitcase and closed the lid. I'd deal with those later.

'We're lucky this is the suitcase that washed up,' I said.

'What was in the other one?'

'Your text books and assignments.' I'd made careful lesson plans, organizing all the work T.J. would need to complete. The novels I'd planned to read over the summer were in that suitcase, too, and I thought longingly of how much they would have helped pass the time. I looked at T.J., my expression hopeful. 'Maybe we'll find your suitcase too.'

'Not a chance. My parents took it with them. That's

why I had some clothes and my toothbrush in my back-pack. My mom wanted me to have something with me in case we got delayed and had to spend the night somewhere.'

'Really?'

'Yeah.'

'Huh. Imagine that.'

I gathered up everything I needed. 'I'm going to take a bath,' I said. 'You can never go down to the water when I'm down there. Are we clear on that?'

T.J. nodded his head. 'I won't. I promise. I'm gonna see if I can make a fishing pole while you're gone. I'll go when you get back.'

'Okay.'

When I reached the shore, I stripped off my clothes, walked into the water, and ducked my head under. I washed my filthy hair, rinsed, and washed it again. The shampoo smelled incredible, but maybe that was because I smelled so bad. After I put the conditioner on, I soaped myself from head to toe and sat on the shore, shaving my legs and underarms. I walked into the water to rinse and floated on my back for a while, content and clean.

I put on my yellow bikini, slicked on deodorant, and untangled my hair, putting it up in a twist and securing it with a hair clip. I chose the black sunglasses, deciding that T.J. should have the Ray-Bans.

He did a double-take when I walked up. When I sat down beside him, he leaned over, sniffed me, and said, 'The mosquitoes are going to eat you alive.'

'I feel so good I don't even care.'

'What do you think?' he asked, holding up the fishing

pole. He had made a hole at the end of a long stick and tied the guitar string to it. He threaded the other end through an open loop in the wire from my earring.

'Looks great. When you get back from cleaning up, let's try it out. I left everything down by the water. Help yourself.'

When T.J. came back, he looked clean and smelled as good as I did. I gave him the Ray-Bans.

'Hey thanks,' he said, putting them on. 'These are cool.' He grabbed the fishing pole.

'What are we going to use for bait?' I asked.

'Worms, I guess.'

We dug in the ground under the trees until we found some. They looked more like large maggots than worms, white and wiggly, and I shuddered. T.J. scooped up a handful, and we went down to the water.

'The line isn't very long,' T.J. said. 'I didn't want to use up all the guitar string in case it snapped or something happened to the pole.'

After wading in waist deep, he threw out his hook. We stayed still.

'Something's nibbling,' T.J. said.

He jerked the pole back and pulled in the line. I cheered at the fish hanging off the end.

'Hey, it worked!' he said.

T.J. caught seven more fish in less than half an hour. When we got back to the lean-to, he left to collect fire-wood, and I cleaned the fish with the knife.

'Where'd you learn to do that?' he asked when he came back. He emptied the backpack full of sticks onto the woodpile in the lean-to.

'My dad. He used to take Sarah and me fishing with him

all the time, at the lake house we had when we were grow-ing up. He always wore this crazy bucket hat with fishing lures all over it. I helped him clean whatever we caught.'

T.J. watched as I scraped the scales with the knife and then cut the head off. I ran the blade horizontally down the length of the fish, separating the filet from the skin. I poured rainwater on my hands to wash off the blood and guts, and then cooked the fish on the flat rock we used for roasting breadfruit. We ate all seven, one after the other. They tasted better than any fish I'd ever eaten.

'What kind of fish do you think this is?' I asked T.J.

'I don't know. It's pretty good though.'

We sat on the blanket after dinner, our stomachs full for the first time in weeks. I reached into my suitcase and pulled out my datebook, smoothing the warped pages.

'How many days have we been here?' I asked T.J.

He walked over to the tree and counted the tally marks he'd made with the knife. 'Twenty-three.'

I circled the date on the calendar. It was almost July. 'I'll keep track from now on.' I thought of something then. 'When are you supposed to go back to the doctor?'

'The end of August. I'm supposed to have a scan.'

'They'll find us by then.'

I didn't really think so. From the look on T.J.'s face, he didn't either.

I was going to the bathroom behind a tree when I heard it. The fluttering, flapping sound startled me, and I almost fell into my puddle of pee. I stood and yanked my under-wear and shorts up, then listened, but I didn't hear the noise again.

'I think I heard an animal,' I said to T.J. when I got back.

'What kind of animal?'

'I don't know. It made a flapping, fluttering noise. Have you heard anything?'

'Yes, I've heard that, too.

We walked back to where I heard the noise, but didn't find anything. We gathered all the firewood we could hold on the way back, and deposited it on our woodpile.

'Do you want to go swimming?' T.J. asked.

'Sure.'

Now that I had a swimsuit, swimming sounded like a great idea.

The clear water in the lagoon would have been perfect for snorkeling. We swam for about a half hour, and right before we got out of the water, T.J. stepped on something. He dove under the surface. When he came up, he held a tennis shoe in his hand.

'Is that yours?' I asked.

'Yep. I figured it would wash up eventually,' he said.

We sat on the beach, the ocean breeze drying our bodies.

'Why did your parents choose these islands?' I asked. 'They're so far away.'

'The scuba diving. It's supposed to be some of the best diving in the world. My dad and I are both certified,' T.J. said, digging his toes into the white sand. 'When I was really sick, he made a big deal out of telling everyone that as soon as I got better, we'd take this major vacation. Like I gave a shit.'

'You didn't want to come here?'

T.J. shook his head.

'Why not?'

'Nobody wants to spend the whole summer with their family. I wanted to stay home and hang out with my friends. Then they told me you were coming and I had to make up all the work I missed or I'd have to do tenth grade over. That really pissed me off.' He looked at me apologetically. 'No offense.'

'None taken.'

'They didn't listen to me, though. My mom and dad convinced themselves that this trip would be the greatest thing ever for our family. But even my sisters were mad. They wanted to go to Disney World.'

'I'm sorry, T.J.'

'It's okay.'

'How old are your sisters?'

'Alexis is nine and Grace is eleven. They drive me nuts sometimes – they never stop talking – but they're okay,' he said. 'Do you have any brothers or sisters?'

'I have one sister, Sarah. She's three years older than I am and she's married to a guy named David. They have two kids – Joe's five and Chloe's two. I miss everyone so much. I can't imagine what they're going through, especially my mom and dad.'

'I miss my family, too,' T.J. said.

I scanned the brilliant blue sky and stared out at the turquoise water, listening to the calming sound of the waves hitting the reef.

'It's actually very beautiful here,' I said.

'Yeah,' T.J. agreed. 'It is.'

Chapter 12
T.J.

One of the hardest things about being on the island was the boredom. It took time to gather food and firewood, and go fishing two or three times a day, but we still had too many hours left over. We explored and we swam, but we also talked and it didn't take long before I felt almost as comfortable with Anna as I did with my friends; she listened to what I had to say.

She asked how I was doing emotionally. Guys are supposed to be tough, and Ben and I sure as hell never sat around talking about how we felt, but I admitted to Anna that I got a weird feeling in my stomach whenever I thought about whether they'd ever find us. I told her I got scared sometimes. I said I didn't always sleep well. She said she didn't either.

I liked sharing a bed with Anna, though. Sometimes she curled up right next to me, with her head on my shoulder, and once when I slept on my side, she pressed her chest against my back and tucked her knees into the space behind mine. She did it in her sleep, and it didn't mean anything, but it felt good. I'd never spent the whole night with a girl before. Emma and I had only slept together for a few hours and that was mostly because she was so sick.

I liked Anna. A lot. Without her, the island would have really sucked.

*

No one rescued us, so I missed my follow-up appointment with the oncologist at the end of August. Anna mentioned it at breakfast one morning.

'I'm worried about you not being able to go to the doctor,' she said, handing me a piece of cooked fish. 'Careful, it's hot.'

'I feel fine,' I told her, blowing on the fish to cool it before putting it in my mouth.

'Yes, but you were pretty sick, right?'

'Yeah.'

She handed me the water bottle. I took a drink and set it down.

'Tell me about it,' she said.

'My mom thought I had the flu. I had a fever, and I started sweating at night. I lost some weight. Then the doctor found a lump on my neck that turned out to be a swollen lymph node. They ran some tests after that: X-rays, biopsy, MRI, and a PET scan. Then they told me I had stage III Hodgkin's lymphoma.'

'Did you start chemo right away?'

'Yeah. It didn't work though. They also found a mass in my chest so I had to have radiation, too.'

'That sounds awful.'

She cut off a piece of breadfruit, and handed the rest to me.

'It wasn't fun. I was in and out of the hospital a lot.'

'How long were you sick?'

'About a year-and-a-half, I guess. For a while, I wasn't doing very well. The doctors didn't know what to think.'

'That had to be really scary, T.J.'

'Well, they tried to keep me in the dark, which I hated. I only knew it was bad because suddenly no one would look me in the eye when I asked questions. Or they'd change the subject. That scared me.'

'I bet it did.'

'At first, my friends visited me all the time, but when I didn't get better, some of them stopped coming around.' I took another drink of water and handed the bottle to Anna. 'You know my friend, Ben?'

'Yes.'

'He came every single day. He spent hours watching T.V. with me, or just sitting in a chair by my hospital bed when I felt too sick to move or talk. My parents and the doctor would have these long conversations, out in the hall or whatever, and I'd ask Ben to try and listen. He'd tell me everything they said, no matter what. He knew I just wanted to hear it straight up, you know?'

'Of course,' she said. 'He sounds like a great friend, T.J.'

'Yeah, he is. Do you have a best friend?'

'Yes, her name is Stefani. We've known each other since kindergarten.'

'That's a long time.'

She nodded. 'Friends are important. I understand why you wanted to spend your summer with them.'

'Yeah,' I said, thinking about everyone back home in Chicago. They probably thought I was dead.

Anna stood up and walked to the woodpile. 'Will you tell me if you notice any symptoms?' She grabbed some wood and threw it on the fire.

'Sure. Just don't ask me if I feel okay all the time. My mom did, and it drove me nuts.'

'I won't. But I'll worry a little.'

'Yeah. Me, too.'

Chapter 13
Anna

The bright sunlight woke me, illuminating the interior of the life raft. T.J. was already gone, out gathering firewood or fishing. I yawned, stretched my arms and legs, and crawled out of bed. My suitcase was in the lean-to, and I reached in and grabbed a bikini, returning to the life raft to change. Dressed, I lifted the nylon flaps to let in some fresh air.

T.J. walked up with the fish he caught for breakfast. He smiled. 'Hey.'

'Good morning.'

I checked the breadfruit and coconut trees, scooping up everything on the ground and bringing them back to the lean-to. T.J. cracked coconuts while I cleaned and cooked the fish.

After breakfast we brushed our teeth, rinsing with rainwater, and I marked off the date in my datebook. September already. Hard to believe.

'Want to go swimming?' T.J. asked.

'Sure.'

Last week, T.J. had spotted two fins, just outside the reef. We panicked and left the water, but as we watched they came all the way into the lagoon. Dolphins. We waded slowly into the water and they didn't swim away, waiting patiently as we approached them.

'They almost act like they're here to introduce themselves,' I said in amazement.

T.J. petted one and laughed when it blew water out its blowhole. I had never seen such social creatures. They swam with us for a while and then left abruptly, on some sort of marine schedule.

'Maybe the dolphins will come back today,' I said, as I followed T.J. down to the shore.

T.J. stripped off his shirt and waded into the lagoon. 'That would be cool. I want to ride one.'

We entertained ourselves by using one of the collapsible plastic containers for a snorkel mask. There were schools of brightly colored fish – purple, blue, orange, and yellow and black striped. We spotted a sea turtle and an eel poking its head up from the ocean floor. I swam away fast when I saw that.

'No dolphins,' I said after T.J. and I had been swimming for at least an hour. 'We must have missed them.'

'We can try again after our nap.' Suddenly, he pointed toward the shoreline. 'Anna, look over there.'

A crab leg stuck out of the sand, the pincer opening, and closing. We ran out of the water.

'I'll grab my sweatshirt,' he said.

'Hurry, it's trying to bury itself.'

T.J. returned in record time, wrapped his sweatshirt around the crab, and pulled it out of the sand. We went back to the lean-to and T.J. shook it out onto the fire.

'Oh God,' I said, thinking for a second about the crab's violent demise.

I got over it fast.

We cracked the legs with the pliers from the toolbox, gorging ourselves. The crabmeat – even without hot melted butter – tasted better than anything I'd eaten since we'd been on the island. Now that we knew where they buried themselves, T.J. and I would have to check the shoreline daily. I was so tired of fish, coconut, and bread-fruit that I could hardly choke them down sometimes, and adding crabmeat would provide a little variety, something that was desperately lacking in our diet.

When the crab was nothing more than a pile of split shells, I took the blanket out of the life raft and spread it under the coconut tree. We stretched out next to each other. The shade from the tree helped keep us cool during the hottest part of the day, and it had become our favorite place to nap.

A big, creepy, hairy spider – its body the size of a quarter – crawled lazily across T.J.'s shoulder and I flicked it off him with my finger. 'That one even freaked me out,' I said.

T.J shuddered. He hated spiders, always shaking our blanket out, checking for them before he put it back in the life raft. Personally, I hated snakes. I'd already stepped on one and the only thing that kept me from being completely traumatized was the fact that I was wearing my tennis shoes. I hated to think about stepping on one bare-foot; whether or not they might be poisonous was too stressful to think about.

I thought T.J. had already fallen asleep, but then he said, 'What do you think's gonna happen to us, Anna?' His voice sounded drowsy.

'I don't know. I think we just keep doing what we're doing and try to hold on until someone finds us.'

'We're not doing too bad,' T.J. said, rolling over onto his stomach. 'I bet that would surprise a lot of people.'

'It surprises me.' My full stomach was making me drowsy, too. 'It's not like we had a choice, T.J. We either figured it out or we died.'

T.J. lifted his head off the blanket and looked at me with a contemplative expression. 'Do you think they had funerals for us back home?'

'Yes.' The thought of our families holding memorials hurt so much that I squeezed my eyes shut and willed myself to sleep, hoping to escape the images of a crowded church, an empty altar, and my parents' tear-stained faces.

After our nap we gathered firewood, an endless, tedious chore. We kept the fire burning constantly, partly so T.J. wouldn't have to make a new one and partly because we both still held out hope that a plane would fly overhead. When it did, we'd be ready, our pile of green leaves sending up smoke signals as soon as we threw them on the flames.

We added the firewood to the pile in the lean-to. Then I filled the container that had held the life raft with seawater, added a capful of Woolite, and swished our dirty clothes around in it.

'It must be laundry day,' T.J. said.

'Yep.'

We strung a rope between two trees and hung the clothes to dry. We didn't have much; T.J. wore shorts and nothing else. I spent my days in a bikini, sleeping in his T-shirt and a pair of shorts at night.

Later that night, after dinner, T.J. asked if I wanted to play cards.

'Poker?'

He laughed. 'What, you didn't get your ass kicked enough last time?'

T.J. had taught me how to play, but I wasn't very good. At least, that's what he thought. I was starting to get the hang of it, and I was about to take him down.

Six hands later – I won four – he said, 'Huh, I must be having an off night. Want to play checkers instead?'

'Okay.'

He drew a checkerboard in the sand. We used pebbles for the checkers and played three games.

'One more?' T.J. asked.

'No, I'm going to take a bath.'

I was already worried about our soap and shampoo supply. I'd packed a lot of each, but T.J. and I had agreed to only bathe every other day. Just in case. We stayed somewhat clean since we swam a lot, but we didn't always smell the greatest.

'Your turn,' I said, when I returned from the shore.

'I miss showering,' T.J. said.

After he bathed, we went to bed. T.J. closed the roll-down door of the life raft and lay down next to me.

'I'd give anything for a Coke,' he said.

'Me too. A big one, with lots of ice.'

'And I want some bread. Not breadfruit. Bread. Like a big sandwich, with potato chips and a pickle.'

'Pizza, Chicago style,' I said.

'A big sloppy cheeseburger.'

'Steak,' I said. 'And a baked potato with cheese and sour cream.'

'Chocolate pie for dessert.'

'I know how to make chocolate pie. My mom taught me.'

76

'The kind with the chocolate shavings on top?'

'Yes. When we get off this island, I'll make you one.' I sighed. 'We're just torturing ourselves.'

'I know. Now I'm hungry. Well, I was already kinda hungry.'

I turned onto my side and got comfortable. 'Good night, T.J.'

'Good night.'

T.J. laid the fish he'd caught on the ground next to me and sat down.

'School's been in session for a couple weeks,' I said. I made an X on the calendar, put the datebook away, and started cleaning our breakfast.

T.J. must have noticed my expression because he said, 'You seem sad.'

I nodded. 'It's hard for me, knowing another teacher is standing in front of my students right now.'

I taught sophomore English, and I loved shopping for school supplies and selecting books for my bookshelves. I always filled a big mug on my desk with pens and there wouldn't be any left by the end of the year.

'So you like your job?'

'I love it. My mom was a teacher – she retired last year – and I always knew I'd be one, too. When I was little I wanted to play school all the time and she used to give me gold stars so I could grade my stuffed animal's homework.'

'I bet you're a really good teacher.'

I smiled. 'I try to be.' I placed the cleaned fish on my cooking rock and positioned it close to the flames. 'Can you believe you'd be starting your junior year?'

'No. It seems like I haven't been to school in a long time.'

'Do you like school? Your mom told me you were a good student.'

'It's okay. I wanted to catch up with my class. I had hoped to get back on the football team, too. I had to quit when I got sick.'

'So you like sports?' I asked.

He nodded. 'Especially football and basketball. Do you?'

'Sure.'

'Do you play any?'

'Well, I run. I ran two half-marathons last year, and I ran track and played basketball in high school. Sometimes I do yoga.' I checked the fish and pulled the rock away from the fire so it could cool. 'I miss exercising.'

I couldn't imagine running now. Even if we had enough food to justify it, running around the island would remind me of a hamster on a wheel. Moving forward but getting absolutely nowhere.

T.J. walked up with a backpack full of firewood. 'Happy birthday,' I said.

'It's September 20th?' He threw a log on the fire and sat down next to me.

I nodded. 'I'm sorry, I didn't get you a present. The island mall sucks.'

T.J. laughed. 'That's okay, I don't need a present.'

'Maybe you can have a big party when we get off this island.'

T.J. shrugged. 'Yeah, maybe.'

78

T.J. seemed older than seventeen. Reserved almost. Maybe facing serious health problems eliminated some of the immature behavior that presented itself when you had nothing more to worry about than getting your driver's license, cutting class, or breaking curfew.

'I can't believe it will be October soon,' I said. 'The leaves are probably starting to change back home.'

I loved fall – football games, taking Joe and Chloe to the pumpkin patch, and feeling a chill in the air. Those were some of my favorite things.

I stared at the palm trees, their green leaves rippling in the breeze. Sweat trickled slowly down the side of my face, and the constant smell of coconut on my hands reminded me of suntan lotion.

It would always be summer on the island.

Chapter 14
T.J.

The rain came down sideways. Thunder crashed, and lightning lit up the sky. The wind shook the life raft, and I worried it might relocate us halfway down the beach. I made a mental note: *anchor life raft to something tomorrow.*

'Are you awake?' I asked Anna.

'Yes.'

The storm raged for hours. We huddled together with the blanket pulled over our heads. The thin nylon covering the roof and hanging down the sides of the life raft was all that protected us from the lightning, which was like having no protection at all. We didn't say much, just waited for it to end and when it finally did, we went back to sleep, exhausted.

The next morning, Anna brought back several small green coconuts blown off the tree by the storm. We split them open. The meat tasted sweet, and the water wasn't bitter like the brown coconuts.

'These are so good,' Anna said.

The lean-to had fallen apart and our fire had gone out so I made another one, this time using my shoelace. I tied it to the opposite ends of a curved stick. Making a loop in the string, I threaded another stick through so that it stood perpendicular to the chunk of wood I rested it on.

'What are you doing?' Anna asked.

'I'm going to use this to spin the stick. That's what the guy on T.V. did.'

I adjusted the tension on the string and held the stick at different angles. It took a while before I could get the stick to spin fast enough, but once it did, I got smoke in about fifteen minutes, and flames pretty soon after that.

'Hey,' Anna said. 'That was a great idea.'

'Thanks.' I piled on tinder and watched the fire grow. Anna and I put the lean-to back together.

I wiped the sweat out of my eyes and said, 'I hope that's the worst storm we ever have.' I leaned the last stick up against the lean-to. 'Because I don't know what we're going to do for shelter if it's not.'

Anna left to take a bath. I looked through her suitcase, trying to find her REO Speedwagon T-shirt. She told me I could wear it – and the Nike one too – since they both fit me. I didn't see the shirt, so I dug a little deeper.

There were two boxes of tampons shoved under some shorts.

What's she going to do when those run out?

I moved some things around and noticed her bras, folded and tucked into a neat pile. The black one was on top. I picked up a bottle of vanilla lotion, flipped open the cap, and sniffed.

That's why she sometimes smells like cupcakes.

I opened a round plastic container. It had tiny pills inside, in a circle marked with days of the week. Five pills remained. It took me a while to figure out they were birth control pills. I found two more unopened packages.

Anna wouldn't mind that I was looking through her suitcase – I kept my clothes in there too because we used my backpack to carry firewood – but she probably wouldn't want me touching all her stuff. I started to shut the lid but then I spotted her underwear. They were at the bottom of the suitcase, next to her tennis shoes. I looked over my shoulder, then grabbed a pink pair and held them up.

I wonder if you can see through these when she's wearing them.

I put them back and picked up a black thong.

Very sexy. But I bet it's totally uncomfortable.

I touched a red pair, and looked closer at the little black bow in the center of the waistband.

Wow. Now that would be a hot present.

Then I scooped up five or six pairs at once, buried my face in them, and inhaled.

'What are you *doing*?' Anna asked.

I whipped around. 'Jesus, you scared the crap out of me!' My heart pounded and my face burned.

How long has she been standing there?

'I'm looking for your REO Speedwagon T-shirt.' I still held a pair of her underwear in my hand, and I dropped them back in her suitcase.

'Really?' she asked. 'Because it kind of looks like you're playing with my underwear.' She put the soap and shampoo away in her suitcase.

She didn't seem mad though, so I pulled out the thong, held it up, and said, 'This looks totally uncomfortable.'

'Give me that.' She snatched it out of my hand and shoved it back in her suitcase, pressing her lips together and trying not to laugh.

When I realized she wasn't pissed at me, I smiled and said, 'You know what, Anna? You're all right.'

'I'm glad you think so.'

'I really *was* looking for your REO Speedwagon T-shirt, but I can't find it.'

'It's hanging on the line. It should be dry.'

'Thanks.'

'Sure. Just don't smell my underwear anymore, okay?'

'You saw that, huh?'

'Yeah.'

Chapter 15
Anna

The dolphins swam alongside me in the lagoon. They dove under my body and surfaced on the other side. They made the funniest squeaking noises, and when I talked to them, they acted like they understood me. T.J. and I liked to grab their fins, laughing as they let us ride them. I could play with them for hours.

T.J. ran down to the lagoon. 'Anna, guess what I found.'

T.J.'s other tennis shoe had washed up, and since he didn't have to worry about injuring his feet anymore, he spent hours in the woods, searching for something interesting. So far, he'd found nothing but mosquito bites, but he kept looking anyway. It gave him something to do.

'What did you find?' I asked, petting one of the dolphins.

'Put your tennis shoes on and come see.'

I said good-bye to the dolphins, followed him back to the lean-to, and put on my shoes and socks.

'Okay, now I'm curious. What is it?'

'A cave. I went to grab a pile of sticks, and when I pulled them away, I saw the opening. I want to see what's in it.'

It only took a few minutes to get to the cave. T.J. knelt at the entrance and crawled through on his hands and knees.

'It's narrower than I thought,' he yelled. 'Lie on the ground and army crawl on your stomach. It's tight, but there's room. Come on in.'

'No way,' I yelled back. 'I am never going in that cave.'

My heart beat faster, and I started sweating just thinking about it.

'I'm feeling around. I can't see anything.'

'Why would you do that? What if there are rats, or a big scary spider?'

'What? You think there might be spiders?'

'No, never mind.'

'I don't think there's anything in here but rocks and sticks. I can't tell though.'

'If the sticks are dry bring them out. We can add them to the woodpile.'

'Okay.'

T.J. crawled out of the cave and stood up with something that looked like a shinbone in one hand and something that was definitely a skull in the other. He dropped them and said, 'Holy shit!'

'Oh my God,' I said. 'I don't know who that is, but it did *not* end well for them.'

'Do you think it's the person who built the shack?' T.J. asked. We stared down at the skull.

I nodded. 'That would be my guess.'

We walked back to the lean-to and grabbed a burning log from the fire to use for a torch. We hurried back to the cave and T.J. got down on his hands and knees and crawled inside, holding the torch in front of him.

'Don't burn yourself,' I called after him.

'I won't.'

'Are you in?'

'Yes.'

'What do you see?'

'It's definitely a skeleton. But there's nothing else in here.' T.J. came out and handed me the torch. 'I'm going to put the bones back in the cave with the rest of it.'

'Good idea.'

T.J. and I walked back to the lean-to. 'Well that was horrifying,' I said.

'How long does it take a body to become a skeleton?' T.J. asked.

'In this heat and humidity? Probably not long.'

'I definitely think it's the guy from the shack.'

'You're probably right. And if it is him, there goes one of our chances for rescue.' I shook my head. 'He's not coming back because he never left. But what killed him?'

'I don't know.' T.J. threw some wood on the fire and sat down beside me. 'Why wouldn't you go in the cave? Before we knew about the skeleton, I mean.'

'I can't stand small, enclosed spaces. They freak me out. You know that lake house I told you about? The one where my dad and I went fishing?'

'Yeah.'

'Sarah and I always played with the other kids who vacationed there with their families. There was a road that went around the whole lake, and it had a long drainage pipe under it. Kids were always daring each other to crawl through it to the other side. One time, Sarah and I decided to do it, and we convinced everyone else to come along. We got halfway in, and I panicked. I couldn't breathe and the person in front of me wouldn't move forward. I couldn't back up because there were kids behind me, too. I was probably seven, and not very big, but the pipe was tiny. We finally made it out the other side, and Sarah had

86

to go find our mom because I wouldn't stop crying. I remember it like it was yesterday.'

'No wonder you wouldn't go in.'

'What I can't understand is why Bones would crawl in there to die.'

'Bones?'

'I feel like he should have a name. Bones sounds better than "guy from the shack."'

'Works for me.' T.J. said.

I sat by the lean-to playing Solitaire. When T.J. walked up, I knew instantly that something was wrong because he held his arm close to his body, and supported it with his other hand. His shoulder slumped downward.

I stood up. 'What happened?'

'I fell out of the coconut tree.'

'Come on.' I put my arm around his waist and led him slowly to the life raft. He winced at the slightest movement, and he tried, unsuccessfully, to suppress a moan when I helped him lay down. The strong, sudden urge to take care of him, to ease his pain, surprised me.

'I'll be right back; I'm going to get the Tylenol.'

I shook two Tylenol into my palm and grabbed the water bottle, filling it at the water collector. I put the pills in T.J.'s mouth and lifted his head so he could take a drink. He swallowed and breathed slowly in and out.

'Why were you climbing the tree?'

'So I could reach those little green coconuts you like.'

I smiled. 'That was very sweet of you, but I think your collarbone is broken. I'm going to wait for the Tylenol to kick in, and then I'll try to rig some kind of sling.'

'Okay,' he said, closing his eyes.

I looked in my suitcase and found a long white tank top. After twenty minutes, I helped him sit up.

'I'm sorry, I know it hurts.'

I bent his arm at the elbow and tucked the sling underneath, tying it gently at his shoulder. Easing him back down, I brushed the hair out of his face and kissed his forehead. 'Try not to move around.'

'Okay, Anna.'

Maybe it didn't hurt that bad though, because when I glanced back at him before leaving the life raft, he had a smile on his face.

I woke up that night to put wood on the fire.

'Anna?'

T.J.'s voice startled me. 'Yes?'

'Can you help me out of here? I have to pee.'

'Sure.'

I helped him through the doorway of the life raft and then built up the fire. When he returned, I gave him more Tylenol.

'Have you been able to sleep at all?' I asked.

'Not really.'

The next morning, a lump and purple bruise showed where the bone had snapped. He grimaced when I tightened the sling, and I gave him a third dose of Tylenol.

He wouldn't let me give him any more pills after that. 'I don't want to take too much, Anna. We might need it again.'

He felt better after three days, and he followed me around like a puppy. He came down to the beach when I was fishing, he tagged along when I went to get breadfruit, and he wanted to help empty the water collector. When he tried to go with me to gather firewood, I sent him back to the blanket under the coconut tree.

'You aren't going to heal if you don't stop moving around, T.J.'

'I'm bored. And I really need a bath. Will you help me when you get back?'

'What? No, I'm not giving you a bath.'

Awkward.

'Anna, you can help me, or you can smell me.'

I sniffed him. 'You've smelled better. Okay, I'll help you, but I'm only washing certain areas and only because you stink.'

He grinned. 'Thanks.'

We went down to the lagoon as soon as I got back with the firewood. T.J. left his shorts on and sat down in water that covered his lower body. I knelt beside him and rubbed the bar of soap in my hands.

'Hold this for me,' I said, handing it to him.

I started by gently washing his face with my soapy hands and then scooped up water in my palm to rinse it off, my fingers touching the stubble on his cheeks and jaw and above his lip.

'That feels good,' he said.

I filled up the plastic container I brought and dumped it on his head, then washed his hair. It had grown a lot, and he constantly flicked it out of his eyes. He preferred my straw cowboy hat for keeping it out of his way which suited me fine; I had long since claimed his baseball cap as my own.

'I wish we had scissors,' I said. 'I'd give you a haircut.'

89

He handed me the soap, and I lathered up my hands again. I washed his neck and moved down to his chest, my fingers gliding over his hardened nipples. He watched me silently.

I washed under his good arm, and his back. He couldn't raise the other arm so I did the best I could, touching him gently near the bruise.

'I'm sorry,' I said, when he winced.

I made the mistake of looking down when I got ready to wash his legs. The water in the lagoon was clear enough to see that he had a hard-on sticking up in his shorts. 'T.J.!'

'Sorry.' He looked at me sheepishly. 'I can't hide this one.'

Wait, how many have there been?

I suddenly didn't know where to look. It wasn't his fault though; I had forgotten what would happen if you rubbed a seventeen-year-old all over with your hands.

Or any man, actually.

'No, it's okay. It just caught me off guard, that's all. I thought you were in pain.'

Appearing genuinely confused, he said, 'Well I didn't break *that*.'

Okay, moving on.

I washed his legs, and when I got to his feet, I discovered he was ticklish. He jerked his foot away, and then said, 'ow' when the movement jostled his upper body.

'Sorry. Okay, you're sorta clean.'

'You're not gonna dry me off?' He gave me a hopeful smile.

'Ha. That's funny. You must be confusing us with people who have towels.'

'Thanks, Anna.'

'Sure.'

I helped him bathe for the next two weeks, until he healed enough to do it on his own. Each time, it got a bit less embarrassing for me. I never glanced down again, to see how it affected him.

'This doesn't totally suck for you, does it?' I asked one day while washing his hair.

'Not at all,' he said, with a big smile on his face. 'But don't worry,' he added with mock seriousness. 'I'll pay you back someday. If you ever get hurt, I will definitely give you a bath.'

'I'll keep that in mind.'

I made a mental note to be extra careful. Bathing him might have been awkward, but it was nothing compared to how I'd feel if it were his soapy hands moving over my skin.

Chapter 16
T.J.

Anna was standing next to the life raft. I handed her the fish I caught and stored my pole in the lean-to. 'Is there anything in the water collector?'

'No.'

'Maybe it'll rain later.'

She looked anxiously at the sky and began cleaning the fish. 'I hope so.'

It was November, and we'd been on the island for six months. Anna said the rainy season wouldn't return until May. It still rained, about every other day, but not for very long. We had coconut water, but we were still thirsty a lot.

'At least we know never to drink from the pond,' Anna said, shuddering. 'That was awful.'

'God, I know. I thought I was gonna crap out my spleen.'

We couldn't control the rain, but the Maldives had plenty of marine life. The coconut and breadfruit barely took the edge off our hunger, but the brightly colored fish I pulled out of the lagoon kept us from starving.

I stood in waist deep water and caught them one after the other. None measured longer than six inches – an earring and a guitar string wouldn't hold much – and I worried about hooking something bigger and snapping the line. It was a good thing Anna packed a lot of earrings because I'd already lost one.

Even though we had enough to eat, Anna said our diet didn't have a bunch of important stuff.

'I'm worried about you, T.J. You still have some growing to do.'

'I'm growing just fine.' Our diet couldn't have been that bad, because my shorts were down to my knees when we crashed, and now they were at least an inch higher.

'The breadfruit must have Vitamin C, otherwise we'd probably have scurvy by now,' she muttered under her breath.

'What the hell is scurvy?' I asked. 'That sounds gross.'

'It's a disease caused by not getting enough Vitamin C,' she said. 'Pirates and sailors came down with it on long voyages. It's not pleasant.'

Anna should have worried more about herself. Her swimsuit bagged in the ass, and her boobs didn't fill out her top like before. Her collarbone stuck out and her ribcage showed. I tried to get her to eat more, and she made an effort, but half the time I ended up finishing her food. Unlike her, eating the same thing every day didn't bother me, and I ate whenever I got hungry.

One morning, a few weeks later, Anna said, 'Today is Thanksgiving.'

'It is?' I didn't pay much attention to the date, but Anna kept track every day.

'Yes.' She closed her datebook and put it down on the ground beside her. 'I don't think I've ever eaten fish on Thanksgiving before.'

'Or coconut and breadfruit,' I added.

'It doesn't matter what we eat. Thanksgiving is about being thankful for what we have.'

She tried to be cheerful when she said it, but then she wiped her eyes with the back of her hand, and put on her sunglasses.

Neither of us mentioned the holiday for the rest of the day. I hadn't thought about Thanksgiving; I'd assumed someone would find us before then. Anna and I hardly ever talked about rescue anymore though – it depressed us both. All we could do was wait and hope someone flew overhead. That was the hardest thing, not having any control over our situation unless we decided to leave on the life raft, and Anna would never agree to that. She was right. It probably would be suicide.

That night in bed she whispered, 'I'm thankful we have each other, T.J.'

'So am I.'

If Anna had died after the plane crash, and I'd been alone all this time, I wondered if I would have made it.

We spent Christmas Day chasing a chicken.

Early that morning, when I bent down to gather some sticks for the woodpile, I screamed like a girl when a chicken shot out of a nearby bush and scared the shit out of me.

I took off after it, but it disappeared into another bush. I thrust my hand in and felt around, but couldn't reach it.

'Anna, that flapping sound we keep hearing is from a chicken,' I said, when I returned with the firewood.

'There are chickens here?'

'Yes. I chased one into the bushes but it got away. Lace up your tennis shoes. We're gonna have chicken for our Christmas dinner.'

'It's over there. I heard it. I'm going to kick the bush so get ready to catch it when it runs out the other side,' Anna said, as Operation Catch a Chicken went into overdrive. We'd been tracking it for over an hour, from one end of the island to the other, and we were finally closing in.

'There it is,' she yelled, when it came flapping out of the bush next to me.

I tried to tackle it and came away with nothing but a handful of feathers. 'Goddammit, you motherfucker!'

I chased after it. Anna caught up to me and we cornered it in a cluster of bushes. It started to wiggle through a gap in the leaves, but Anna lunged and held onto it. I grabbed its legs, pulled it out of the bush, and slammed it down on the ground.

Anna didn't miss a beat. 'Good job, T.J.' She patted me on the back.

I slit its throat and hung it upside down until most of the blood drained out, then pulled the feathers off, trying not to look at its head.

Anna cut it apart with the knife.

'This is not at all what it looks like at the grocery store,' she said.

'It looks fine,' I said. She totally mangled it, but we put the pieces on several rocks and placed them close to the fire.

She sniffed the air. 'Smell that,' she said, as the chicken cooked.

When it looked done, we let it cool and then pulled the meat apart with our fingers. It was burned in some spots, and a little under-cooked in others, but it tasted awesome.

'This chicken rocks,' I said, licking my fingers.

Anna finished her drumstick and said, 'Yes, it does.' She threw her chicken bone in the growing pile next to the fire, wiped her mouth with the back of her hand, and said, 'I wonder how many more chickens there are.'

'I don't know. But we're going to find every one of them.'

'This is the best chicken I've ever eaten, T.J.'

I burped and laughed. 'No doubt.'

We picked the bones clean and spread our blanket on the ground, away from the fire.

'Do you open your presents on Christmas Eve, or Christmas Day?' I asked her.

'Christmas Eve. What about you?'

'Same. Sometimes Grace and Alexis beg to open them on the twenty-third, but my mom makes them wait.'

We lay side by side, relaxing. I thought of Grace and Alexis, and my mom and dad. They were probably having a hard time, celebrating their first Christmas without me.

If they only knew that Anna and I were alive and holding our own.

The rain returned in May, and Anna and I relaxed a little. But it stormed more often, and we couldn't do anything but huddle in the life raft, listening to the crash of thunder while we waited for it to stop.

We had a bad one that brought down a tree, so I cut it

into firewood with the handsaw. It took me two days, but by the time I finished, the woodpile filled the lean-to.

I went down to the beach afterward to cool off. Anna splashed in the water, playing with six dolphins. Wading in, I petted one of them on the head, and I swear it smiled at me.

'Six, wow. That's a record,' I said.

'I know. They all came at once today.' The dolphins swam into the lagoon like clockwork, late morning and late afternoon. There were always at least two, but this was the first time there had been so many at once.

'You're sweating,' she said. 'Were you sawing again?'

I ducked my head under and shook like a dog when I came back up. 'Yeah, it's all done though. We won't have to gather wood for a while.' I stretched, my arms aching. 'Rub my shoulders, Anna. Please?'

'Come on.' She led me out of the water. 'I'll give you a back rub. Mine are world-famous.'

I sat in front of her and almost groaned when she touched my shoulders. She wasn't kidding about being good at it, and I wondered if she rubbed the boyfriend down a lot. Her hands were stronger than I would have guessed, and she massaged my neck and back for a long time. I thought about her hands touching me other places, and if she'd been able to read my mind she probably would have freaked.

'There,' she said when she finished. 'Did that feel good?'

'You have no idea,' I said. 'Thanks.'

We walked back to the lean-to. Anna poured a capful

of Woolite into the rainwater she collected in the life raft container, and swished it around with her hand.

'Laundry time, huh?'

'Yep.'

I had offered to split laundry duty, but she said she'd do it. She probably didn't want me messing with her underwear.

She put our dirty clothes in the container and washed them. When she took them out one at a time and set them aside for rinsing, she said, 'Hey T.J., where's all your underwear?'

Speaking of underwear.

'It doesn't fit anymore, and it mostly fell apart.'

'So you don't have any?'

'No. I didn't have a whole suitcase full like some people.'

'Isn't that uncomfortable?'

'It was at first, but now I'm used to it.' I grinned and pointed at my shorts. 'Totally commando here, Anna.'

She laughed. 'Whatever, T.J.'

Chapter 17
Anna

We had been on the island a little over a year when the plane flew over.

I was gathering coconuts that afternoon, and the roar of the engines, so loud and unexpected, startled me. I dropped everything and ran to the beach.

T.J. exploded out of the trees. He raced toward me, and we waved our arms back and forth, watching as the plane flew right over our heads.

We screamed and hugged and jumped up and down, but the plane banked to the right and kept flying. We stood there, listening to the sound of the engines fading away.

'Did it tip its wings?' I asked T.J.

'I'm not sure. Did it?'

'I couldn't tell. Maybe it did.'

'It had floats, right?'

'It was a seaplane,' I confirmed.

'So, it could have landed out there?' he asked, motioning toward the lagoon.

'I think so.'

'Did they see us?' he asked.

T.J. wore gray athletic shorts with a thin blue stripe down each side and no shirt, but I was wearing my black bikini which should have been visible against the white sand.

'Sure, I mean, wouldn't you notice two people waving their arms?'

'Maybe,' he said.

'They wouldn't have seen our fire, though,' I pointed out. We hadn't knocked down the lean-to, or thrown any green leaves on the flames to create extra smoke. I wasn't sure we even *had* any green leaves in the lean-to.

We sat on the beach for the next two hours, not talking, straining to hear the sound of approaching airplane engines.

Finally, T.J. stood up. 'I'm gonna go fishing.' His voice sounded flat.

'Okay,' I said.

After he left, I walked to the coconut tree and gathered the ones I'd dropped on the ground. I stopped at the breadfruit tree on my way back, and scooped up two, then put everything in the lean-to. I stoked the fire and waited for T.J.

When he returned, I cleaned and cooked the fish for our dinner, but neither of us ate. I blinked back tears and sighed in relief when T.J. wandered off toward the woods.

I lay down in the life raft, curled myself into a ball, and cried.

All the hope I'd clung to since our plane went down splintered into a million tiny shards that day, like a glass block someone pounded with a sledgehammer. I thought that if we could manage to be on the beach when the next plane flew over, we'd be rescued. Maybe they didn't see us. Maybe they did, but they didn't know we were missing. It didn't matter now because they weren't coming back.

My tears ended, and I wondered if I'd finally run out of them.

I crawled out of the life raft. The sun had gone down, and T.J. was sitting by the fire, his right hand resting limply on his thigh.

I took a closer look. 'Oh, T.J. Is it broken?'

'Probably.'

Whatever his fist connected with – my guess would be the trunk of a tree – had left his knuckles bloody and his hand horribly swollen.

I went to the first-aid kit and brought back two Tylenol and some water.

'I'm sorry,' he said, not making eye contact. 'The last thing you need is another broken bone to take care of.'

'Listen,' I said, kneeling down in front of him. 'I will never criticize anything you do if it helps you cope, okay?'

He finally looked at me, nodded, and took the Tylenol from my outstretched hand. I handed him the water bottle, and he swallowed them down. I sat cross-legged next to him, staring at the sparks that drifted into the air when I dropped a log on the fire.

'How do you cope, Anna?'

'I cry.'

'Does it work?'

'Sometimes.'

I stared at his broken hand and fought the urge to wash the blood off and hold it in my own. 'I give up, T.J. You once said, "It's easier if you don't think they're coming back" and you were right. This one's not coming back either. A plane will have to land in the lagoon for me to believe we might actually get off this island. Until then, it's just you and me. That's the only thing I know for sure.'

'I give up, too,' he whispered.

I looked at him, so broken, both physically and mentally, and it turned out I had some tears left after all.

I checked his hand the next morning. The swelling had doubled the size of it.

'It needs to be immobilized,' I said. I grabbed a short stick from the woodpile and rummaged in my suitcase for something to wrap around it. 'I won't put it on tight, but it's going to hurt a little, T.J.'

'That's okay.'

I put the stick under his palm, and gently pulled the black fabric over the back of his hand, winding it around twice, and tucking it underneath.

'What did you wrap my hand with?' he asked.

'My thong.' I looked up at him. 'You were right; it's totally uncomfortable. Awesome for first-aid though.'

The corners of T.J.'s mouth turned up slightly. He looked at me, his brown eyes showing a trace of the spark that had been missing the night before. 'It'll make for a funny story someday,' I said.

'You know what, Anna? It's kinda funny now.'

T.J. turned eighteen in September of 2002. He didn't look like the same boy I crash-landed in the ocean with fifteen months ago.

For one thing, he really needed to shave. The hair was much longer than a five o'clock shadow but shorter than a full beard and moustache. It looked good on him, actually. I wasn't sure if he liked the facial hair, or if he just didn't want to bother with shaving.

The hair on his head was almost long enough to pull

back in one of my ponytail holders, and the sun had bleached it light brown. My hair had grown, too. It hung past the middle of my back and drove me nuts. I tried to cut it with our knife but the blade – dull and non-serrated – wouldn't saw through hair.

Although very lean, T.J. had grown at least two inches taller, bringing him to about six feet.

He looked older. Having turned thirty-one in May, I probably did, too. I wouldn't know; the only mirror I had was in the makeup bag in my purse, which was floating around in the ocean somewhere.

I forced myself not to ask him how he felt, or if he had any cancer symptoms, but I watched him closely. He seemed to be doing okay, growing and thriving, even under our less than desirable conditions.

The man in my dream moaned when I kissed his neck. I slid my leg between his and then kissed my way from his jaw down to his chest. He put his arms around me and rolled me onto my back, bringing his mouth down to mine. Something about his kiss startled me, and I woke up.

T.J. was on top of me. We were on the blanket under the coconut tree where we'd laid down to take a nap. I realized what I'd done and wriggled out from underneath him, my face on fire. 'I was dreaming.'

He flipped onto his back, breathing hard.

I scrambled to my feet, then went down to the water's edge and sat cross-legged on the sand. *Way to go, Anna. Attack him while he's asleep.*

T.J. joined me a few minutes later.

'I am completely mortified,' I said.

He sat down. 'Don't be.'

'You must have wondered what the hell I was doing.'

'Well, yeah, but then I just rolled with it.'

I looked over at him, my mouth hanging open. 'Are you insane?'

'What? You're the one that said I was adaptable.'

Yes, and apparently quite opportunistic.

'Besides,' T.J. said. 'You like to cuddle. How am I supposed to know what it means? It's confusing.'

My humiliation level kicked up another notch. I often woke up in the middle of the night way too close to T.J., my body curled around his, and I had assumed he slept right through it.

'I'm sorry. This was completely my fault. I didn't mean to give you the wrong idea.'

'That's okay, Anna. It's no big deal.'

I kept my distance for the rest of the day, but that night, in bed, I said, 'It's true. What you said about the cuddling. It's just that I'm used to sleeping with someone. I slept next to him for a really long time.'

'Is that who you were dreaming about?'

'No. It was one of those weird dreams that didn't make sense. I don't know who it was, actually. But I'm really sorry.'

'You don't have to keep apologizing, Anna. I said it confused me. I never once said I didn't like it.'

The next day, when I came back from the lagoon, I discovered T.J. sitting beside the lean-to prying his braces off with the knife.

'Do you need help with that?'

He spit a piece of metal out of his mouth. It landed on the ground next to several more.

'Nope.'

'When were you supposed to get them off?'

'Six months ago. I kinda forgot about it until yesterday.'

That's when I realized what woke me up, during the dream. A boy with braces hadn't kissed me since high school.

Chapter 18
T.J.

I was standing in front of Bones' shack when Anna found me. Sweat ran down her face.

'I chased a chicken all over the island, but it ran too fast. I will catch it if it's the last thing I do.' She leaned over and put her hands on her knees, trying to catch her breath. She looked up at me. 'What are you doing?'

'I want to tear down this shack, then bring the wood back to the beach to build us a house.'

'Do you have any idea how to build a house?'

'No, but I've got plenty of time to figure it out. If I'm careful, I can re-use all the wood and nails. I can make an awning with the tarp so the fire won't go out.' I examined the hinges on the door, wondering if they were salvageable. 'I need something to do, Anna.'

'I think it's a great idea,' she said.

It took us three days to knock down the shack and carry the pieces back to the beach. I pulled all the old nails out and put them in the toolbox with the others.

'I don't want to be too near the woods,' Anna said. 'Because of the rats.'

'Ok.' I couldn't build on the beach, though, because the sand was too unstable. We chose a spot between the two, where the sand ended and the dirt began. We dug a foundation, which sucked because we didn't have a shovel. I used the claw end of the hammer to pull chunks of dirt out of the ground, and Anna followed along behind me, scooping it up in one of our plastic containers.

I used the rusty saw to cut the wood into the right size. Anna held the boards while I pounded in the nails.

'I'm glad you decided to do this,' she said.

'It's going to take me a while to finish it.'

'That's okay.'

She walked to the toolbox to get me some more nails. After she handed them to me she said, 'Let me know if you need more help.'

She stretched out on the blanket nearby and closed her eyes. I watched her for a minute, my eyes moving from her legs to her stomach to her boobs, wondering if her skin felt as soft as it looked. I thought about the other day, when she kissed my neck under the coconut tree. I remembered how good it felt. Suddenly, she opened her eyes and turned her head toward me. I looked away quickly. I'd lost track of how many times she'd caught me staring at her. She never said anything about it, or told me to knock it off, which was just one more reason why I liked her so much.

It would have been my senior year, and Anna hated that I missed so much school.

'You're probably going to have to get a GED. I wouldn't blame you at all if that's what you wanted to do, instead of going back and finishing high school.'

'What's a GED?'

'A general education diploma. Sometimes when kids drop out of school, they choose that option instead of going back. But don't worry, I'll help you.'

'Okay.' I didn't give two shits about my high school diploma right then, but it seemed important to her.

The next day, when we were working on the house, Anna said, 'Are you ever going to shave?' She felt my beard with the back of her hand. 'Isn't that hot?'

I hoped there was enough hair to hide my red face. 'I've never shaved before. What little I had fell out when I started chemo. When we left Chicago everything was just starting to grow back.'

'Well it's all there now.'

'I know. But we don't have a mirror, and I don't know what I'm doing.'

'Why didn't you say something? You know I would help you.'

'Uh, because it's embarrassing?'

'Let's go,' she said. She grabbed my hand and pulled me back to the lean-to. She opened her suitcase and took out a razor and the shaving cream she used on her legs, and we went down to the water.

We sat cross-legged facing each other. She squirted shaving cream into her hand and dabbed it on my face, then spread it around. She put her hand behind my head, pulling me toward her until I was at the right angle, and then shaved the left side of my face with slow, careful strokes.

'Just so you know,' she said. 'I've never shaved a man before. I'll try not to cut you, but I can't promise.'

'You'll do a better job than I would.'

Only a few inches separated our faces, and I looked into her eyes. Sometimes they were gray, and sometimes blue. Today was a blue day. I never realized how long her eyelashes were. 'Do people notice your eyes?' I blurted.

She leaned over and swished the razor around in the water. 'Sometimes.'

'They're amazing. They look even bluer because you're so tan.'

She smiled. 'Thanks.'

She scooped up water in her hand and ran it over my cheeks, rinsing the shaving cream away.

'What's that look for?' she asked.

'What look?'

'You've got something on your mind.' She pointed at my head. 'I can practically see the wheels turning up there.'

'When you said you'd never shaved a man before. Do you think of me as a man?'

She paused before she answered. 'I don't think of you as a boy.'

Good, because I'm not.

She squirted more shaving cream into her palm and shaved the rest of my face. When she finished, she held my chin and turned my face side to side, running the back of her hand along my skin.

'Okay,' she said. 'You're all done.'

'Thanks. I feel cooler already.'

'You're welcome. Let me know when you want me to do it again.'

Anna and I lay in bed one night, talking in the dark.

'I miss my family,' she said. 'I have this daydream I play out in my mind all the time. I imagine that a plane has landed in the lagoon and you and I are right on the beach when it does. We swim out to it and the pilot can't believe it's us. We fly away and as soon as we find a phone, we call our families. Can you imagine what that would be like for them? Being told someone has died and having their funeral, and then they call you on the phone?'

'No, I can't imagine what that's like.' I turned onto my stomach and adjusted the seat cushion under my head. 'I bet you wish you never took this job.'

'I took the job because it was a great opportunity to go someplace I'd never been. No one could have predicted this would happen.'

I scratched a mosquito bite on my leg. 'Did you live with that guy? You said you slept next to him.'

'Yes.'

'I wouldn't think he'd want you to be away for so long.'

'He didn't.'

'But you did?'

She didn't say anything for a minute. 'I feel weird talking about it with you.'

'Why, because you think I'm too young to possibly understand?'

'No, because you're a guy. I don't know if you can relate.'

'Oh, sorry.' I shouldn't have said that. Anna was really good about not treating me like a kid.

'His name is John. I wanted to get married, but he wasn't ready, and I was tired of waiting. I thought it would be good for me to get away for awhile. Make some decisions.'

'How long have you been together?'

'Eight years.' She sounded embarrassed.

'So he doesn't ever want to get married?'

'Well. I think he just doesn't want to marry me.'

'Oh.'

'I don't want to talk about him anymore. What about you? Do you have someone back in Chicago?'

'Not anymore. I used to go out with this girl named Emma. I met her at the hospital.'

'Did she have Hodgkin's too?'

'No, leukemia. She was sitting in the chair next to mine when I had my first chemo treatment. We spent a lot of time together after that.'

'Was she your age?'

'A little younger. She was fourteen.'

'What was she like?'

'She was kinda quiet. I thought she was really pretty. She'd already lost her hair though, and she hated that. She always wore a hat. When mine fell out she finally stopped being embarrassed. Then we just sat around like two baldies, and we didn't care.'

'Losing your hair has to be hard.'

'Well, it's probably worse for girls. Emma showed me some old pictures, and she had long blond hair.'

'Did you ever get to spend time together when you weren't having chemo?'

'Yeah. She knew her way around the hospital. The nurses always looked the other way when they caught us making out somewhere. We went up to the rooftop garden at the hospital, and sat in the sun. I wanted to take her out, but her immune system couldn't handle being in a crowd. One night the nurses let us watch a video in an empty room. We got in the bed together and they brought us popcorn.'

'How sick was she?'

'She was doing okay when we first met, but after about

six months, she got a lot sicker. One night on the phone, she told me she'd made a list of things she wanted to do, and she told me she thought she might be running out of time.'

'Oh, T.J.'

'She'd turned fifteen by then, but she wanted to make it to sixteen so she could get her driver's license. She wanted to go to prom, but she said any school dance would do.' I hesitated, but lying in the dark next to Anna made it easier to talk about things. 'She told me she wanted to have sex, so she could know what it felt like. Her doctor had put her back in the hospital by then and she had a private room. I think the nurses knew, maybe she told them, but they left us alone and we managed to check one thing off that list. She died three weeks later.'

'That's so sad, T.J.' Anna sounded like she was trying not to cry. 'Were you in love with her?'

'I don't know. I cared about her a lot, but it was such a weird time. My chemo stopped working, and I had to start radiation. It scared me when she died. Wouldn't I know if I loved her, Anna?'

'Yes,' she whispered.

I hadn't thought about Emma in a while. I'd never forget her though; it had been my first time, too.

'What did you decide about that guy, Anna?'

She didn't answer. Maybe she didn't want to tell me, or maybe she'd already fallen asleep. I listened to the waves crashing into the reef, the sound relaxing me, and I closed my eyes and didn't open them until the sun woke me up the next morning.

Chapter 19
Anna

'Do you want to play poker?' T.J. asked.

'Sure, but I left the cards down by the water.'

'I'll go get them,' he said.

'That's okay. I have to go to the bathroom. I'll grab them on my way back.' I hated going anywhere near the woods after dark, and I had about two minutes before the sun went down.

I had just grabbed the cards when it happened. I never saw it coming, and it must have swooped out of the sky with some speed behind it, because when the bat collided with my head, it almost knocked me off my feet. It took me a second to figure out what hit me, and then I started screaming. I panicked, my hands raking through my hair to get the bat out.

T.J. ran to me. 'What's wrong?' Before I could answer him, the bat sank its teeth into my hand. I screamed louder. 'There's a bat in my hair,' I said, as stinging pain radiated across my palm. 'It's biting me!'

T.J. sprinted off. I shook my head back and forth, trying to dislodge the bat. When he returned, he pushed me down onto the sand until I was flat on the ground.

'Don't move,' he said, cupping his hand around my head. Then he drove the blade of the knife through the bat's body. It stopped wiggling. 'Just hold on. I'm going to get it out of your hair.'

'Is it dead?' I asked.

'Yes.'

I lay still. My heart raced, and I wanted to freak out, but I forced myself to remain calm while T.J. untangled the bat from my hair.

'It's out.'

We couldn't see it very well in the sliver of moonlight, so T.J. went back to the fire and grabbed a burning log. He bent down and held it over the bat's body.

It was disgusting, light brown with big black wings, pointy ears, and jagged teeth. Its body was covered with open sores. The fur around its mouth looked wet and slimy.

'Come on,' T.J. said. 'Let's get the first-aid kit.'

We walked back to the lean-to and sat down by the fire.

'Give me your hand.'

He cleaned the bite with the alcohol wipes, dabbed on antibiotic cream, and covered it with a band-aid. My hand throbbed.

'Does it hurt?'

'Yes.'

I could handle the pain, but the thought of what might be incubating in my bloodstream terrified me.

T.J. must have been thinking about it too, because before we went to bed he stuck the blade of the knife in the fire and left it there all night.

Chapter 20
T.J.

Anna was awake and sitting by the fire when I got back from fishing the next morning.

'How's your hand?'

She held out her palm, and I peeled back the band-aid.

'It doesn't look too bad,' I said. 'The jagged wound seeped blood, and her hand had swollen a little overnight. 'I'll clean it again, and put another band-aid on it, okay?'

'Okay.'

I swiped another alcohol pad across the bite. 'You look tired,' I said, noticing the dark circles under her eyes.

'I didn't sleep very well.'

'Do you want to go back to bed?'

She shook her head. 'I'll nap later.'

I put a fresh band-aid on her hand. 'There. You're good as new.'

She must not have heard me though, because she stared off into space and didn't say anything.

Later that morning, I finished framing the house and began putting up the walls. The breadfruit trees gave off a milky sap, and I patched the cracks with it.

Anna worked silently beside me, holding boards or handing me nails.

'You're quiet,' I said.

'Yeah.'

I pounded a nail into the board, securing it into the frame and said, 'You're worrying about the bite?'

She nodded. 'That bat looked sick, T.J.'

I put down the hammer and wiped the sweat out of my eyes. 'It didn't look good,' I admitted.

'Do you think it had rabies?'

I positioned the next board and picked up the hammer. 'No, I'm sure it didn't.' I knew bats sometimes carried the disease, though.

Anna took a deep breath. 'I'll have to wait it out, I guess. If I don't get sick within a month, I'm probably okay.'

'What are the symptoms?'

'I don't know. Fever, maybe? Convulsions? The disease attacks the central nervous system.'

That scared the shit out of me. 'What do I do if you get sick?' I tried to remember what was in the first-aid kit.

Anna shook her head. 'You don't do anything, T.J.'

'Why not?'

'Because without rabies shots the disease is fatal.'

I couldn't breathe for a second, like the wind had been knocked out of me. 'I didn't know that.'

She nodded, tears filling her eyes. I dropped my hammer and put my hands on her shoulders. 'Don't worry,' I said. 'You're going to be okay.'

I had no idea if she would, but I needed both of us to believe it.

I counted forward five weeks and circled the date in Anna's datebook. She wanted to wait longer than a month, just to be sure.

'So if nothing happens by then,' I said, 'and you don't have any symptoms, you're okay, right?'

'I think so.'

I closed the datebook and put it back in Anna's suitcase.

'Let's just get back to our regular routine,' she said. 'I don't want to dwell on it.'

'Sure, whatever helps.'

She should have been an actress instead of a teacher. By day, she put on quite a show, smiling like nothing bothered her. She kept busy, spending hours playing with the dolphins or helping me with the house. But she wasn't eating, and she was so restless in bed I knew she was having trouble sleeping.

I woke up when she crawled out of the life raft one night two weeks later. She always got up at least once to throw wood on the fire, but she usually came right back. She didn't this time, so I went to check on her. I found her in the lean-to, staring at the flames.

'Hey,' I said, sitting down next to her. 'What's wrong?'

'I can't sleep.' Anna poked at the fire with a stick.

'Do you feel okay?' I tried not to sound anxious. 'You're not running a fever, are you?'

She shook her head. 'No. I'm fine, really. Go back to bed.'

'I can't fall back to sleep unless you're beside me.'

She looked surprised. 'You can't?'

'No. I don't like it when you're out here alone. It makes me nervous. You don't have to put wood on the fire every night. I told you it's no big deal for me to make one in the morning.'

'It's just a habit.' She stood up. 'Come on. At least one of us should be able to sleep.'

I followed Anna into the life raft and after we lay down, she covered us with the blanket. She wore shorts and my T-shirt, and as she settled into a comfortable position, her bare leg brushed mine. She didn't pull it away when she stopped moving, and neither did I.

We lay in the dark, legs touching, and neither of us slept for a long time.

She agreed to stop getting up in the middle of the night and one morning a couple weeks later, after I built the fire, I said, 'Anna, I wish you could time me. I bet I made this in less than five minutes.'

'Well, now you're just showing off.'

She laughed when she said it though, and as we got closer to the date I circled in the datebook, she seemed to relax a little.

When five weeks had passed, I held her open palm in my hand, and traced the scar left behind with my thumb. 'I think you're going to be just fine,' I said. And this time, I really meant it.

She smiled at me. 'I think so, too.'

She polished off three fish for lunch that day.

'Are you still hungry? I can catch more.'

'No thanks. I was starving, but I'm full now.'

We swam for a long time and we worked on the house until dinnertime. Again, she ate more than she'd eaten in weeks. At bedtime, she could hardly hold her eyes open, and she fell asleep seconds after I lay down next to her. I fell asleep too, but I woke up when Anna curled up next to me and rested her head on my shoulder.

I put my arm around her and pulled her closer.

If she had gotten sick, the only thing I could have done was watch her suffer. Bury her next to Mick when she died. I didn't know if I could make it without her. The sound of her voice, her smile, *her* – those were the things that made living on the island bearable. I held her a little tighter and thought if she woke up I might tell her that. She didn't though. She sighed in her sleep, and eventually I drifted off.

She had moved back to her side of the bed by the time I woke up the next morning. I was building a fire when she climbed out of the life raft.

She smiled at me, stretching her arms over her head. 'I had a great night's sleep. The best I've had in a long time.'

'I slept pretty good too, Anna.'

A few nights later, we were lying in bed debating our favorite top ten classic rock albums of all time.

'The Rolling Stones' *Sticky Fingers* is my number one. I'm knocking *Led Zeppelin IV* back to the fifth spot,' she said.

'Are you high?' As I started listing the reasons why I disagreed – everyone knew Pink Floyd's *The Wall* should be number one – I farted. The breadfruit had that effect on me sometimes.

She shrieked and immediately tried to escape through the door of the life raft, but I grabbed her around her waist, yanked her backward, and pulled the blanket tight over her head.

It was a little game I liked to play with her.

'Oh no, Anna, oh my God, you better get out from under there,' I teased, laughing. 'It must smell horrible.'

She struggled to free herself, and I held the blanket down even tighter.

When I finally let her out, she made gagging noises and said, 'I'm gonna kick your ass, Callahan.'

'Really? You and what army?' She probably weighed about a hundred pounds. We both knew she wasn't kicking anyone's ass.

'Don't get too cocky. One of these days, I'll figure out a way to take you down.'

I laughed and said, 'Oooh, I'm scared, Anna.'

What I didn't admit, though, was that she could have brought me to my knees with one touch of her hand, if she put it in the right place.

I wondered if she knew that.

'I'm going to take a bath,' Anna said, when I got back from the beach. She gathered the soap and shampoo and her clothes.

'Okay.'

After she left, I noticed we were running low on firewood. I took my backpack and shoved all the sticks I could find inside it. The sun dipped lower in the sky and the mosquitoes buzzed around me. I walked away from the thick canopy of leaves, not paying attention.

I stepped out of the trees and looked up in time to see Anna walking into the ocean, naked.

I froze.

I knew I should go, just get the hell out of there, but I couldn't. I ducked behind a tree and watched her.

She dipped below the water to get her hair wet, then turned around and walked back out. She looked incredible, and her tan lines framed the parts of her body I liked the most. I slid my hand inside my shorts.

She stood on the beach and washed her hair, then waded in to rinse the shampoo. She walked back out, rubbed the soap between her hands, and washed her body. After sitting down on the sand, she shaved her legs and then went into the water one more time to rinse.

What she did next blew my mind.

When she came out, she looked around and then sat down facing the shore. She had brought the baby oil, and she poured some in the palm of her hand and put her hand between her legs.

Oh, Jesus Christ.

She lay back with one leg straight and one leg bent at the knee. I watched her touch herself, my own hand moving a little faster.

Though I did it almost every day, when I was alone in the woods, it never occurred to me that she might be doing it, too. I kept watching, and after a few minutes she straightened out her bent leg and arched her back. I knew she was coming and so was I.

She stood up, brushed the sand off, and stepped into her underwear. She pulled on the rest of her clothes and gathered her things. When she turned to leave she stopped suddenly and looked in my direction. Hidden behind the tree, I didn't move, waiting for her to walk away. Then I fled, sprinting through the trees, away from the beach.

'Oh, hey,' I said when I walked up. She was standing next to the lean-to brushing her teeth.

She took the toothbrush out of her mouth and looked at me, tilting her head to the side. 'Where were you?'

'Getting wood.' I unzipped my backpack and dumped the sticks onto the woodpile.

'Oh.' She finished brushing her teeth and yawned. 'I'm going to bed.'

'I'll be in soon.'

Later, as she slept beside me, I replayed the images of her naked body and her touching herself in my head like a movie I could watch as many times as I wanted. I wished I could kiss her, touch her, do whatever I wanted to her, but I couldn't. The movie played in my head, over and over, and I didn't get any sleep that night.

Chapter 21
Anna

T.J. climbed onto the roof of the house and spread a layer of breadfruit sap over the palm fronds. 'I don't know if this will keep us dry. I guess we'll find out when it rains.'

The house was nearing completion. I sat cross-legged on the ground, watching as he jumped off the roof, grabbed the hammer, and drove in the last few nails.

He had pulled his hair back in a ponytail, and he wore my cowboy hat and aviator sunglasses. His face was so tan he looked like he'd been born on the island. He had a great smile, with straight white teeth, prominent cheekbones, and a solid square jaw. I needed to shave him again.

'You look good, T.J. Very healthy.' He was lean, but he had well-defined muscles, probably from building our house by hand, and he didn't show any outward signs of malnutrition, at least not yet.

'Really?'

'Yes. I'm not sure how, but you've grown here.'

'Do I look older?'

'You do.'

'Am I good-looking, Anna?' He knelt down in front of me and grinned. 'Come on, you can tell me.'

I rolled my eyes. 'Yes, T.J.,' I said, smiling at him. 'You're very good-looking. If we ever get off this island you'll be quite popular with the ladies.'

He pumped his fist in the air. 'Yes.' Then he put down

the hammer and took a drink of water. 'I can't remember what I looked like before the crash, can you?'

'Sort of. But I probably haven't changed as much.'

T.J. sat down in front of me. 'God, I'm sore. Will you please rub my back?'

'Sure.' I massaged his shoulders, which were considerably broader than they were two years ago. His chest was wider too, and his arms were solid. I lifted his ponytail, kneading the back of his neck.

'That feels good.'

I gave him an extra-long massage and near the end he said, 'You're still beautiful, Anna. In case you were wondering.'

My face got hot, but I smiled. 'I wasn't, T.J. But thanks.'

Two nights later, we slept in our new house for the first time. We had decided on one large room, instead of two, which gave us plenty of space. I could dress inside the house, instead of wiggling into my clothes in the life raft. My suitcase and the toolbox sat in the corner, and the guitar case next to it held our first-aid kit, knife, and rope.

T.J. had removed the life-raft canopy – we had a real roof now – and made windows out of the mesh roll-down doors, which let in light and air. He used the nylon sides for shades that we closed at night. He nailed the tarp to the front of the house, stretched it out, and attached it to tall sticks he drove into the ground, then dug a fire pit underneath.

'I'm proud of you, T.J. Bones would be, too.'

'Thanks, Anna.'

We'd come a long way since our days of sleeping on the ground. Just a couple of castaways playing house.

A seaplane landed in the lagoon while T.J. and I swam. The pilot opened the door, stuck his head out, and said, 'We finally found you. We've been looking forever.'

I was fifty-two years old.

I woke up, drenched in sweat and stifling a scream, seconds before it flew out of my mouth.

T.J.'s side of the bed was empty. He'd been spending a lot of time in the woods lately, gathering firewood in the morning and again in the afternoon.

I dressed, brushed my teeth, and walked to the coconut tree. While I gathered them, one fell off a branch and almost hit me on the head. Startled, I jumped and yelled, 'Dammit.'

When I returned to the house, I checked the water collector. It was February, the middle of the dry season, and there wasn't much. I dropped it and burst into tears when the water spilled on the ground.

T.J. walked up with his backpack full of firewood. 'Hey,' he said, putting down his backpack. 'What's wrong?'

I wiped my eyes with the back of my hand. 'Nothing, I'm just tired and mad at myself. I spilled the water.' Then I started crying again.

'It's okay. It'll probably rain again later.'

'It might not. It barely rained yesterday.' I flopped down on the ground, feeling stupid.

He sat beside me. 'Um, is this like PMS or something?'

I squeezed my eyes shut, willing the tears to stop. 'No. I'm just having a bad morning.'

'Go back to bed,' he said. 'I'll come get you when I'm done fishing, okay?'

'Okay.'

I woke up when T.J. rubbed my arm. 'The fish are ready,' he said, stretching out next to me.

'Why didn't you wake me so I could clean them?'

'I thought you'd feel better if you slept a little longer.'

'Thanks. I do.'

'I'm sorry I asked if you had PMS. I don't really know anything about that.'

'No, it was a fair question.' I hesitated. 'I don't get my period anymore. I haven't for a long time.' I still had tampons in my suitcase.

T.J. looked confused. 'Why?'

'I don't know. I'm underweight. Stress. Malnutrition. Take your pick.'

'Oh,' he said.

We lay on our sides, facing each other. 'I had a bad dream this morning. A seaplane landed in the lagoon while we were swimming.'

'That sounds like a good dream.'

'I was fifty-two when they found us.'

'Then we were missing a really long time. Is that why you were so upset?'

'I want to have a baby.'

'You do?'

'Yes. Two or three, actually. That was another thing John didn't want. If they don't find us until I'm fifty-two, it'll be too late. Forty-two might be cutting it close. I can always adopt, but I really wanted to give birth to at least one.' I picked at a thread on the blanket. 'It's stupid, thinking about a baby when there are so many others things to worry about here. And I know having kids isn't on your radar yet, but I really want them someday.'

'I have thought about kids. I'm sterile.'

His words were so unexpected I didn't know what to say at first. 'Because of the cancer?'

'Yep. I had a shitload of chemo.'

'Oh God T.J., I'm sorry. I wasn't thinking.' Nothing like going on about having kids in front of someone whose fertility had been exchanged for survival.

'It's okay. The doctor talked to me before chemo started. He explained that if I ever wanted to have kids someday, I had to bank sperm immediately because once I started the treatment it would be too late. I decided I wanted the option to have them.'

'Wow. That's not a decision most boys have to make when they're fifteen.'

'No, we're pretty much thinking about *not* getting anyone pregnant. This next part might cheer you up. So my mom told me she was gonna drive me to my appointment at the sperm bank, and she handed me one of my dad's *Playboys* – I had something way dirtier stashed in my closet, by the way – and she asked me, all serious, if I knew what to do.'

'You've got to be kidding.'

'No, I'm not.' He started laughing. 'I was fifteen, Anna. I was an expert at it, and I did not want to talk about jacking off *with my mom*.'

'Oh my God, I'm dying here,' I said, laughing so hard tears ran down my face.

'Yeah, the next time I had to bank sperm my dad drove me.'

I wiped my eyes as one last giggle escaped. 'Do you want to know what your very best quality is?'

'Is it that I'm so good-looking?' he deadpanned.

I started laughing again. 'I see the compliment I paid you went straight to your head. No, that's not it. I want you to know that it's almost impossible not to be happy when you're around.'

'Really? Thanks.' He patted my arm. 'Don't worry, Anna. They'll find us someday and you'll have that baby.'

'I hope so.'

Tick tock, you know.

Chapter 22
T.J.

I was in the woods when Anna screamed. It came from the direction of the house, and when I cleared the trees I ran toward the sound.

She staggered up and collapsed on the ground. Gasping, she said, 'Jellyfish.'

The outline of its tentacles had left red welts on her legs, stomach, and chest. I didn't know what to do.

'Get them off me,' she yelled. When I looked down, I saw a few clear tentacles still attached to her stomach and chest. I pulled on one, and it stung me.

I ran to the water collector and grabbed the plastic container on the ground next to it. I filled it, ran back to Anna, and doused her with the fresh water. The tentacles didn't rinse off and she screamed in pain, as if the fresh water made it worse.

'T.J., try seawater,' she said. 'Hurry!'

Still holding the container, I ran down to the shore and filled it with water from the ocean. I sprinted back and this time, when I poured seawater on her, she didn't scream.

She whimpered on the ground while I tried to figure out what to do next. I knew she still felt pain by the way she moved back and forth, struggling to find a comfortable position.

I remembered the tweezers and hurried to Anna's

suitcase to get them. When I returned, I pulled off the tentacles as fast as I could. She closed her eyes and moaned.

I had removed almost all of them when Anna's skin started turning red, not only where she had been stung, but all over. Her eyelids and lips puffed up. I panicked and poured more seawater on her, but it didn't help. Her eyes swelled shut.

I ran into the lean-to and found the first-aid kit, then flung myself back down on the sand next to her, opening the lid and dumping everything out. When I picked up the bottle with red liquid inside, I heard her voice in my head.

This can save your life. It'll stop an allergic reaction.

Anna's face resembled a balloon by then and her lips were so swollen the skin had split. I struggled with the childproof cap, but once I got it off I put my arm under her, lifted her head up, and poured the Benadryl down her throat. She coughed and sputtered; I had no idea how much I'd given her.

Her bikini top shifted when I lifted her. It was too big on her, since she'd lost weight, and when I looked down I saw a few tentacles inside it, still stinging her.

I yanked her top off, wincing at the marks on her chest. I laid her back down, poured the last of the seawater on her, and removed the tentacles with the tweezers.

I took off my T-shirt and covered her with it, tucking it gently underneath her. 'You'll be okay, Anna.' Then I held her hand and waited.

When her skin wasn't as red and the swelling had gone down a little, I looked through the contents of the first-aid kit scattered on the ground. After reading all the labels, I chose a tube of cortisone cream.

I started with her legs and worked my way up, rubbing the cream onto the welts. 'Does this help?'

'Yes,' she whispered. Her eyes weren't swollen shut anymore, but she didn't open them. 'I'm so tired.'

I didn't know if I should let her fall asleep, afraid I'd accidentally overdosed her. When I checked the bottle of Benadryl, there was still a lot left, and the label said it would cause drowsiness. 'It's okay, go to sleep.' She passed out before I finished speaking.

I rubbed the cream on her stomach, but when I got to her chest I hesitated. I didn't think she realized I took her top off, or maybe she didn't care.

I lifted my T-shirt off her chest and cringed.

Her boobs were a mess. Raised welts covered her skin, some of them already crusting over with dried blood.

I stayed focused, thinking only about helping her, and I applied the cream carefully with my fingertips. When I finished, I checked her over to see if I'd missed any welts.

Her skin color was back to normal and the swelling had disappeared. I waited a bit longer, and then I picked her up and carried her to the life raft.

Chapter 23
Anna

I opened my eyes and sighed in relief at the absence of burning, stinging pain. T.J. slept beside me, his breathing deep and steady. Naked from the waist up, something soft covered my chest like a blanket. I sat up and slipped the T-shirt over my head, inhaling the familiar smell of T.J. I rolled over on my side and slept again.

In the morning, I woke up alone. I pulled the hem of my T-shirt up. The faint red outline of the tentacles remained and probably would for quite some time. Raising it higher, I cringed at the condition of my breasts. Dark red streaks covered them, crusted and bloody. I let the T-shirt fall, stepped into shorts, and left the house to go to the bathroom.

T.J. was making a fire when I returned.

He stood up. 'How do you feel?'

'Almost back to normal.' I lifted my T-shirt a little and showed him my stomach. He traced the marks with his finger.

'Does it hurt?'

'No, not really.'

'What about?' He pointed at my chest.

'Not as good.'

'I'm sorry. There were some tentacles inside your top, stinging you, and I didn't notice right away.'

I had no recollection of him taking off my top, only the burning pain. 'That's okay, you didn't know.'

'You turned red and swelled up.'

'I did?' I didn't remember that either.

'I gave you Benadryl. It knocked you out.'

'You did exactly the right thing.'

He walked into the house and returned with the tube of cortisone cream. 'I rubbed this on your skin. It seemed to help. You told me it did before you fell asleep.'

I took the tube from his outstretched hand. Had he rubbed it on my breasts, too? I pictured myself lying on the sand, wearing only the bottom half of my swimsuit while T.J. rubbed the cream onto my skin, and suddenly I couldn't look at him.

'Thanks,' I said.

'Did you see the jellyfish before it stung you?'

'No, I just felt the pain.'

'I've never seen one in the lagoon.'

'Me neither. That one must have taken a wrong turn at the reef.' I walked into the house to get my toothbrush, squeezing a miniscule amount of toothpaste onto it. When I came out, I said, 'At least it wasn't one of the deadly ones.'

T.J. looked at me with an alarmed expression. 'Jellyfish can kill you?'

I pulled the toothbrush out of my mouth. 'Some of them.'

We stayed out of the water that day. I walked along the shore, squinting into the distance and checking for jelly-fish, reminding myself that just because we couldn't see the dangers of the ocean didn't mean they weren't there. I also wondered if the first-aid kit would someday cease to contain the one thing we needed to save either of our lives.

In June of 2003, T.J. and I had been living on the island for two years. I had turned thirty-two in May, and T.J. would be nineteen in a few months. He stood at least six-two by then, and there was nothing boyish about him. Sometimes, when I watched him fish, repair the house, or emerge from the woods that he knew like the back of his hand, I wondered if he thought of the island as his own. A place where he could do whatever he wanted and anything was acceptable, as long as we stayed alive.

We sat cross-legged, facing each other near the water's edge so I could shave him. He leaned forward, resting his hands on my thighs for balance.

'How did I become your personal groomer?' I teased. 'I've bathed you. I shave you.' I spread the shaving cream, which was almost gone, on his cheeks.

He gave me a big smile. 'I'm lucky?'

'You're spoiled. When we get off this island, you're going to have to shave yourself.'

'That won't be any fun at all.'

'You'll manage.'

I finished shaving him and we walked back to the house, ready for a nap under the awning.

'You know, I would be happy to give you a bath or shave you, Anna. Just say the word.'

I laughed. 'I'm fine, really.'

'Are you sure?' He was lying on the blanket beside me

and he reached over and pulled my arm up, then ran the back of his hand along my underarm. 'Wow, you are smooth.'

'Stop! I'm very ticklish.' I swatted his hand away.

'What about your legs?' he asked, and before I could answer, he leaned toward me and ran a hand slowly up my leg, from ankle to thigh.

The heat that flooded my body took me by surprise. I made a noise, a cross between a gasp and a moan, and it slipped out before I could stop it. T.J.'s eyes widened and he stared at me with his mouth hanging open. Then he smirked, clearly pleased with the effect his touch had on me.

I took a deep breath and said, 'I can handle my own grooming.'

'I'm just trying to pay you back for helping me out all the time.'

'That's very nice of you, T.J. Go to sleep.' He laughed and turned on his side, facing away from me. I lay on my back and closed my eyes.

He's only eighteen. That's too young.

A voice in my head said, *technically it's old enough.*

A few days later, in the afternoon, T.J. and I swam with the dolphins. There were four of them, and we watched as they frolicked around us. I wanted to name them, but I couldn't tell them apart.

When the dolphins swam away, T.J. and I sat on the shore. I dug my toes into the soft, white sand.

'Didn't you say you were going to take a bath?' he asked.

'Yes. I didn't bring anything with me though.' Our supplies were dwindling fast. We only washed with soap once a week now. I no longer noticed the way we smelled.

'I'll get everything for you,' he said.

'You will?'

'Sure.'

'Okay, but I need clothes, too.'

'No problem.'

He brought it all down and left it on the sand. I waited until he walked away and then got undressed.

When I finished bathing, I stood for a minute drying in the sun. I walked over to the pile of clothes, expecting to find a tank top and shorts, or a bikini. What he picked out surprised me. He chose a dress, the only one I'd packed. It was one of my favorites, short and light blue with thin straps. He also selected a lacy, pink pair of bikini underwear, and I felt the heat on my cheeks. He'd forgotten a bra, or maybe he hadn't, but I never wore one with that dress anyway.

I stepped into the underwear and slipped the dress over my head. When I reached the house, T.J. stared openly.

'Do we have dinner reservations I don't know about?' I asked.

'I wish,' he said.

I stopped in front of him. 'Why a dress?'

He shrugged. 'I thought you'd look good in it.' He took his sunglasses off and looked me up and down. 'And you do.'

'Thanks,' I said, feeling the heat on my cheeks again.

He left to go fishing, and I sat on the blanket under the awning waiting for him to come back.

I often caught T.J. staring at me, but he'd never been so blatant about it. He was getting bolder, testing the waters. If he had been trying to hide his feelings before, he wasn't as concerned with that now. I didn't know of his intentions, or even if he had any, but living with him was about to get complicated.

That much I knew.

'I wish we had scissors.' I was sitting on the blanket outside the house a week later, trying to brush the knots out of my hair. It hung almost to my butt and drove me nuts. 'I should have had you hack off some of my hair before the knife got so dull,' I said.

I glanced over at the fire.

'You're thinking of burning some of it off, aren't you?' T.J. asked.

I looked at him like he was crazy. 'No.'

Maybe.

I continued brushing.

T.J. walked over and held out his hand. 'Give me the brush. I'll do it. See? I'm paying you back for shaving me.'

I handed him the brush. 'Knock yourself out.'

He leaned back against the outside wall of the house, and I sat in front of him. He started brushing. 'You have a ton of hair,' he said.

'I know. It's way too long.'

'I like long hair.'

T.J. patiently dealt with the tangles, working on one section at a time. The sun beat down, but the awning shaded us. A cool breeze blew off the ocean. The omnipresent sound of the waves crashing into the reef, and the feel of the brush moving gently through my hair lulled me into a state of relaxation.

He lifted my hair off my neck, and then pulled me toward him so that my back rested against his chest. I

137

turned my head, and he pulled my hair to the side, laying it over my right shoulder. He continued brushing and it felt so good that after a while I closed my eyes and fell asleep.

When I woke up, I knew by the sound of T.J.'s breathing that he'd fallen asleep, too. His arms encircled my waist from behind, his clasped hands resting on the bare skin above my bikini bottom. I closed my eyes again, thinking about how nice it felt with T.J.'s arms around me.

He stirred, whispering in my ear, 'Are you awake?'

'Yeah. I had a nice nap.'

'Me, too.'

Though I didn't really want to, I sat up and his hands slid off my stomach. My hair fell in a smooth sheet down my back. I looked over my shoulder and smiled. 'Thanks for brushing my hair.'

His eyes were heavy with sleep and something else. Something that looked unmistakably like desire.

'Anytime.'

My heart rate increased. My stomach filled with butterflies and a warm feeling spread over me.

Thinking that our relationship was about to get complicated might have been an understatement.

Chapter 24
T.J.

I watched Anna walk away after I brushed her hair. I thought about the other day, when she made that sound when I ran my hand up her leg. I wondered what kind of noise she'd make if I did something else with my hand. The urge to slip it inside her bikini bottom and find out had been almost uncontrollable. If we were in Chicago, I wouldn't stand a chance with her. But I was starting to wonder if, here on the island, I might.

Anna and I swam back and forth in the lagoon, waiting for the dolphins. 'I'm bored,' I said.

'Me too,' she said, floating on her back. 'Hey, let's see if we can do that lift like Johnny and Baby.'

'I seriously have no clue what you're talking about.'

'You've never seen *Dirty Dancing*?'

'No.' The title didn't sound half-bad, though.

'It's a great movie. I saw it in high school. 1987, I think.

'I was two years old.'

'Oh. Sometimes I forget how young you are.'

T.J. shook his head. 'I'm not that young.'

'Well anyway, Patrick Swayze played this dance instructor named Johnny Castle at a resort in the Catskills. Jennifer Grey played Baby Houseman, and she was there with her family.' Anna paused for a second and then said, 'Hey, I just thought of something. Baby and her family were spending *their* whole summer vacation away from home, just like you.'

'Was she pissed about it, too?' I asked.

Anna shook her head and laughed. 'I don't think so. She got together with Johnny and they spent *a lot* of time in bed.'

Why have I never seen this movie? It sounds awesome.

'But then Penny, Johnny's dance partner got pregnant, and Baby had to fill in. There was this tricky lift, and Baby couldn't do it at first, so they practiced in the water.'

'And that's what you want to do?' If it meant touching her, I was all for it.

'I've always wanted to try it. It can't be that hard.'

She stood in front of me and said, 'Okay, I'm going to run toward you, and when I jump, put your hands here.' She took my hands and put them on her hips. 'Then lift me straight up over your head. Do you think you can lift me?'

I rolled my eyes at her. 'Of course I can lift you.'

'For some reason, Baby wore pants in the water when she did this, which I never understood. Okay, are you ready?'

I said yes, and Anna ran toward me and jumped. The minute my hands touched her hips, she collapsed on me because she said it tickled. My face ended up in her crotch.

We untangled ourselves and she said, 'Don't tickle me next time.'

I laughed. 'I didn't tickle you. I put my hands where you told me to.'

'Okay, let's do it again.' She backed up to get a running start. 'Here I come.'

This time, when I lifted her, the water was too deep and I couldn't stay on my feet. I fell backward and she landed on top of me, which didn't suck.

'Shit, that was my fault,' I said. 'We need to move into shallower water. Try again.'

This time we did it perfectly. I lifted her up and she stretched out her arms and legs and arched her back.

'We did it,' she yelled.

I held her as long as I could, and then lowered my arms. I had taken a few steps backward beyond a slight drop-off, and as soon as her feet touched the bottom, her head went under. I reached down and lifted her up. She took a breath and put her arms around my neck. A few seconds later, she wrapped her legs around my waist and held on.

She looked surprised, maybe because she didn't expect the water to be over her head, or maybe because I had her ass in my hands.

'I'm not bored at all now, Anna.' In fact, if I moved her a little lower, she'd feel exactly how not bored I was getting.

'Good.' She still had her arms and legs wrapped around me, and I was thinking about kissing her when she said, 'We have company.'

I looked behind me as four dolphins swam into the lagoon, poking us with their snouts and begging us to play with them. Disappointed, I moved into shallower water and set her down, making sure she had her footing on the ocean floor.

I liked playing with the dolphins, but I liked playing with Anna a whole lot more.

Chapter 25
Anna

We sat under the awning playing poker, watching the storm roll in. Lightning zigzagged across the sky, and the humid air pressed down on me like a blanket. The wind picked up and scattered our cards.

'We better go in,' T.J. said.

Once inside, I stretched out beside him in the life raft and watched the interior of the house light up with each lightning strike.

'We won't get much sleep tonight,' I said.

'Probably not.'

We lay next to each other, listening to the rain beat against the house. Only a few seconds separated the crash of thunder.

'There's never been so much lightning before,' I said. Even more unsettling, the hair on my arms and the back of my neck stood on end from the electrically-charged air. I told myself the storm would end soon, but as the hours passed, it only intensified.

When the walls started shaking, T.J. climbed out of the life raft and reached into my suitcase. He turned around and threw my jeans at me. 'Put these on.' He grabbed his own jeans and stepped into them. Then he shoved the fishing pole into the guitar case.

'Why?'

'Because I don't think we can ride this out here.'

I got out of bed and pulled my jeans on over my shorts. 'Where else would we go?' As soon as I asked, I knew. 'No! There's no way I'm going in there. We've made it through other storms okay. We can stay here.'

T.J. grabbed his backpack and stuffed the knife, rope, and first-aid kit inside. He tossed me my tennis shoes and jammed his feet into his Nikes without untying the laces first. 'There's never been one this bad,' he said. 'And you know it.'

I opened my mouth to argue with him, and the roof blew off.

T.J. knew he had won. 'Let's go,' he said, barely audible over the howling wind. He slipped his arms through the backpack and handed me the guitar case. 'You'll have to carry this.' He picked up the toolbox in one hand and my suitcase in the other, and we hurried through the woods to the cave. The rain pelted us and the wind blew so violently, I thought it might knock me off my feet.

I hesitated at the entrance of the cave.

'Get in, Anna,' he yelled.

I bent down, trying to work up the courage to crawl inside. The sudden cracking of a tree branch sounded like a gunshot, and T.J. put his hand on my butt and shoved. He pushed the guitar case, toolbox, and suitcase in after me, and followed behind right before the tree fell, blocking the entrance to the cave and plunging us into darkness.

I collided with Bones like a bowling ball into ten pins. The skeleton scattered across the floor of the cave, and a few seconds later, T.J. landed in a heap beside me.

The two of us — and everything we owned — barely fit in the small space. We had to lay flat on our backs, shoulder to shoulder, and if I stretched my arm out, I could have touched the cave wall, inches to my right; T.J. could have done the same on his left. The cave smelled like dirt, decaying plants, and animals I hoped weren't bats. Grateful to be wearing jeans, I crossed my feet at the ankles to prevent anything from crawling up my pant legs. The ceiling was less than two feet above our heads. It was like being in a coffin with the lid closed, and I panicked, heartbeat thundering, gasping, feeling like I couldn't get enough air.

'Try not to breathe so fast,' T.J. said. 'As soon as it stops, we're out of here.'

I closed my eyes and concentrated on inhaling and exhaling. *Just block everything out. Leaving the cave now is not an option.*

T.J. took my hand and laced his fingers through mine, squeezing gently. I squeezed back, holding onto his hand like a lifeline.

'Don't let go,' I whispered.

'I wasn't going to.'

We stayed in the cave for hours, listening as the storm raged outside. When it finally stopped, T.J. shoved the tree branches away from the entrance. The sun was up and we crawled out, gazing in shock at the devastation.

The storm toppled so many trees it was like picking our way through a maze to get back to the beach. When we finally made it out of the woods, we both stared.

The house was gone.

T.J. looked at the ground where it once stood. I hugged him and said, 'I'm sorry.' He didn't respond, but he put his arms around me and we stayed like that for a long time.

We scoured the area and found the life raft shoved against a tree. We checked it carefully for holes, and I listened for the hiss of escaping air, but didn't hear anything. The water collector floated in the ocean several yards offshore, and the tarp and roof canopy lay tangled amid the piles of wood that were once our home.

The seat cushions, life jackets, and blanket were scattered across the sand. We left them to dry in the sun. We attached the roof canopy to the life raft, but T.J. had cut away the nylon sides and the roll-down door to use on the house. The canopy would shield us from rain but we no longer had any protection from the mosquitoes.

We spent the rest of the day constructing another lean-to and gathering firewood, piling it inside so it could dry. T.J. went fishing, and I collected coconut and breadfruit.

Later, we sat by the fire eating fish, barely keeping our eyes open. Thankfully, the life raft continued to hold air and when the sun went down T.J. and I went to bed. I fell asleep instantly, my head resting on my slightly damp seat cushion.

I swam back and forth in the lagoon. T.J. was working on rebuilding the house, but he promised to join me as soon as he finished nailing a few more boards.

His desire to get a roof over our heads again consumed him, and in the six weeks since the storm, he'd made remarkable progress. He'd finished the framing and shifted his focus to putting up the walls. Having already built the house once his pace was faster this time around, and he would have worked around the clock if I didn't convince him to take a break.

I was treading water when he appeared on the beach. Suddenly, he ran toward the shore, yelling and motioning for me to get out. I couldn't figure out why he was so upset, so I turned around.

I spotted the fin seconds before it disappeared below the surface. I knew by the size and shape of it that it wasn't a dolphin.

T.J. ran into the water yelling, 'Swim Anna, swim!'

Afraid to look over my shoulder, I swam faster than I thought possible. I still couldn't touch the ocean floor, but T.J. reached me, yanked me by the arm, and pulled me to shallower water. I found my footing, and we ran.

I shook all over. T.J. grabbed me by my shoulders and said, 'You're okay.'

'How long do you think that's been swimming around in our lagoon?' I asked.

T.J. scanned the turquoise water. 'I don't know.'

'What kind do you think it was?'

'Reef maybe?'

'You can't go fishing, T.J.' He often stood in waist deep water, since our fishing line wasn't very long.

'I'd get out if I saw the fin.'

'Unless you didn't see it.'

We spent the next few days by the shore, watching for the shark. The surface of the lagoon remained unbroken, and the water stayed calm and still. The dolphins came, but I wouldn't go in. We took turns bathing, but we agreed to stay near the shore, only going in a few feet to rinse ourselves.

A full week passed without either of us seeing the shark. We thought it had gone away for good, that its appearance in the lagoon had been an anomaly, like the jellyfish.

T.J. started fishing again.

A few days later, I sat near the shore shaving my legs. T.J. walked up with the fish he'd caught, watching as I dragged the razor slowly up my leg, nicking my knee and drawing blood. He winced.

'The blade is dull,' I explained.

He sat down next to me. 'You can't go near the water right now, Anna.' And that's how I knew the shark was back.

He told me he had just pulled the last fish in when he spotted it. 'It swam back and forth parallel to the shore, with just the tip of its fin sticking out of the water. It looked like it was hunting.'

'Don't fish anymore, T.J. Please.'

There were days I could hardly choke down the fish that made up the bulk of our diet. We checked the shore daily for crab, hoping for a little variety, but we almost never found them and neither of us could figure out why. The breadfruit and coconut would sustain us, but I realized how hungry we would be as long as the shark lurked in the lagoon.

Another two weeks passed without either of us seeing it. I still wouldn't go near the water, except to bathe and then only up to my knees. Our stomachs growled constantly. T.J. wanted to fish, but I begged him not to.

I pictured the shark, waiting patiently for one of us to venture in too far. T.J. believed the shark had moved on, that it had finally decided there was nothing in the lagoon it wanted. Our conflicting theories caused more than one disagreement between us.

I had long since abandoned the notion that I held any kind of rank over T.J. I may have been older and had more life experience, but that didn't matter on the island. We took each day as it came, addressing and solving problems together. But placing yourself in the natural habitat of an animal that could eat you struck me as the epitome of stupid, and I told T.J. so which is probably why, when I saw him fishing near dinnertime two days later, in waist deep water, I went ballistic.

I waved my arms back and forth to get his attention, jumping up and down on the sand. 'Get out right now!'

He took his time getting out of the water, walked up to me, and said, 'What is your deal?'

'What do you think you're doing?'

'I'm fishing. I'm hungry, and so are you.'

'Hungry is not dead T.J., and you are not invincible!' I poked him hard in the chest after each word, and he grabbed my hand to stop me from poking him again.

'Jesus Christ, calm down!'

'You told me not to go in the water the other day and now you're standing in it up to your waist like it's no big deal.'

'You were bleeding, Anna! And you wouldn't go near the water now if I begged you to, so don't act like you need my permission,' he yelled.

'Why are you so determined to put yourself in danger, even after I asked you not to?'

'Because whether or not I get in the water is *my* decision, Anna, not yours.'

'Your decisions have a direct effect on me, T.J., so I think I have every right to weigh in when those decisions are asinine!' Tears sprang to my eyes, and my lip quivered. I turned my back on him and stomped away. He didn't follow.

T.J. had finished rebuilding the house the week before. I walked in the door and lay down in the life raft. When I was done crying, I took deep, calming breaths, and I must have dozed because when I opened my eyes, T.J. was lying on his back beside me, awake.

'I'm sorry,' we both said at the same time.

'Jinx. You owe me a Coke,' I said. 'I want a big one, with extra ice.'

He smiled. 'It's the first thing I'll do when we get off this island.'

I propped myself up on one elbow, facing him. 'I freaked out. I'm just so scared.'

'I really do think the shark is gone.'

'It's not just the shark, T.J.' I took a deep breath. 'I care about you, very much, and I can't bear the thought of you getting hurt, or dying. I can only handle being here because you're with me.'

'You could survive, Anna. You can do everything I can, and you'd be okay.'

'I would not be okay. I'm fine being on my own back home, but not here, T.J. Not on this island.' Tears welled up in my eyes as I imagined the isolation and pain I would feel if T.J. was gone. 'I don't know if you can die of loneliness, but after a while I might want to,' I whispered.

He sat up a little and put his hand on my forearm. 'Don't ever say that.'

'It's true. Don't tell me you've never thought about it.'

He didn't say anything at first, but he wouldn't look directly at me. Finally, he nodded and said, 'After the bat bit you.'

Tears poured from my eyes and ran down my face. T.J. pulled me down onto his chest and held me while I cried, rubbing my back and waiting for me to finish. Neither of us wore much – a pair of shorts for him and a swimsuit for me – and the skin-on-skin contact soothed me in a way I didn't expect. He smelled like the ocean and that was a scent I'd forever associate with him.

I sighed, content in the release that came with a good cry. It had been so long since anyone held me I didn't want to move. Finally, I raised my head. He cupped my face in his hands and wiped my tears with his thumbs.

'Better?'

'Yes.'

He looked into my eyes and said, 'I'll never leave you alone, Anna. Not if I can help it.'

'Then please don't go in the water.'

'Okay.' He wiped a few more tears. 'Don't worry. We'll figure something out. We always do.'

'I'm just so tired, T.J.'

'Then close your eyes.'

He misunderstood me. I meant tired in general, from always having a new problem to solve and constantly worrying about one of us getting sick or hurt. It would be dark soon, though, and it felt so good being in his arms. I put my head back down and shut my eyes.

He tightened his hold on me. One of his hands stroked from my shoulder down to the small of my back, and the other rested on my arm.

'You make me feel safe,' I whispered.

'You are safe.'

I gave in to the pull of sleep and the escape it offered, but seconds before I drifted off completely, I could have sworn T.J.'s lips brushed mine in the sweetest and softest of kisses.

I woke up in his arms just before sunrise, hungry, thirsty, and needing to go to the bathroom. I climbed out of bed, left the house, and walked into the woods, stopping to gather coconuts and breadfruit on my way back. The sky filled with morning light as I brushed my teeth and combed my hair, then prepared our breakfast.

While I waited for him to wake up, I replayed last night's events in my mind. His desire had been palpable, radiating off him like heat from a fire. His breathing had changed, growing louder, and his heart had pounded under my cheek. He'd shown remarkable restraint, and I wondered how long he'd be satisfied with only holding me in his arms.

I wondered how long I would be.

He came out of the house a few minutes later, scraping his hair back into a ponytail.

'Hey.' He sat down beside me and gave my shoulder a squeeze. 'How're you doing this morning?' His knee rested against mine.

'Much better.'

'Did you sleep okay?'

'Yes. Did you?'

He nodded, smiling. 'I slept great, Anna.'

We sat on the shore after breakfast.

'So, I've been thinking,' he said, scratching one of his

mosquito bites. 'What if I take the life raft out into the lagoon to fish?'

His suggestion terrified me. 'No way,' I said, shaking my head back and forth. 'What if the shark bites the raft? Or capsizes it?'

'It's not *Jaws*, Anna. Besides, you said you didn't want me standing in the water.'

'I might have made my feelings clear on that,' I admitted.

'If I fish from the raft, we won't be hungry.'

My stomach growled like Pavlov's dog when he mentioned fish. 'I don't know, T.J. It seems like a bad idea.'

'I won't go out very far. Just deep enough to catch some fish.'

'Fine. But I'm going with you.'

'You don't have to.'

'Of course I do.'

We had to deflate the life raft to get it through the doorway of the house. We re-inflated it with the carbon dioxide canister and carried it down to the beach.

'I changed my mind,' I said. 'This is insane. We should stay on the beach where it's safe.'

T.J. grinned. 'Now what would be the fun in that?'

We paddled the life raft out to the middle of the lagoon. T.J. baited his hook and pulled the fish in one by one, throwing them in a plastic container filled with seawater. I couldn't sit still or stop looking over the side of the raft. T.J. pulled me down beside him.

'You're making me nervous,' he said, putting his arm around me. 'I'll catch a couple more fish, and we'll go back.'

The life raft no longer had the roof canopy attached

and the sun beat down on us. I wore only a bikini, but I was still sweltering in the heat. T.J. was wearing my cowboy hat and he took it off and plunked it down on my head.

'Your nose is turning red,' he said.

'I'm burning up. It's hot out here.'

T.J. reached his hand over the side, scooped up some water, and poured it on my chest, watching as it ran in a lazy trickle down to my bellybutton. My body tingled and my core temperature shot up ten degrees. He started to dip his hand in again, and then stopped abruptly. 'There it is.' He pulled his fishing pole out of the water.

I looked over my shoulder and every muscle in my body tensed. The fin glided through the water twenty yards away, moving toward us. When it got close enough for us to get a good look, I reached instinctively for the paddles and handed one to T.J. We watched the shark circle the raft, neither of us saying anything.

'I want to go back to shore,' I said.

T.J. nodded, and we paddled away, the shark following us into shallow water. When it was only knee high, T.J. jumped out and pulled the raft onto the sand with me still sitting in it. I climbed out.

'What the fuck are we gonna do about that?' he asked.

'I don't know.'

Because really, I had no idea what T.J. and I were going to do about the nine-foot tiger shark living in our lagoon.

We walked back to the house. T.J. made a fire, and I cleaned and cooked our lunch. We ate all the fish, stuffing ourselves after going without them for so long. T.J. started pacing as soon as he finished his last bite.

'I can't believe you were in the water with that thing.' He stopped, turning to look at me. 'You don't have to worry about me standing in the ocean anymore. I'll fish from the raft. I just hope it doesn't decide to take a bite out of it.'

'Here's the problem, T.J. We can't keep re-inflating the life raft every time we take it in, or out, of the house. I don't how much CO_2 we have left. As long as you use the raft for fishing, we'll have to keep it outside. We'll have the canopy overhead, but that's it. No protection from the mosquitoes without the nylon sides.' T.J. already had multiple bites from being in the woods all the time.

'So the shark gets to decide if we eat and where we sleep?'

'Pretty much.'

'That's bullshit. The shark can call the shots in the water, but not on land. We'll have to kill it.'

He's got to be kidding. Taking on a known man-eater didn't seem very realistic, and I thought it might also get us killed. T.J. went into the house and returned with the toolbox. He removed the rope, unraveled it, and separated it into individual strands.

'What are you thinking?' I asked, afraid of what his answer might be.

'If I can bend a few nails, and attach them to this rope, maybe we can hook the shark and pull it out of the water.'

'You want to try and catch it?'

'Yes.'

'From the raft?'

'No, from the beach. If we're on land, we might actually have a chance. We'll have to get the shark into shallow water,' he said.

'Well, we know that's possible. I was surprised how close it got to shore.'

T.J. nodded. Neither of us mentioned that the shark had been perfectly capable of swimming in waist-deep water.

T.J hammered three nails halfway into the side of the house and then used the claw end of the hammer to bend them before pulling them back out. He tied the individual strands of the rope around the head of each nail, making a three-pronged hook.

'I'm not sure what to use for bait,' T.J. said.

'You want to try and catch the shark *today*?'

'I want our lagoon back, Anna.' He had a determined look in his eye, and I figured there was no talking him out of it.

'I know what we need.' I couldn't believe I was about to contribute to this insane plan.

'What?'

'A chicken. If we put it on the hook alive, it'll thrash around and attract the shark.'

He patted me on the back. 'Glad to see you're on board.'

'Reluctantly.' But I agreed with T.J. that we had to try. Despite the shark, and the jellyfish, and the other dangers we probably didn't even know about, the lagoon was ours, and I could understand why T.J. wanted to fight for it. I only hoped we didn't pay for it with our lives.

We had caught and eaten two more chickens since the one we'd found on our first Christmas. We thought there was at least one left, two if we were lucky. We hadn't heard or seen one for a while though. It was like they knew we were picking them off one by one.

We scoured the island and had almost given up when

we heard the flapping. It took another half hour to catch it. I looked away when T.J. put it on the hook.

He waded into chest deep water, threw the chicken as far as he could, and got the hell back out, taking the slack out of the rope so he could feel any change in the tension.

The chicken flapped on the surface, trying to escape. We watched, horrified, as the shark launched itself out of the water and engulfed the chicken in its mouth. T.J. yanked on the rope as hard as he could to set the hook. 'I think it worked, Anna. I can feel it pulling.'

He took several steps backward and dug his heels in, holding the rope with both hands.

Suddenly, the rope jerked and T.J. flew forward, landing face down as the shark swam in the opposite direction from shore. I threw myself onto his back and clawed at the sand, snapping back two of my fingernails. The shark dragged us both as if we weighed nothing at all. When we managed to regain our footing and stand, we were knee deep in the water.

'Get behind me,' T.J. said. He wrapped the rope around his forearm twice. I grabbed onto the end. We took a few steps backward and held our ground. The shark thrashed back and forth, trying to simultaneously eat the chicken and dislodge our hook.

It jerked us forward again. T.J. pulled back on the rope as hard as he could, forearms bulging. Sweat poured down my face as we continued our tug-of-war, the water now up to our thighs.

My arms burned and as the minutes passed, I knew with absolute certainty that T.J. and I could never land it.

I thought the only reason we'd held any ground at all was because the shark *let us*. It would have taken three grown men to have any kind of fighting chance, and it was time to give up.

'Drop the rope, T.J. We need to get out now.'

He didn't argue, but the rope was wrapped so tight around his forearm he couldn't unwind it. He struggled to free himself as the shark pulled him into deeper water, and he was in well over his head when the rope went slack. Relieved, I thought it had snapped, but then I realized the shark was swimming toward us.

'Get out of the water, Anna!'

I froze, watching T.J. frantically untangle his arm from the rope. The fin slipped below the surface, and I knew he'd never make it to shore in time.

I screamed. But then, out of the corner of my eye, I noticed more fins, moving so fast they sped by in a blur. The dolphins had arrived, two or three of them swimming close together in a group.

I scrambled out of the water and watched as they surrounded T.J., protecting him while he swam toward the shore. When he joined me on the sand, I threw my arms around him, sobbing.

Four more dolphins joined the others and now there were at least seven. They charged the shark, battering it with their snouts, pushing it into shallow water.

T.J. spotted the end of the rope floating next to the school of dolphins. He waded in and quickly grabbed it. We pulled, and with some help from the dolphins, the shark ended up on the beach shaking its head back and forth, a few chicken feathers protruding from its mouth.

T.J. scooped me up in a bear hug. I wrapped my legs around his waist and we screamed and cheered.

The dolphins swam back and forth excitedly. T.J. and I ran into the water and though hugging dolphins wasn't an easy thing to do, we managed. They dispersed a few minutes later. T.J. and I left the water and stood next to the shark, which lay still on the sand.

'I don't know what would have happened if the dolphins hadn't shown up,' I said.

'We were getting our asses kicked, that's for sure.'

'I've never been so scared in my life. I thought that shark was going to eat you.'

T.J. hugged me, resting his chin on the top of my head. 'It didn't, though.'

'We're going to eat him now, aren't we?' I asked.

'Oh, hell yes,' he said, a big grin on his face.

T.J. cut the shark apart with the handsaw, and it was the most disgusting thing I'd ever seen. I carved chunks of it into steaks with the knife. The saw and the knife weren't ideal implements for filleting a shark and the blood covered us, soaking my yellow bikini and his shorts in an oily residue. The smell overpowered me, a sharp metallic assault every time I inhaled. We'd have to bury the carcass somewhere, but we decided to worry about that later.

I surveyed our work. We had more shark steaks than we could eat and we'd have to throw most of it out, but dinner would be a feast.

Blood streaked T.J.'s chest. 'Do you want to get cleaned up first?' he asked, after we walked back to the house.

'No, you go ahead. I'm going to make mashed breadfruit. I'll go after you.' It had been days since I felt truly clean. I looked forward to using soap and taking a long bath in more than one foot of water.

He went into the house and came out carrying his clothes and the soap and shampoo.

'Just leave your shorts down there. I'll try to wash them out later.'

'Okay,' he said over his shoulder.

I made mashed breadfruit. I'd invented the recipe one long, boring day, first grating coconut on a rock and then squeezing it through a T-shirt to make coconut milk. I roasted the breadfruit and grated that too, adding the coconut milk and heating it near the fire in an empty coconut shell. T.J. loved it.

I impaled the shark on sticks, so we could cook it over the fire.

'Your turn,' T.J. said when he returned, smelling a lot better than I did. 'I'll start cooking while you're gone. We can eat as soon as you get back.'

'Okay.' I pointed at T.J. 'Hands off that breadfruit.'

I went inside the house and reached into my suitcase for my clothes. Something blue caught my eye.

Why not?

I had every reason to dress up. Dinner was always special when you killed it, instead of the other way around.

Chapter 26
T.J.

I spread the blanket out next to the fire and checked the shark, making sure it wasn't burning. Not that it mattered because we had plenty, but my stomach growled, and I couldn't wait for it to be done so we could eat.

Anna walked up wearing the blue dress, her wet hair combed back. She smelled like vanilla. I smiled and raised my eyebrows at her when she sat down beside me, and she blushed.

'You look very nice,' I said.

'Thanks. I thought I should dress up. Since we're celebrating.'

We ate as much shark as we could hold. The texture of the steaks reminded me of beef, and the flavor was stronger than the small fish we usually ate.

'Do you want some more breadfruit?' I asked. Instead of answering me, she burped. 'Anna, I'm *shocked*,' I teased. 'I have never heard you burp.'

'That's because I'm a *lady*. And I never have enough food in my stomach to make me burp.' She grinned. 'Wow. That felt really good.'

'So, do you want some? It's almost gone.'

'Sure,' she said, laughing. 'I have room now.'

I had already scooped some of the breadfruit onto my fingers. Without thinking, I held them out to her. She stopped laughing, and looked at me like she wasn't quite sure what I meant. I waited, and she leaned toward me and opened her mouth. I slid my fingers inside, wondering if my eyes were as big as hers. When she sucked the breadfruit off, my breathing got all messed up.

'More?'

She nodded, just barely, and her breathing didn't sound right either. I scooped up some breadfruit and this time, when I put my fingers in her mouth, she put her hand on my wrist.

I waited for her to swallow and then I lost my shit completely.

I grabbed her face with both hands, and I kissed her, hard. She opened her mouth and I slipped my tongue inside. I could have kissed her for days, and if she told me to stop I wasn't sure I'd be able to.

But she didn't tell me stop. She put her arms around my neck, pressed herself against me, and kissed me back just as hard. I pulled her onto my lap so she straddled me, and I moaned into her mouth when she sat down on my hard-on, her dress pushed up to her waist.

She kissed my neck, licking and sucking her way down to my shoulder. It felt incredible. I pulled her dress over her head, and lifted her off me, easing her onto her back. I hooked my fingers under the waistband of her underwear, and she raised her hips so I could take them off. I kissed her frantically, my hands roaming because I couldn't decide where I wanted to touch her most.

'Slow down, T.J.' she whispered.

'I can't.'

She reached between us and tugged on my shorts. I pulled them off and as soon as I was naked, she wrapped her hand around me. I came twenty seconds later, surprised it took that long.

When my head cleared I kissed her and ran my hands over every inch of her, slowly this time. I touched her in places I never thought I would and listening to the noises she made, I guess it must have felt pretty good.

When I was ready again, which was very soon, I pulled her on top of me. Being inside her was like nothing I'd ever felt before. Emma had been nervous and tense, and I'd worried about hurting her, but Anna seemed relaxed, like she knew what she was doing. She sat straight up, her hands flat on my stomach, moving at her own pace. The view was amazing. I watched as she closed her eyes and arched her back, and a few minutes later, when her expression changed and she cried out, I held her hips tight and came harder than I ever had in my life.

Afterward, I put my arms around her and whispered, 'Was this just a one-time thing, you and me?'

'No.'

Chapter 27
Anna

We went into the house when darkness fell and the mosquitoes descended. T.J. lay down beside me and covered us with the blanket. He wrapped his naked body around mine and fell asleep seconds later.

I was wide awake.

When he kissed me, I hadn't stopped to think before I kissed him back. We were two consenting adults, but no matter how I spun it in my head I knew if we ever got off the island, and people found out what we'd done, there would be repercussions for my actions. As I lay there in the dark with T.J. spooning me I justified that what we had done felt good, and if anyone deserved that, it was us. What we did was our business and no one else's.

At least that's what I told myself.

I knelt on one knee wearing T.J.'s baseball cap, my hair pulled back so it wouldn't get in my way. The curved stick T.J. used to start fires, two small chunks of wood, and a dry nest of coconut husks and grass were spread out on the ground in front of me.

A week or so after we killed the shark, T.J. pointed out that there was one thing I didn't know how to do. He always made our fires, and he wanted to make sure I could make one, too. He'd been teaching me, and I was starting to get the hang of it, although I had yet to produce anything other than a lot of smoke and my own sweat.

'Are you ready?' T.J. asked.

'Yes.'

'Okay, go ahead.'

I picked up a stick, threaded it through the loop in the shoelace, and used the bow to spin it. After ten minutes, I had smoke.

'Keep going,' he said. 'You're getting close. You have to spin the stick as fast as you can.'

I spun my stick faster and twenty minutes later, arms aching and sweat running down my face, I noticed a glowing ember. Digging it out, I nudged it into the flammable nest beside me. I picked up the nest, held it in front of my face, and blew gently into it.

It burst into flames, and I dropped it. 'Oh my God!'

T.J. high-fived me. 'You did it!'

'I know! How long do you think it took?'

'Not too long. I don't care how *fast* you can make one, though. I just want to know that you can.' He took my hat off and kissed me. 'Good job.'

'Thanks.'

The accomplishment was bittersweet, because even though I could start a fire by myself, the only reason I'd ever need to was if something happened to T.J.

Chapter 28
T.J.

We were eating lunch when a chicken walked out of the woods.

'Anna, look behind you.'

She turned around. 'What the heck?'

We watched as the chicken came closer. It pecked the ground, not in any kind of hurry.

'There was one more after all,' I said.

'Yeah, the stupid one,' Anna pointed out. 'Although it's the last one standing, so it's done something right.'

It came right up to Anna and she said, 'Oh, hi. Do you not know what we did to the rest of your kind?'

It tilted its head and looked up at her as if it were trying to figure out what she said. My mouth watered. I thought about the chicken dinner Anna and I would have. But then she said, 'Let's not kill this one, T.J. Let's see if it lays eggs.'

I built a small pen. Anna picked the chicken up and put it inside. It sat down and looked at both of us like it was happy with its new house. Anna put some water in an empty coconut shell. 'What do chickens eat?' she asked.

'I don't know. You're the teacher. You tell me.'

'I taught *English*. In a major metropolitan area.'

That cracked me up. 'Well, I don't know what it eats.' I bent down by the pen and said, 'You better lay eggs because right now you're just another mouth to feed, and if you don't like coconut, breadfruit, and fish, you may not like it here.'

I swear to God that chicken nodded its head.

It laid an egg the next day. Anna cracked it into an empty coconut shell and scrambled it with her finger. She put the coconut shell near the flames and waited for the egg to cook. When it looked done, she divided it between us.

'This is fantastic,' Anna said.

'I know.' I finished my share in two bites. 'I haven't had a scrambled egg in so long. It tastes just like I remember.'

The chicken laid another egg two days later. 'That was a good idea you had, Anna.'

'Chicken probably thinks so, too,' she said.

'You named the chicken, Chicken?'

She looked embarrassed. 'When we decided not to kill it, I got attached.'

'That's okay,' I said. 'Something tells me Chicken probably likes you, too.'

Anna and I walked down to the water to take a bath. When we reached the shore, I dropped my shorts and waded in, turning around to watch her undress.

She took her time, first taking off her tank top and then slowly pulling down her shorts and underwear.

I wish she could do that to music.

She joined me in the water, and I washed her hair.

'We are dangerously low on shampoo,' she said, ducking under the water to rinse.

'How much do we have?'

'I don't know, maybe enough for a few more months. Our soap supply isn't much better.'

We switched places, and she washed my hair. I soaped up my hands and rubbed them all over her and she did the same for me. After we rinsed, we sat on the sand letting the breeze dry our skin. Anna settled in front of me and leaned back on my chest, relaxing as the sun sank lower on the horizon.

'I watched you take a bath once,' I admitted. 'I was out looking for firewood, and I wasn't paying attention. You walked into the ocean naked, and I hid behind a tree and watched you. I shouldn't have. You trusted me, and I did it anyway.'

'Did you ever watch me again?'

'No. I wanted to, lots of times, but I didn't.' I took a deep breath and let it out. 'Are you mad?'

'No. I always wondered if you would try to watch. Did I, um . . .'

'Yes.' I stood up and took her by the hand. We went back to the house and lay down in the life raft, and afterward she told me I was so much better than baby oil and her hand.

Chapter 29
Anna

I sat near the shore painting my toenails pink. It was silly, considering our circumstances, but I had the polish in my suitcase, and I definitely had the time, so I painted them anyway.

T.J. walked up. 'Nice toes.'

'Thanks,' I said, starting another coat. 'Did I ever tell you about Lucy, my manicurist?'

He laughed. 'I don't even know what that is.'

'The girl who does my nails.'

'Oh. No, you never told me about her.'

'I used to go to Lucy every other Saturday.'

T.J. raised an eyebrow.

'Yes, I might have been slightly more high maintenance in Chicago than I am here. Anyway, English wasn't Lucy's first language, and I never knew what was, only that I couldn't speak it. But that didn't stop us from having these long conversations, even though neither of us understood all of what the other said.'

'What did you talk about?'

'I don't know, just stuff. She knew I taught school and that I had a boyfriend named John. I learned she had a thirteen-year-old daughter and loved reality TV. She was so nice. She called me honey and always hugged me hello and goodbye. Every single visit, she asked me when John and I were getting married. One time we had

168

a huge communication breakdown and, apparently, I promised her she could do my bridesmaid's manicures for the wedding.'

I screwed the cap back on the nail polish and checked out my toes. I hadn't done the greatest job. 'Lucy would shit if she saw my feet right now.' I looked up at T.J. He had a strange expression on his face, one I couldn't read. 'What's wrong?'

'Nothing.'

'Are you sure?'

'Yeah. I'm gonna go fishing. You better let those toes dry.'

'Okay.'

He seemed back to normal by the time he returned with the fish, so whatever had bothered him, he got over it fast.

'Why aren't you naked all the time?' T.J. asked. 'Why even get dressed?'

'I'm naked right now.'

'I know. That's what made me think of it.'

T.J. and I stood near the shore attempting to wash our dirty clothes, including the ones we'd been wearing.

'Does this still smell?' T.J. asked, holding out a T-shirt for me to sniff.

'Eh, maybe a little.' It was hard to get anything clean, considering we ran out of Woolite over a year ago. Now we swished everything back and forth in the water and called it good.

'If we were naked all the time we wouldn't have to do any laundry, Anna,' he said with a big smile on his face. We walked out of the water, throwing the clothes over the rope we'd strung between two trees.

'If I was naked all the time you wouldn't even notice after a while.'

He snorted. 'Oh, I'd notice.'

'You think that now, but in time, you might not.'

He looked at me like I was crazy. When we got back to the house, he stretched out on the blanket.

I didn't get dressed either because everything we owned was wet. I lay on my side facing him, propped up on my elbow.

'Oh, now that's a nice pose,' he said. 'I like that.'

'It would be like eating your favorite food all the time,' I said. At first, it would be great but after a while, you wouldn't want it anymore. It wouldn't taste as good.'

'Anna. You will *always* taste good.' He leaned over and kissed my neck.

'But eventually you'd get tired of it,' I insisted.

'Never.' By then he had moved a little lower with his kisses.

'It could happen,' I said, but by then even I didn't believe it.

'Nope,' he said, moving lower still until finally he stopped answering me because it was almost impossible to talk when you were doing what he was doing.

Chicken walked over and plopped down in my lap.

T.J. laughed, reached over, and ruffled her feathers. 'It cracks me up when she does that,' he said.

We didn't have to keep Chicken penned up anymore. I let her out once and forgot to put her back in, and she wandered around but didn't try to leave.

'I know, it's so weird. She really likes me for some reason.' I gave Chicken a gentle pet on the head.

'It's because you take care of her.'

'I love animals. I always wanted a dog, but John was allergic.'

'Maybe you can get one when we get home,' T.J. said.

'A golden retriever.'

'That's the kind of dog you want?'

'Yes. One that's full-grown, that nobody wants. From a shelter. I'm going to get my own apartment, and I'll adopt it and bring it home.'

'You've thought about this.'

'I've had time to think about a lot of things, T.J.'

A few nights later when we were in bed, T.J. groaned and collapsed on top of me, breathing hard.

'Wow,' I said, feeling his body relax.

He kissed my neck and whispered, 'Did that feel good?'

'Yes. Where did you learn that?'

T.J. laughed, still trying to catch his breath. 'I have an excellent teacher. She lets me practice all the time until I get it just right.'

He rolled off me, pulling me toward him so I could lay my head on his chest. I snuggled closer, content and drowsy. He rubbed my back.

It wasn't until I was twenty-six or twenty-seven that I even figured out what I wanted in bed. When I tried to tell John, he didn't seem all that thrilled about taking direction. T.J. hadn't been shy about asking what I liked, though, so I decided not to be shy about telling him, which was working out spectacularly.

I sighed. 'You'll make a woman very happy someday, T.J.'

His body tensed and he stopped rubbing my back. 'I only want to make you happy, Anna.' The way he said it, and the rejection I heard in his voice made me wish I could take it back.

'Oh you do, T.J.' I said, quickly. 'You do.'

He didn't talk much the next day. I waded into the water while he fished and stood next to him. 'I'm sorry. I hurt your feelings and that's the last thing I wanted to do.'

He kept his eyes on the fishing line. 'I know this never would have happened between us in Chicago, but please don't talk about saying goodbye to me while we're still here.'

I put my hand on his arm. 'When I said that, about you making another woman happy, it wasn't because I was the one who said goodbye, T.J. You were.'

He turned to me, confused. 'Why would I say goodbye?'

'Because I'm thirteen years older than you are. This might be our world, but it isn't the real world. You still have a lot of things you haven't experienced. You won't want to be tied down to anyone.'

'You don't know what I want, Anna. Besides, I don't think about the future anymore, and I haven't since that plane didn't come back. All I know is that you make me happy, and I want to be with you. Can't you just be with me, too?

'Yes,' I whispered. 'I can do that.'

I wanted to tell him I'd never do anything to hurt him again. But I was afraid it was a promise I might not be able to keep.

T.J. turned nineteen in September. 'Happy birthday,' I said. 'I made you mashed breadfruit.' I handed him the bowl and leaned in to give him a kiss. He pulled me onto his lap and insisted on sharing.

'Why don't we ever celebrate your birthday?' He gave me a sheepish look and said, 'And when is it, again?'

'It's May twenty-second. I'm just not into birthdays, I guess.'

I used to love celebrating my birthday until John ruined it for me. When I turned twenty-seven I was convinced he was going to propose because he'd made reservations, told me to dress up, and invited our friends to join us for drinks before dinner. I pictured him down on one knee holding a ring, and I could hardly contain my excitement when the cab dropped us off in front of the restaurant. We went inside and everyone was already there, almost like a surprise party. When the champagne came, John pulled the Tiffany box out of his jacket and presented me with a pair of diamond stud earrings. I kept a smile on my face for the rest of the night, but Stefani pulled me into the bathroom later and hugged me. I set my expectations as low as possible after that which turned out to be a smart move because for the next three birthdays he didn't even buy me jewelry.

'I want to celebrate your next birthday, Anna.'

'Okay.'

The rainy season ended in November. Thanksgiving came and went like any other day, but on Christmas T.J. found a huge crab near the shore. My mouth watered as he poked and prodded it toward the fire, one giant claw pinching the end of his stick, the other snapping at him the whole way. He dropped it onto the flames and soon we were gorging ourselves, cracking the legs with the pliers and pulling the meat out with our fingers.

'This reminds me of our first Christmas, when we caught the chicken and celebrated with something other than fish,' T.J. said.

'That seems like such a long time ago,' I said, blinking back tears.

'Are you okay?'

'Yeah. I just thought we might be home for Christmas this year.'

T.J. put his arm around me. 'Maybe next year, Anna.'

In February, I woke up from a nap. A bouquet of flowers gathered from the various bushes and shrubs scattered around the island lay on the blanket beside me, a small length of rope wound around their stems.

I found T.J. down at the shore. 'Someone's been checking the calendar.'

He grinned. 'I didn't want to miss Valentine's Day.'

I kissed him. 'You're sweet to me.'

Pulling me closer, he said, 'It's not hard, Anna.'

I stared into T.J.'s eyes, and he started to sway. My arms went around his neck and we danced, moving in a circle, the sand soft and warm under our feet.

'You don't need music, do you?'

'No,' T.J. said. 'But I do need you.'

A few days later, T.J. and I walked along the shore at sunset. 'I miss my mom and dad. I've been thinking about them a lot lately. My sister and brother-in-law, too. And Joe and Chloe. I hope you get to meet them all someday, T.J. They'd like you.'

'I hope so, too.'

By then, I knew if we were ever rescued, T.J. would have to be a part of my life in Chicago. In what capacity, I didn't know. He'd missed so much, and it wouldn't be fair of me to take up too much of his time. The selfish part of me, however, couldn't fathom not falling asleep in his arms or being with him every day. I needed T.J., and the thought of being away from him bothered me more than I wanted to admit.

Chapter 30
T.J

'Anna.' I whispered her name. 'Are you awake?'

'Hmm,' she said.

'Do you still love that guy?' I knew his name, but I didn't want to say it. I was wrapped around her, my chest against her back. She rolled over to face me.

'John? No. I don't love him anymore. I haven't thought about him in a long time. Why?'

'I was just wondering. Never mind, go to sleep.' I kissed her forehead and settled her onto my chest.

But she didn't go to sleep. She made love to me instead.

Anna turned thirty-three in May, and we celebrated her birthday for the first time on the island. A light rain was falling, and we lay next to each other in the life raft listening to the steady rhythm of the drops hitting the roof of the house.

'I didn't actually get you anything. You told me a long time ago that the island mall sucked,' I said.

She smiled. 'It's a little low on merchandise.'

'Yes. So we'll have to pretend. If we were home, I'd take you out for dinner and then I'd give you these gifts. But since we're not home, I'm just going to tell you all the awesome stuff I got you, okay?'

'You shouldn't have,' she teased.

'You're worth it. Okay, your first gift is books. All the current bestsellers.'

Anna sighed. 'I miss reading.'

'I know you do.'

She snuggled closer. 'You're great at this. What else did you get me?'

'Ah, someone is enjoying her birthday. Your next gift is music.'

'Did you make me a *mix tape*?' she asked.

I grinned and started tickling her. 'With all your favorite classic rock songs.'

She squirmed and giggled, rolling over on top of me trying to trap my hands underneath her so I'd stop tickling. 'I love it,' she said. 'Books and music. My two favorite things. Thank you.' She kissed me. 'This was the best birthday I've had in a long time.'

'I'm glad you liked it.'

I pulled my arms out from underneath her body and tucked her hair behind her ears. 'I love you, Anna.'

The surprised look on her face told me she hadn't seen that coming.

'You weren't supposed to fall in love,' she whispered.

'Well, I did,' I said, looking into her eyes. 'I've been in love with you for months. I'm telling you now because I think you love me too, Anna. You just don't think you're supposed to. You'll tell me when you're ready. I can wait.' I pulled her mouth down to mine and kissed her and when it ended, I smiled and said, 'Happy birthday.'

Chapter 31
Anna

I should have known he was falling in love. All the signs were there, and had been for quite some time. It was only after he got sick that I regretted not telling him he was absolutely right.

I loved him, too.

A week after my birthday I lay down in bed next to him only to discover he was already asleep. I had gone to the bathroom and filled our bottle at the water collector, but I'd only been a few minutes behind him, and T.J. never went to sleep without making love first.

He was still sleeping the next morning when I woke up, and he wasn't awake by the time I'd gone fishing and gathered the coconut and breadfruit.

I crawled into bed. His eyes were open, but he looked tired. I kissed his chest. 'Do you feel okay?' I asked.

'Yeah, I'm just tired.'

I kissed his neck, the way I knew he liked, but then I pulled back suddenly.

'Hey, don't stop.'

I put my hand on his neck. 'T.J., there's a lump here.'

He reached up and felt it with his fingertips. 'It's probably nothing.'

'You said you would tell me if you noticed anything.'

'I didn't know it was there.'

'You seem really tired.'

'I'm fine.' He kissed me and tried to take my shirt off.

I sat up, just out of reach. 'Then what's with the lump?'

'I don't know.' He got out of bed. 'Don't worry about it, Anna.'

After breakfast, he reluctantly agreed to let me feel his neck again. I pressed my fingers gently under his jaw, discovering swollen lymph nodes on both sides. Had he been sweating at night? I wasn't sure. He didn't look like he'd lost any weight; I would have noticed if he had. Neither of us said anything about what the lumps might mean. He seemed exhausted so I sent him back to bed. I walked down to the lagoon, waded into the water, and floated on my back, staring up at the cloudless blue sky.

The cancer is back. I know it, and so does he.

He woke up for lunch, but after we ate, he fell asleep again and he was still sleeping at dinnertime. I went into the house to check on him. When I bent down to kiss his cheek, his skin scorched my lips.

'T.J.!' He moaned when I placed the back of my hand against his hot forehead. 'I'll be right back. I'm going to get the Tylenol.'

I found the first-aid kit and shook two Tylenol into the palm of my hand. I helped him swallow the Tylenol with water, but he threw up all over himself a few minutes later.

I cleaned him up with a T-shirt and tried to shift him over a little, to a drier part of the blanket. He cried out when I touched him.

'Okay, I won't move you. Tell me what hurts.'

'My head. Behind my eyes. Everywhere.' He stayed still and didn't say anything else.

I waited a while and then I tried some more Tylenol. I worried that he would throw up again, but they stayed down this time. 'You'll feel better in a little while,' I said, but when I checked a half hour later, his forehead felt even hotter.

All through the night, he burned with a fever. He threw up again, and he couldn't stand for me to touch him because he said it felt like his bones were breaking.

The next day, he slept for hours. He wouldn't eat and he'd barely drink. His forehead felt so hot I worried the fever would fry his brain.

This wasn't cancer. The symptoms had come on too suddenly.

But if it isn't cancer, what is it? And what the hell am I going to do about it?

His fever didn't go down, and I never wished for ice more than I did then. He was so hot and the T-shirt I dipped in water and wrung out was probably too warm to cool his forehead, but I didn't know what else to do.

His lips were dry and cracked, and I managed to get some water and Tylenol down his throat. I wanted to hold him in my arms, comfort him, smooth the hair out of his eyes, but my touch caused him pain so I didn't.

He broke out in a rash on the third day. Bright red dots covered his face and body. I thought maybe the fever was close to breaking, that the rash signaled his body was fighting the illness, but by the next morning the rash was worse, and he felt hotter. Restless and irritable, he slipped in and out of consciousness leaving me panic-stricken when I couldn't rouse him.

The blood started trickling from his nose and mouth

on the fifth day. The fear washed over me in waves as I wiped the blood away with my white tank top; by late afternoon it was red. I told myself the bleeding had slowed down, but it hadn't. Bruises covered his body where the blood pooled under the skin. I lay next to him for hours, crying and holding his hand. 'Please don't die, T.J.'

When the sun rose the next morning, I gathered him in my arms. If he felt pain at my touch he didn't show it. Chicken scratched at the side of the life raft, and I leaned over and picked her up. She plopped down next to T.J. and wouldn't leave his side. I let her stay.

'You are not alone, T.J. I'm right here.' I brushed the hair back from his face and kissed his lips. Drifting in and out of sleep, I dreamed that T.J. and I were at a hospital and the doctor told me I should be happy because at least it wasn't cancer.

When I woke up, I put my ear to his chest, crying in relief when I heard his heartbeat. Throughout the day, his rash faded, and the bleeding tapered off and finally stopped. That evening I started to think that maybe he would live.

The next morning his forehead was cool when I touched it. He made a sound when I tried to rouse him, which I thought meant he was sleeping and not unconscious. I left the house to gather coconut and breadfruit, filling several containers with water from the water collector and stopping frequently to check on him.

I made a fire. I didn't have any way to time myself but if I had to guess, I'd say it took less than twenty minutes.

Not bad for a city girl.

I brushed my teeth. I really needed a bath – I hadn't

been near the water in days – but I didn't want to leave T.J. alone that long. In the late afternoon I lay beside him, holding his hand. His eyelids fluttered, then opened all the way. I gave his fingers a gentle squeeze and said, 'Hi there.'

He turned toward me and blinked, trying to focus. He wrinkled his nose. 'You stink, Anna.'

I started laughing and crying at the same time. 'You don't smell so hot either, Callahan.'

'Can I have some water?' His voice was scratchy. I helped him sit up so he could drink from the water bottle I had waiting for him.

'Don't drink too fast. I want it to stay down.' I let him drink half the bottle and then eased him back down on the bed. 'You can have the rest in a few minutes.'

'I don't think the cancer is back.'

'No,' I agreed.

'What do you think it was?'

'Something viral, otherwise you and I wouldn't be having this conversation. Are you hungry?'

'Yeah.'

'I'll get you some coconut. Sorry, there's no fish. I haven't been down to the water lately.'

He looked surprised. 'How long was I out?'

'A few days.'

'Really?'

'Yes.' Tears filled my eyes. 'I thought you were going to die,' I whispered. 'You were so sick and there was nothing I could do except stay by your side. I love you, T.J. I should have told you before.' The tears ran down my cheeks.

He pulled me close and said, 'I love you too, Anna. But you already knew that.'

Chapter 32
T.J.

I drank water while Anna went fishing. When she came back, she cooked the fish and fed them to me in bed.

'You made a fire,' I said.

She looked proud. 'I did.'

'Did you have any trouble?'

'Nope.'

I wanted to shovel the food in but Anna wouldn't let me.

'Don't eat too fast,' she said.

I paced myself, letting my stomach get used to having something in it.

'Why is Chicken in bed with us?' I asked. I hadn't noticed her at first, but she sat in the corner of the life raft not making a sound and looking very comfortable.

'She was worried about you, too. Now she just likes being up here.'

Later, Anna and I walked down to the beach to take a bath, stopping twice so I could rest.

She led me into the water and soaped up her hands, running them over my skin. When I was clean, she washed herself. Her hipbones poked out, and I counted every rib.

'Didn't you eat while I was sick?'

'Not really. I was afraid to leave you.' She rinsed and then helped me to my feet. 'Besides, you weren't eating either.'

She held my hand and we headed back to the house. I stopped walking.

'What is it?' she asked.

'That boyfriend you had must have been a complete dick.'

She smiled. 'Come on. You need to rest.'

Taking a bath wore me out so much I didn't argue. When we reached the house, she helped me into bed and stretched out beside me, holding my hand until I fell asleep.

I didn't have much energy for the next week and Anna worried about a relapse. She constantly checked my forehead to see if I had a fever and made sure I drank plenty of water.

'Why do I have so many bruises?' I asked.

'You were bleeding from your nose and mouth and apparently under your skin. That scared me the most, T.J. I knew you could only lose a certain amount of blood, and I didn't know how much.'

Hearing that freaked me out. I stopped thinking about it and concentrated on nicer things, like kissing Anna and pulling her T-shirt off.

'You really are feeling better,' she said.

'Yeah. You might have to be on top, though. I don't have the strength for anything else.'

'Lucky for you I like being on top,' she said, kissing me back.

'Lucky's my middle name.'

Afterward, when I held her I said, 'I love you.'

'I love you, too.'

'What did you say?'

'I said "I love you, too."' She snuggled closer and laughed. 'You heard me the first time.'

In June of 2004, Anna and I had been on the island for three years. We hadn't seen any more planes since the one that had flown over two years before. I worried they would never find us, but I hadn't given up completely. I wasn't sure if Anna could say the same.

'This is the last of the soap.'

Anna held a bottle of shower gel in her hand. Only a few ounces remained. The shampoo and the shaving cream were long gone. She still shaved me, but we were on our last blade and it was so dull it took a toll on my skin, drawing blood no matter how careful she was. We rubbed sand on our scalps – our version of dry shampoo – and it sort of helped. Anna talked me into burning off some of her hair. I torched the ends and doused her head with water, shortening it by eight inches. The smell of singed hair lingered for days.

We didn't have any toothpaste either. We used sea salt to brush our teeth, scooping water out of the lagoon and waiting for it to evaporate. The chunks of salt left behind were rough enough to clean our teeth but nothing compared to toothpaste for making our mouths taste good. Anna hated that the most. Now we'd be without soap, too.

'Maybe we should divide this into thirds,' Anna said, studying the bottle of shower gel. 'Wash all our clothes, wash our hair, and wash ourselves. What do you think?'

'Sounds like a plan.'

We took everything down to the lagoon and filled the life raft container with water. Anna squeezed some shower gel into it. When all the clothes were submerged, she washed them thoroughly. I was down to one pair of shorts, a sweatshirt that didn't really fit me anymore, and Anna's REO Speedwagon T-shirt. I went naked a lot. Anna had enough to wear but I sometimes convinced her to have a naked day, too.

I turned twenty in September. I started getting dizzy when I stood up too fast, and I didn't always feel the greatest. Anna worried a lot and I didn't want to tell her, but I wanted to know if she was getting dizzy, too. She said she was.

'It's a sign of malnutrition,' she said. 'It happens when the body finally uses up its stored nutrients. We aren't putting enough of them back in.' She reached for my hand and looked at my fingers, running her thumb over the brittle nails. 'That's another sign.' She held out her hand and examined it. 'Mine look like that, too.'

We braced ourselves for the approaching dry season and the end of regular rainfall. And somehow, we kept on surviving.

Chapter 33
Anna

I threw up my breakfast one morning in November. I was sitting on the blanket next to T.J. eating a scrambled egg, and the nausea came out of nowhere. I barely got three steps away before I puked.

'Hey, what's wrong?' T.J. asked. He brought me some water, and I rinsed my mouth.

'I don't know but that was *not* staying down.'

'Do you feel okay?'

'I feel much better now.' I pointed at Chicken who was walking around by us. 'Chicken, that was a bad egg.'

'Do you want to try some breadfruit?'

'Maybe later.'

'Okay.'

I felt fine the rest of the day but the next morning, right after I ate a piece of coconut, I threw up again.

In a repeat of the day before, T.J. brought me water, and I rinsed out my mouth. He led me back to the blanket.

'Anna, what's wrong?' he asked, a worried expression on his face.

'I don't know.' I lay down and curled up on my side, waiting for the nausea to subside.

T.J. sat down beside me and smoothed the hair away from my face. 'This is going to sound crazy, but you're not pregnant are you?'

I looked down at my stomach, nearly concave since I

hadn't gained back the weight I'd lost when T.J. was sick. I still didn't have my period.

'You're sterile though, right?'

'They said I was. That I probably always would be.'

'What did they mean by probably?'

He thought about it for a minute. 'I remember something about a slight chance fertility could come back but not to count on it. That's why everyone wanted me to bank my sperm. They said it was the only way to be sure.'

'That sounds pretty sterile to me.' I sat up, feeling a little less nauseous. 'There's no way I'm pregnant. Between the two of us, it's probably impossible. I'm sure it's just a stomach bug. God knows what's living in my digestive tract.'

He took my hand. 'Okay.'

Later that night, right before we fell asleep he said, 'What if you were pregnant, Anna? I know you want a baby.' He wrapped his arms around me tighter.

'Oh, T.J. Don't say that. Not here. Not on the island. The baby would have horrible odds for survival. When you were sick, and I thought you might die, it was almost more than I could take. If we had to watch our baby die I'd want to die, too.'

He exhaled. 'I know. You're right.'

I didn't throw up the next morning, or any mornings after that. My stomach stayed flat, and I didn't have to worry about having a baby on the island.

T.J. walked up to the house carrying the fishing pole.

'Something big just snapped my line.' He went inside

and came back out. 'This is your last earring. I don't know what we're gonna do when I lose this one.'

He shook his head and turned to go, heading back to the water to catch enough fish for our next meal.

'T.J.?'

He looked over his shoulder. 'Yeah, sweetie?'

'I can't find Chicken.'

'She'll turn up. I'll help you look for her when I get back, okay?'

We searched everywhere. She'd wandered away before, but never for very long. I hadn't seen her since early morning and she still hadn't come back by the time T.J. and I went to bed.

'We'll look again tomorrow, Anna.'

I was sitting under the awning the next day peeling breadfruit when T.J. walked up. I knew by the look on his face that he had bad news.

'You must have found Chicken. Is she dead?'

He nodded.

'Where?'

'Out in the woods.'

T.J. sat down, and I put my head in his lap, blinking back tears.

'She'd been dead at least a day,' T.J. said. 'I buried her next to Mick.'

T.J. and I ate our food as soon as we killed it because we worried about food poisoning. Knowing that Chicken had been dead too long to eat saved us from making a meal out of our pet.

T.J. and I were, after all, extremely pragmatic.

I didn't feel like getting out of bed a few days later,

on the morning of Christmas Eve. Curled up on my side, I pretended to be asleep whenever T.J. checked on me. I cried some. He let me get away with it that day, but the next morning he insisted I get up.

'It's Christmas, Anna,' he said, bending down beside the life raft until his head was level with mine. I looked into his eyes, alarmed by how lifeless they appeared. The color surrounding his pupils appeared a shade duller than I remembered.

Getting out of that bed was one of the hardest things I'd ever done. I only succeeded because I sensed it wouldn't take much to bring T.J. down to my level and that was something I simply couldn't handle.

He convinced me to go down to the water with him. 'It'll make you feel better.'

'Okay.'

I floated on my back, feeling weightless and insubstantial, as if my body was breaking down from the inside out, which it likely was. The dolphins joined us and brought a genuine smile to my face, if only for a minute.

We sat on the sand afterward, as we had so many times. T.J. sat behind me, and I leaned back against his chest. He wrapped me in his arms. I pictured my family back home, gathered around the big oak table in my mom and dad's dining room, eating Christmas dinner. My mom would have spent the day cooking and my dad would have been right alongside her, getting in her way.

'I wonder if Santa Claus was good to Chloe and Joe,' I said. I missed watching my niece and nephew grow up.

'How old are they now?' T.J. asked.

'Joe's eight. Chloe just turned six. I hope they still

believe in Santa.' Unless someone spoiled it for them, they probably did.

'I promise you and I will spend Christmas together in Chicago next year, Anna.' He squeezed me, hard, and didn't let go. 'But you have to promise *me* that you won't give up, okay?'

'I won't,' I said. And now both of us were full of shit.

The calendar in my datebook ran out at the end of the month, and I'd have to find another way to keep track of the date in 2005.

Maybe I wouldn't bother.

Chapter 34
T.J.

Anna and I walked hand in hand on the beach the day after Christmas. Neither of us had slept well the night before. She wasn't very talkative, but I hoped she might cheer up now that the holidays were over.

I noticed something strange about the lagoon. The water had receded almost to the reef, leaving a huge area of dry seabed behind.

'Look at that, Anna. What's going on?'

'I don't know,' she said. 'I've never seen that before.'

Stranded fish flopped back and forth. 'This is weird.'

'Yeah. I don't get it.' She shielded her eyes with her hand. 'What's that out there?'

'Where?' I squinted, trying to figure out what she was looking at. Something blue had formed in the distance but it confused me because the size was all wrong.

And whatever it was, it was roaring.

Anna screamed, and I understood. I grabbed her hand, and we ran.

My lungs burned. 'Hurry Anna, come on, faster, faster!' I looked over my shoulder at the wall of water coming toward us and realized it wouldn't matter how fast we ran. Our low-lying island didn't stand a chance.

Seconds later, the wave arrived, ripping Anna's hand from my grasp. It swallowed her, and me, and the island.

It swallowed everything.

Chapter 35
Anna

When the wave hit it pushed me forward and then pulled me under. I spun and somersaulted under the water for so long I thought my lungs would explode. Knowing I wouldn't be able to hold my breath much longer, I kicked and clawed with everything I had toward the sunlight shimmering above me. My head broke the surface and I coughed and gasped, struggling to get enough air.

'T.J.,' I screamed his name but as soon as I opened my mouth, water poured down my throat. Tree trunks, large pieces of wood, bricks, and chunks of concrete floated in the water, and I didn't understand where any of it came from.

I thought of sharks, and I panicked, flailing and hyperventilating. My heart beat so violently I thought it might burst through my chest. My windpipe constricted and it felt like trying to suck air through a straw. I heard T.J.'s voice in my head.

Slow down your breathing, Anna.

I inhaled slowly, dodging the debris. Fighting to keep my head above water, I floated on my back to conserve energy. I yelled T.J.'s name again, screaming for him until I lost my voice, my pained cries reduced to nothing more than a hoarse whisper. I strained to hear his voice calling for me, but there was only silence.

Another wave came then, not as powerful as the first,

but it pulled me under, spinning and turning my body in circles. Again, I swam toward the sunlight. When I surfaced, gasping, I spotted a large, plastic bucket floating in the water. My fingers stretched toward the handle and I grabbed it, its buoyancy barely keeping me afloat.

The sea calmed down. I looked around, but there was nothing but blue.

Hours passed, and gradually my body temperature dropped. I shivered, tears pouring from my eyes, wondering when the sharks would come because I knew, eventually, they would. Maybe they were already circling below.

The bucket kept my head above water, but the effort required to constantly shift position, so it remained at an angle that wouldn't cause it to submerge, exhausted me.

I would have given anything – paid any price – to be back on the island with T.J. I'd have lived there forever, as long as we could have been together.

I dozed, jerking awake when the water covered my face. The bucket slipped from my grasp and floated a few yards away. I tried to swim toward it, but my limbs no longer functioned. My head went under, and I fought my way back up.

I thought of T.J., and I smiled through my tears.

You like Pink Floyd?

I was trying to reach those little green coconuts you like.

You know what, Anna? You're all right.

I cried, letting it all out. My head went under, and I thrashed about, using the last of my strength to come back up.

I'll never leave you alone Anna. Not if I can help it.

I think you love me too, Anna.

I went under again and when I surfaced I knew it was for the last time, and the panic, the panic and fear were running neck and neck, and I screamed, but I was so tired it sounded like a whimper. And just when I thought, *this is it, this is the end of my life*, I heard the helicopter.

Chapter 36
T.J.

When the wave hit, it tore Anna from my grasp and tossed me up and down and around. I coughed and choked and couldn't breathe, and the waves pulled me back under every time I managed to get my head above water.

'Anna!' I yelled her name repeatedly, fighting to keep the water from going down my throat. I spun in a circle, but I couldn't see her anywhere.

Where are you, Anna?

The trunk of a tree crashed into my hip and pain shot through my body. Endless debris swirled around me, but there was nothing big enough to grab onto before it passed by, carried along by the churning waves.

I slowed my breathing, trying not to panic.

She has to fight. She can't give up.

I floated on my back to conserve my strength, yelling her name and listening carefully for a reply. Nothing but silence.

A second wave hit, smaller this time, and I went under again. A large tree branch bobbed next to me when I surfaced, and I clung to it. The thought of Anna trying to keep her head above water killed me. She was terrified of being alone on the island but being alone in the water was a nightmare neither of us had ever thought about. She said she felt safe with me, but I couldn't protect her now.

I only left you alone, Anna, because I couldn't help it.

I called her name again, pausing for a full minute to listen before trying again. My voice grew weak and my throat ached with thirst. The sun, high in the sky, beat down on me, my face already stinging with sunburn.

The waterlogged tree branch sank. There wasn't anything else to hold onto, so I alternated between treading water and floating on my back.

I fought to keep my head above water. The time passed and my exhaustion grew. Squinting into the distance, I spotted a wooden beam floating. My arms and legs barely had enough strength left to propel me toward it. I grabbed it, grateful that it supported my weight without sinking. My cheek rested on the wood, and I weighed my options.

It didn't take long to realize I didn't have any.

Chapter 37
Anna

The man in the wet suit splashed into the water next to me. He spoke, but I couldn't hear him over the sound of the helicopter blades. He held my head out of the water and motioned with his free hand for someone to lower a basket.

I wasn't sure if it was real, or a dream. The man put me in the basket; it rose and another man pulled it into the helicopter. They lowered it again and pulled the man in the wet suit back up.

I shivered uncontrollably in my T-shirt and shorts. They wrapped me in blankets and I struggled in the midst of exhaustion more profound than I'd ever experienced to form the words I wanted to say.

'T.J.' It came out no louder than a whisper, and no one in the helicopter heard me. 'T.J.,' I said, a little louder.

The man lifted my head and put a water bottle to my lips. I drank, satisfying my raging thirst. The cool water soothed my throat, and I found my voice.

'T.J! T.J. is down there. You've got to find him.'

'We're low on fuel,' the man said. 'And we need to get you to the hospital.'

I struggled to understand what he was saying. 'No!' I sat up, grabbing his shoulders. 'He's down there. We can't leave him here.'

Hysteria overwhelmed me, and I screamed, the sound filling the helicopter. The man tried to calm me down.

'I'll have the pilot alert the other helicopters. They'll look for him. Everything's going to be okay,' he said, squeezing my shoulder.

I couldn't get the image of T.J. slipping under the surface, and not coming back up, out of my head. I shut down, and went to a place deep inside myself where I didn't have to think or feel. The homecoming with my family, the scene I'd played out in my head hundreds of times over the last three-and-a-half years, failed to elicit any emotion at all.

The helicopter banked sharply and we headed for the hospital, leaving T.J behind.

Chapter 38
T.J.

I couldn't identify the noise at first. It hit me suddenly, when my brain figured out that the thwack-thwack-thwack sound was helicopter blades echoing in the distance.

The sound grew fainter until I couldn't hear it anymore. *Come back. Please turn around.*

It didn't. My hope turned to despair, and I knew I was going to die. My strength was fading, and I had a hard time holding on to the beam. My body temperature had dropped, and I ached everywhere.

I pictured Anna's face.

How many people can say they've been loved the way she loved me?

My fingers slipped off the beam, and I struggled to grab it again. I held on, drifting in and out. A dream about sharks jerked me awake. A faint sound in the distance became louder.

I know that sound.

My hopes soared, but I had used up the very last of my strength and I lost my grip on the beam, my fingers sliding down the wet surface. My head went under and I drifted downward. I instinctively held my breath as long as I could until, eventually, I couldn't.

I floated in a sea of nothing, weightless, until another sensation overpowered me. Death wouldn't be peaceful after all. It hurt, the crushing weight of it pounding on my chest.

Suddenly, the pressure vanished. Seawater spewed from my mouth, and I opened my eyes. A man in a wetsuit knelt beside me, his hands hovering above my chest. My back rested on something solid, and I realized I was inside a helicopter. I breathed in deeply and as soon as I had enough air in my lungs, I said, 'Go back. We have to find her.'

'Who?' he asked.

'Anna! We have to find Anna!'

Chapter 39
Anna

I nestled deeper into my numb place. The man gently shook my shoulder, and I didn't want to talk, but he wouldn't stop asking if I could hear him. I turned toward his voice and blinked, trying to focus my swollen, tear-filled eyes.

'What's your name?' he asked. 'One of the other helicopters just pulled a man out of the water.'

I struggled to sit up, wanting to hear clearly what he was about to say.

'They said he's looking for someone named Anna.'

It took a moment for his words to register but when I comprehended their meaning, I experienced elation, pure and true, for the first time in my entire life.

'I'm Anna.' I wrapped myself in my arms and rocked back and forth, sobbing.

We landed at the hospital and they loaded me onto a stretcher and brought me inside. Two men transferred me from the stretcher to a hospital bed, neither of them speaking English. They wheeled me past a pay phone hanging on the wall.

A phone. There's a phone.

I turned my head toward it as we went by and panicked when I couldn't immediately recall my parents' phone number.

The hospital was overflowing with patients. People sat

on the floor in the lobby, waiting to see a doctor. A nurse approached me and spoke soothingly in a language I didn't understand. Smiling and patting my arm, she pierced the skin on the back of my hand with a needle and hung the IV bag on a pole next to my bed.

'I need to find T.J.,' I said, but she shook her head and, noticing my shivering, pulled the sheet up to my neck.

The chaos of so many voices, only some of them speaking in English, thundered in my ears, louder than anything I'd heard in the last three and-a-half years. I inhaled the smell of disinfectant and blinked at the fluorescent lights that hurt my eyes. Someone pushed my bed into a hallway around the corner. I lay on my back fighting to stay awake.

Where is T.J.?

I wanted to call my parents, but I didn't have the strength to move my body. I fell asleep for a minute, jerking awake when footsteps approached. A voice said, 'The Coast Guard just brought her in. I think she's the one he's looking for.'

A few seconds later a hand pulled back the sheet covering me, and T.J. climbed from his hospital bed into mine, trying not to tangle the lines of our IVs. He wrapped his arms around me and collapsed, burying his face in my neck. Tears ran down my face at the sheer relief of holding the solid weight of him in my arms.

'You made it,' he said, trembling all over. 'I love you, Anna,' he whispered.

'I love you, too.' I tried to tell him about the pay phone, but exhaustion overtook me and my garbled words didn't make sense.

I slept.

'Can you hear me?' Someone gently shook my shoulder. I opened my eyes and for a moment, I had no idea where I was.

'English,' I whispered, comprehending that the man looking down at me was a blond-haired, blue-eyed American in his mid-thirties. I glanced over at T.J. but his eyes were still closed.

Phone. Where is that phone?

'My name is Dr Reynolds. I'm sorry no one has checked on you for a while. We're not equipped to handle extra casualties. A nurse took both of your vital signs a few hours ago and they were good, so I decided to let you sleep. You've been out for almost twelve hours. Are you in any pain?'

'Just a little sore. And thirsty and hungry.' The doctor motioned to a passing nurse and made a pouring gesture. She nodded and returned with a small pitcher of water and two plastic cups. He filled one and helped me sit up. I drank it all and looked around in confusion. 'Why are there so many people here?'

'The Maldives is currently in a state of emergency.'

'Why?'

He looked at me strangely. 'Because of the tsunami.'

T.J. stirred beside me and opened his eyes. I helped him sit up and hugged him while the doctor poured a glass of water and handed it to him. He drank it down without stopping.

'T.J., it was a *tsunami*.'

He seemed confused for a minute, but then he rubbed his eyes and said, 'Really?'

'Yes.'

'Did the Coast Guard bring you in?' Dr Reynolds asked, pouring each of us another glass of water.'

We nodded.

'Where did you come from?'

T.J. and I looked at each other.

'We don't know,' I said. 'We've been missing for three-and-a-half years.'

'What do you mean, missing?'

'We've been living on one of the islands ever since our pilot had a heart attack and crashed into the ocean,' T.J. said.

The doctor scrutinized us, looking back and forth at our faces. Maybe it was T.J.'s hair that finally convinced him.

'Oh my God, you're them, aren't you? The ones who went down in the seaplane.' His eyes were wide. He took a deep breath and blew it out. 'Everyone thought you were dead.'

'Yeah, that's what we figured,' T.J. said. 'Do you think you could find us a phone?'

Dr Reynolds handed T.J. his cell. 'You can use mine.' A nurse removed our IVs and T.J. and I climbed carefully off the hospital bed. My legs wobbled, and T.J. steadied me, putting an arm around my waist.

'There's a small supply room down the hall. It's quiet and you can have some privacy.' He stared at us and shook his head. 'I can't believe you're alive. You were all over the news for weeks.'

We followed him but before we reached the supply room, we came to the women's bathroom.

'Can you wait, please?' I asked. They stopped, and I

pushed open the door, closing it behind me and plunging into darkness. My hand fumbled for the switch and when the lights came on, my eyes darted from the toilet to the sink and finally to the mirror.

I had completely forgotten what I looked like.

I went up to the mirror and studied myself. My skin was the color of coffee beans and T.J. was right, my eyes did look bluer because of it. There were a few lines on my face that hadn't been there before. My hair was a mess of tangles and two shades lighter than I remembered. I looked like an island girl, savage, unkempt, and wild.

I tore my gaze away from the mirror, pulled my shorts down, and sat on the toilet. I reached for the toilet paper. Unspooling some, I rubbed it against my cheek, feeling the softness. When I finished, I flushed and washed my hands, marveling at the water that flowed from the tap. T.J. and Dr Reynolds were standing in the hall waiting for me when I opened the door. 'I'm sorry I took so long.'

'That's okay,' T.J. said. 'I went to the bathroom, too.' He smiled at me. 'That was weird.' He took my hand and we followed Dr Reynolds into the supply room.

'I'll be back in a bit. I have to check on some patients and then I'll call the local police. They'll want to talk to you. I'll also see if I can find you something to eat.'

My stomach growled at the mention of food.

'Thanks,' T.J. said. When he left we sat down on the floor. Shelves of medical supplies surrounded us. It was cramped but quiet.

'You call yours first, Anna.'

'Are you sure?'

'Yes.'

He handed me the phone. It took me a minute, but I finally remembered my parents' phone number. My hand shook, and I held my breath as it rang. There was a click on the line. I started to say hello but then a recorded voice said, 'The number you are trying to reach has been disconnected or is no longer in service.'

I looked at T.J. 'Their number has been disconnected. They must have moved.'

'Call Sarah.'

'Do you want to try your parents first?'

'No, go ahead.' T.J. buzzed with anticipation. 'I just want someone to answer.'

I called Sarah's number, my heart hammering in my chest. It rang four times before someone answered.

'Hello?'

Chloe!

'Chloe, can you put your mommy on the phone right away please?'

'May I ask who's calling?'

'Chloe honey, just get your mom, okay?'

'I have to ask who it is and if they don't tell me, I'm supposed to hang up.'

'No! Don't hang up, Chloe.' *Would she even remember me?* ' It's Aunt Anna. Tell your mommy it's Aunt Anna.'

'Hi, Aunt Anna. Mommy showed me pictures of you. She told me you live in heaven. Do you have angel wings? Mommy's grabbing the phone so I gotta go now.'

'Listen,' Sarah said. 'I don't know who you are, but that's a sick thing to do to a child.'

'Sarah! It's Anna, don't hang up, it's me, it's really me.' I started crying.

'Who is this? What do you get out of these kinds of calls? Do you think they don't hurt?'

'Sarah, T.J. and I didn't die in the plane crash. We've been living on an island and if it weren't for the tsunami, we'd still be there. We're at a hospital in Malé.' Now that I'd gotten the words out, my crying intensified. 'Please don't hang up!'

'What? Oh my God. Oh my God!' She screamed for David but she was crying and talking so fast I couldn't understand anything that was coming out of her mouth.

'Anna? You're alive? You're really alive?'

'Yes.' I was bawling and T.J. was jumping up and down he was so excited. 'Sarah, I called Mom and Dad first but their number was disconnected. Did they sell the house?'

'The house was sold.'

'What's their number?' I looked around to see if there was a pen or something to write on but came up empty-handed. 'Call them, Sarah, call them the minute we hang up. Tell them I tried to call them first. I'll call you back and get their number as soon as I can find something to write it down with. Tell them to wait by the phone.'

'How are you getting home?' she asked.

'I don't know. Listen, T.J. hasn't even called his parents yet. I don't know anything at this point, but I'm going to give his mom and dad your number so they can coordinate with you. Wait for their call, okay?'

'I will. Oh, Anna, I don't even know what to say. We had your *funeral*.'

'Well, I'm alive. And I can't wait to get home.'

Chapter 40
T.J.

Anna handed me the cell phone. I dialed my number and waited for someone to answer. *Pick up, pick up, pick up.*

'Hello?' It was my mom. A wave of emotion washed over me when I heard her voice. I hadn't realized until that very moment how much I'd missed her. Tears filled my eyes and I blinked them back. Anna put her arm around me. 'Mom, it's T.J. Don't hang up.' There was silence on the other end, so I kept talking. 'Anna and I didn't die in the plane crash. We've been living on an island. The Coast Guard rescued us after the tsunami and we're at the hospital in Malé.'

'T.J.?' She sounded weird, like she was in a trance. She started crying. 'Mom, put Dad on!'

'Who is this?' my dad yelled into the phone.

I felt a second wave of emotion when I heard my dad's voice and I wanted to hold onto it, but my desire to make someone understand what had happened and where we were, won out. My voice was steady when I said, 'Dad, it's T.J. Don't hang up. Just listen. Anna and I made it to an island after we crashed. The Coast Guard pulled us out of the water after the tsunami. We're at the hospital in Malé, and we're both fine.' There was silence on the other end. 'Dad?'

'Oh my God,' he said. 'It's you? It's really you?'

'Yes, it's me.'

'You've been alive this whole time? How?'

'It wasn't easy.'

'Are you okay? Are you hurt?'

'We're okay. Tired and sore. Hungry.'

'Is Anna okay?'

'Yeah, she's sitting here next to me.'

'I don't know what to say, T.J. I'm overwhelmed. I need to think for a minute. I need to figure out how to get you out of there,' he said.

For the first time in a long time, nothing weighed heavy on my shoulders. My dad would take over and bring us home. 'Dad, Anna wants you to call her sister, too and make sure she knows what's going on.'

Anna gave me the phone number, and I repeated it for my dad.

'The last thing I want to do is hang up, T.J., but it's 8:00 p.m. here, and I need to start making calls before it gets much later. Getting you on a plane might be difficult because of nine-eleven. If I can't get you and Anna on a commercial flight, I'll charter one. It will probably be tomorrow before I can get you out of there. Are you both able to leave the hospital?'

'Yeah, I think so.'

'Can someone take you to a hotel?'

'I can check. Maybe someone can give us a ride.'

'Once you get to a hotel, call me and I'll give them my credit card number.'

'Okay, Dad. Is Mom all right?'

'Yeah, she's right here. She wants to talk to you.'

I could hardly understand my mom. As soon as she heard my voice, she started crying again.

'It's okay Mom, I'll be home soon. Don't cry. Put Dad back on the phone, okay?'

When my dad came back on the line I told him we were going to talk to the local police and then we'd try to get to a hotel, and I'd call him from there.

'Okay, T.J. I'll be waiting.'

'He's going to start making calls,' I said after I snapped the phone shut. 'He said getting us on a commercial flight might be hard because of nine-eleven.

'What's nine-eleven?'

'I don't know. He said he might have to charter a plane. If we can find a ride to a hotel, we can call him and he'll give them his credit card number. We probably can't get out until tomorrow though, Anna.'

She smiled. 'We've waited this long. I can wait one more day.'

I pulled her close and hugged her. 'We're going home.'

We walked out of the supply closet and looked around for Dr Reynolds. He was standing in the hallway waiting for us with two police officers. There was another man waiting with them. He wore a khaki shirt with the name of the seaplane charter stitched on the pocket.

Dr Reynolds held a brown paper bag with a big grease stain down the side. Smiling, he handed it to me and I looked inside. Tacos. I pulled one out and handed it to Anna, then took one for myself.

The deep fried tortilla was wrapped around shredded beef and onions. A spicy sauce dripped down my hand. I wasn't used to so many different flavors at one time. Starving, I ate the whole thing in under a minute.

The officers wanted to talk to us so we followed them

to an empty corner of the lobby. I reached into the bag and got both of us another taco.

The officers spoke English but their thick accents made them hard to understand. We answered their questions, telling them about Mick and his heart attack, and then crashing and making it to the island.

'The search and rescue team found parts of the plane but no bodies,' one of the officers said. 'We assumed you had drowned.'

'Mick knew we might not land safely so he told us to put on life jackets. Otherwise we would have,' Anna said.

'They searched for bodies,' the other officer said. 'But they didn't expect to find any. There are sharks.'

Anna and I glanced at each other.

'Some of the wreckage from the plane washed ashore. My backpack, Anna's suitcase, and the life raft. Mick's body washed up, too,' I said. 'We buried him on the island.'

The man from the seaplane charter had some questions.

'If the life raft washed up, why didn't you trigger the emergency beacon?'

'Because there wasn't one,' I said.

'All life rafts have a beacon. They're mandated by the Coast Guard when a plane flies over water.'

'Well, ours didn't,' I said. 'And believe me, we looked.'

He wrote down our contact information and then handed me a business card.

'Please have your attorney call me when you get back to the states.'

I put the card in the pocket of my shorts. 'There's one more thing,' I said, turning back to the two police officers. 'Someone was living there before us.' Anna and I told

them about the shack and the skeleton. 'If you were looking for a missing person, we may have found him.'

When we finished talking to them, we asked Dr
Reynolds if someone could drive us to a hotel.

'I can,' he said.

Dr Reynolds drove a beat up Honda Civic. He didn't
have air conditioning so we rolled our windows down.
He pulled out of the parking lot and roads, cars, and
buildings – things I hadn't seen in so long – amazed me. I
inhaled car exhaust fumes, so different from the smell of
the island. When I saw the sign for the hotel I smiled
because it finally hit me that Anna and I would have a
room, a shower, and a bed.

'Thanks for all your help,' we told Dr Reynolds when
he dropped us off in front of the hotel.

'Good luck to both of you,' he said, shaking my hand
and giving Anna a hug.

The hotel hadn't suffered much damage. Someone was
sweeping debris away from the sidewalk in front when
Anna and I walked through the revolving door. Hotel
guests had gathered in the lobby, some of them standing
next to piles of luggage.

Everyone stared at us. If there was a no shoes, no shirt,
no service rule, I was currently violating it. I caught our
reflection in a large mirror hanging on the wall. We didn't
look so great.

I followed Anna to the reception desk where a woman
stood typing on a computer.

'Are you checking in?' she asked.

'Yes. One room, please,' I said. 'And could I borrow
your phone?'

She turned the phone toward me, and I called my dad collect. 'We're at the hotel,' I said.

'Get a couple rooms and charge everything to them,' my dad said.

'We only need one room, Dad.'

He paused for a second. 'Oh. Okay.'

I handed the phone to the woman and waited while my dad gave her his credit card information. She handed it back to me and finished typing.

'Is there a gift shop at the hotel?' my dad asked.

'Yeah, I can see it from here.' The gift shop was just around the corner from the front desk. From what I could tell, it looked pretty high-end.

'Buy whatever you need. I'm working on getting you and Anna out of there. Malé Airport sustained some damage, but they told me they haven't had to cancel too many flights. A commercial flight isn't going to work so I'm working on chartering a plane. Your mom wanted to fly over and get you, but I convinced her that you'd get home sooner if you didn't have to wait for her to come to you first. I'll call your room as soon as I have the details but be ready to leave by morning.'

'Okay, Dad. We will.'

'I don't even know what to say, T.J. Your mom and I are still in shock. Your sisters haven't stopped crying, and the phone is ringing off the hook. We just want to get you and Anna home. I've already talked to Sarah, and I'll make sure she gets all the information as soon as I have it.'

We said goodbye, and I handed the phone back to the woman behind the desk.

'We're pretty full,' she said. 'But we do have a suite available. Will that be okay?'

I smiled and said, 'That will be just fine.'

Anna and I walked into the gift shop and looked around, unsure where to start. It was divided in two. One side had racks of clothes – everything from souvenir T-shirts to formal wear – and one side had nothing but food. Candy, chips, crackers, and cookies lined the shelves.

'Oh my God,' Anna said, and took off.

I grabbed two shopping baskets from a pile near the front door and followed her.

I handed her one and laughed as she tossed Sweet Tarts and Hot Tamales into it. I picked up a bag of Doritos and threw them in, followed by three Slim Jims.

'Really?' she asked, raising one eyebrow.

'Oh, yeah,' I said, smiling at her.

After we filled one basket with junk food, we headed to a rack of toiletries.

'There's probably soap and shampoo in the room, but I'm not taking any chances,' Anna said, grabbing more and adding toothbrushes and toothpaste, deodorant, lotion, razors, shaving cream, and a brush and comb.

Next, we picked out a T-shirt and pair of shorts for me. Anna waved a package of boxer briefs in my direction, and I shook my head but she nodded, laughed, and threw them in the basket. I reached into a barrel full of men's flip-flops and picked out a black pair.

A nearby rack held sundresses and I selected a blue one for Anna. She found a pair of sandals to go with it.

Anna scooped up some underwear, and a pair of shorts

and a T-shirt and we carried the baskets to the counter, charging everything to our room.

We rode the elevator to the third floor. I slid the key card in, and when we entered the room, the first thing I noticed was a huge king-sized bed piled high with pillows. A large flat screen T.V. hung on the wall across from the bed and four dining chairs and a table sat next to a roll top desk and mini refrigerator. The living room area had a coffee table, couch, and two chairs arranged in front of another T.V. The air conditioner blasted frigid air into the room. A tray of four plastic-covered glasses sat on a low table by the door. I unwrapped two, walked into the bathroom, and filled them at the sink. Anna followed me, and I handed one to her. She stared at it for a few seconds before she raised it to her lips and drank.

We checked out the rest of the bathroom. A giant glass-walled shower occupied one corner of the room and a marble counter with two sinks and a basket of soap and shampoo stood between the shower and a deep Jacuzzi tub. Two white robes hung on a hook by the door.

'I'm going to call Sarah, so I can get my mom and dad's number. I told her to have them wait by the phone. How many hours behind Chicago are we?'

'I think eleven. When I talked to my dad he said it was already 8:00 p.m there.'

Anna sat down on the bed and grabbed the pad of paper and a pen from the nightstand. She picked up the phone and dialed. 'It's busy. I'll try her cell.' Dialing again, she waited and then hung up the phone. 'It just kept ringing.' Anna frowned. 'Why isn't she answering?'

'Because she's probably calling everyone you know and

they're calling her back. Her phone will probably be ringing for the next several days. Let's get in the shower. You can try again as soon as we get out.'

We stayed in the shower for almost an hour, scrubbing and laughing. Anna couldn't stop washing, even after I told her she was definitely clean.

'I'm never going to take another bath for as long as I live. I'm officially only taking showers,' Anna said.

'Me, too.'

When we finished, we dried off and put on the bathrobes. Anna squeezed toothpaste onto two toothbrushes and handed one to me. We stood in front of the double sinks brushing, rinsing, and spitting. She put her toothbrush down and said, 'Kiss me right now, T.J.'

I picked her up and set her on the counter, then took her face in my hands. We kissed for a long time.

'You taste incredible,' I said. 'You smell pretty good, too. Not that I ever minded when you didn't.'

'This is better, though,' she said, resting her forehead on mine

'Yes.'

We left the bathroom, and I stretched out on the bed with a room service menu in one hand and the T.V. remote in the other. 'Anna, take a look at this.' She was tearing into a package of sweet-tarts but she plopped down next to me and checked out the menu. She handed me the bag of Doritos and I opened them and crammed a handful into my mouth. Nacho cheese had never tasted so good.

It was hard deciding what to order because we wanted everything. We finally narrowed it down to steak and

French fries, spaghetti and meatballs, garlic bread, and chocolate cake.

'Oh, and two giant Cokes,' Anna said.

I called room service and placed our order. Anna grabbed the key card and something off the low table by the door and said she'd be right back.

'You're naked under that robe,' I reminded her.

'It won't take long.'

I channel-surfed. Every station was broadcasting tsunami coverage. Anna came back into the room carrying a small bucket. I sat up. 'Is that ice?' I asked.

She put a piece in her mouth and said, 'Yep.' She lay down on the bed next to me and I watched her suck on it. She sat up and untied my robe. Opening it, she ran her hand gently along my side. Despite the pain, my body responded to her touch immediately.

'You have some spectacular bruises developing here,' she said. 'What happened?'

'There was a huge tree trunk in the water.'

'You don't get along well with those,' she pointed out.

'This one hit me.'

Anna put another ice cube in her mouth and kissed my neck and my chest.

'How long until room service gets here?' she asked.

'They didn't say.'

Anna kissed my stomach and moved lower. When I felt her mouth on me, I gasped because it had never been cold before. I closed my eyes and rested my hands on her head.

When room service knocked on the door a little later, I tied my robe and answered it. The man that delivered the food put everything on the table and as soon as I added a tip and signed the check, we spread it out, taking the lids off.

'We have silverware,' Anna said. She held up a fork and stared at it for a second before spearing a meatball.

'And chairs.' I said, pulling one out and sitting down next to her. I handed her some garlic bread and cut a piece of steak. I groaned when I put it in my mouth. We fed each other bites off our forks and drank our Cokes. Our stomachs filled up fast; we weren't used to such heavy food, or so much. Anna carefully wrapped up all the leftovers and put them in the refrigerator.

We stretched out on the bed afterward, to let our food settle. Anna played with a piece of my hair and put her head on my shoulder, tangling her legs with mine.

'I've never been so content in my life,' she said.

I muted the T.V. We had been watching coverage of the tsunami while we ate, amazed at the amount of devastation. Indonesia seemed to have been hit the hardest and the death toll had already reached the tens of thousands.

'I feel terrible saying this because so many people have died, but if it hadn't been for the tsunami, we'd still be on that island,' Anna said. 'I don't know how much longer we would have lasted.'

'I don't either.' I stretched my fingers toward the nightstand and turned the clock radio on, fiddling with the dial until I found an American music station. Boston's 'More Than a Feeling' was playing, and I smiled.

Anna sighed. 'I love this song.'

She snuggled closer, and I held her tight.

'Has it hit you yet, T.J.? That we're safe and we're going to see our families again?'

'It's starting to.'

'What time is it?' she asked.

I turned my head toward the clock. 'It's a little past two.'

'It's one in the morning in Chicago. I don't care. I'm going to try Sarah again. There's no way she or my parents are sleeping anyway.'

Anna sat up and reached for the phone, pulling the cord across my body. 'I'll try her home number first.' She dialed and waited. 'It's busy,' she said. 'Maybe she'll answer her cell.' Anna dialed the number and waited. 'It went straight to voice mail. I'll leave her a message,' she said, but then she hung up without saying anything. 'Her mailbox was full.'

'Try again in a little while. You'll get through eventually.' She handed me the phone and I put it back on the nightstand. 'Anna?'

She snuggled back into my arms. 'Yeah?'

'What about John? Don't you think Sarah probably called him?'

'I'm sure she did.'

'What do you think he'll do when he finds out you're alive?'

'He'll be happy for my family, of course. Other than that, I don't know. He's probably living in the suburbs with a wife and a kid by now.' She paused for a minute and said, 'I hope he gave my stuff to my parents.'

'Where will you live?'

'With my mom and dad. Wherever that is. They'll want me to stay with them for a while. Then I'll get my own place. I still can't believe they sold their house, T.J. They always talked about buying something smaller someday, maybe a condominium, but I didn't think they'd actually do it. I grew up in that house. It makes me sad to know they don't own it anymore.'

I kissed her, and then I untied her robe and slipped it off her shoulders. We made love and fell asleep afterward. When I woke up it was 5:00 p.m. Anna slept soundly beside me. Staring at the ceiling, I thought about our conversation. I had asked her about John, but I hadn't asked the only question I really wanted an answer to.

What about us?

Chapter 41
Anna

I opened my eyes and stretched. T.J. was leaning back against the headboard with the T.V. on low, eating a Slim Jim.

'That was a good nap.' I kissed him and swung my legs out of bed. 'I have to pee. Do you know what I love the most about this bathroom?' I said, looking over my shoulder as I walked toward the door.

'Toilet paper?'

'Yep.'

When I got back from the bathroom, T.J. made me try a bite of his Slim Jim.

'Admit it. It's not bad,' he said.

'It's okay, but I'm a lot less picky than I used to be. Where did I leave those Sweet Tarts?'

I found them on the dresser. I wasn't used to air conditioning so I wrapped my robe tighter around my body and snuggled back under the covers next to T.J.'s body. I was stiff and sore, more than I'd been when they first pulled me from the water, and I was thankful for such a soft bed.

At 10:00 p.m. I tried Sarah. It was 9:00 a.m. in Chicago, but I got a busy signal on her cell phone. 'I still can't get through,' I said. I called her home number but it just rang. 'Her machine isn't picking up either.'

'I'll try my dad. Maybe he's talked to her.' T.J. dialed his home number and waited. He shook his head. 'Their line's busy, too. I guess they're both getting a lot of calls. We can try again in the morning.'

T.J. put the phone back and stroked my hair. 'I don't know how I'm going to get used to not sharing a bed with you every night.'

'Then let's not get used to it,' I said. I propped myself up on my elbow and looked down at him. I wasn't ready to let him go, no matter how selfish it made me feel.

He sat up. 'Do you mean that?'

'Yes.' My heart pounded and my brain screamed that it was a bad idea, but I didn't care. 'We'll be apart for a while. You need to be with your family and I do, too. But after that, if you want to come back, I'll be waiting.'

He exhaled, a relieved expression on his face. He pulled me into his arms and kissed my forehead. 'Of course I want that.'

'It won't be easy, T.J. People won't understand. There will be lots of questions.' A knot formed in my stomach just thinking about it. 'You might want to mention you were almost nineteen before anything happened between us.'

'You think someone will ask?'

'I think everyone will ask.'

I woke up in the middle of the night to go to the bathroom. We had fallen asleep with the T.V. on and when I crawled back into bed, I picked up the remote and scrolled through the channels, stopping to watch the news for a while.

I sat straight up when CNN announced breaking news and there on the screen, under the caption "TWO FROM CHICAGO LOST AT SEA, RESCUED AFTER

THREE-AND-HALF YEARS" were pictures of T.J. and me, frozen at sixteen and thirty.

I reached over and gently shook T.J.'s shoulder.

'What, what is it?' he asked, still half asleep.

'Look at the T.V.'

T.J. sat up, blinked, and stared at the screen.

I turned the volume up just in time to hear Larry King say, 'I think I speak for everyone when I say there's a story there.'

'Holy shit,' T.J. said.

Here we go.

Chapter 42
T.J.

I woke up before Anna and ordered eggs, pancakes, sausage, bacon, toast, hash browns, juice, and coffee. When it arrived, I kissed her until she woke up.

She opened her eyes. 'I smell coffee.'

I poured her a cup. She took a drink and sighed. 'Oh, that's good.'

We ate breakfast in bed and then Anna took a shower. I stayed by the phone in case my dad called. As soon as she was done in the bathroom, we switched places. When I walked out, drying myself with a towel, she stared at me.

'You shaved.'

She rubbed the back of her hand against my skin.

I laughed. 'You told me if we were ever rescued I'd have to do it myself.'

'I didn't really mean it.'

The phone rang at 11:00 a.m. My dad had chartered a plane and said we needed to be at the airport in one hour.

'Other than refueling, you'll fly straight through. We'll be waiting for you at O'Hare.'

'Dad, Anna's been trying to reach her sister. Have you talked to her?'

'I got through to her twice. Her line has been busy, but ours has been, too, T.J. The news spread fast. The airport made special arrangements, and they're allowing us to be at the gate when you land, but the media will be there too. I'll do what I can to keep them at a reasonable distance.'

'Okay. I better go so we can get to the airport.'

'I love you, T.J.'

'I love you too, Dad.'

I dressed in the T-shirt and shorts we bought in the gift shop. Anna wore the blue dress. I fished the business card for the seaplane charter out of the pocket of my shorts and threw our filthy old clothes in the trash. We stuffed everything else into two plastic bags we found in the room.

After checking out, we took the hotel shuttle to the airport. Anna could barely sit still. I laughed and wrapped my arms around her.

'You're wired.'

'I know. I'm excited and I drank a lot of coffee.'

The shuttle slowed to a stop at the airport entrance and Anna and I stood.

'You ready to get out of here?' I asked, taking her hand.

She smiled and said, 'Absolutely.'

The flight crew – pilot, co-pilot, and one flight attendant – cheered and clapped when Anna and I ducked our heads and walked through the door of the plane. They shook our hands and we smiled and introduced ourselves.

I checked out the cabin. There were seven seats; five single seats separated by a narrow aisle and two attached seats. A narrow couch stretched along the wall. I couldn't imagine what this must have cost my dad.

'What kind of plane is this?' I asked.

'It's a Lear 55,' the pilot said. 'It's a mid-sized jet. We'll have to stop several times to refuel but we should be in Chicago in about eighteen hours.'

Anna and I put our plastic bags in the overhead compartment and settled into the side-by-side leather reclining seats. A large floor-mounted table sat in front of us.

The flight attendant walked over to us as soon as we buckled our seat belts.

'Hi. My name is Susan. What would you like to drink? I have soft drinks, beer, wine, cocktails, bottled water, juice, and champagne.'

'Go ahead, Anna.'

'I'll have water, champagne, and juice, please,' she said.

'Would you like me to make that a mimosa? I have fresh orange juice.'

Anna smiled at Susan. 'I would *love* a mimosa. Thank you.'

'I'll take water, beer, and a coke,' I said. 'Thanks.'

'Certainly. I'll be right back.'

We had zero tolerance for alcohol, and we got kind of hammered. Anna drank two mimosas and I had four beers. She couldn't stop giggling, and I couldn't stop kissing her; we were loud, too, and Susan did an awesome job pretending not to notice. She brought over a huge plate of cheese, crackers, and fruit, probably hoping it would sober us up. We inhaled it, but not before I insisted on trying to throw several grapes into Anna's open mouth. I missed every time, which cracked us up.

When it got dark, Susan brought over blankets and pillows.

'Oh, good,' Anna said, hiccupping. 'I'm a little sleepy.'

I spread the blankets over us and slipped my hands under Anna's dress.

'Stop that,' she said, trying to deflect my hands. 'Susan is right over there.'

'Susan won't care,' I said, pulling the blanket over our heads so we could have some privacy. I was all talk, though, because five minutes later, I passed out.

I woke up with a headache. Anna was still asleep, her head resting on my shoulder. When she woke up, we took turns cleaning up and brushing our teeth in the bathroom. Susan set a plate of turkey and roast beef sandwiches on the table along with potato chips and Cokes. She also handed me two individually wrapped packages of Tylenol and two bottles of water.

'Thanks.'

'You're welcome,' she said, patting me on the shoulder.

We tore open the Tylenol and swallowed the pills with a drink of water.

'What day is it, Anna?'

She thought about it for a minute before she answered. 'December twenty-eighth?'

'I want to spend New Year's Eve together,' I said. 'I'll be missing you a lot by then.'

Anna gave me a quick kiss. 'It's a date.'

We ate our sandwiches and chips and passed the rest of the time talking.

'I've thought about this day for so long, T.J. I can picture my mom and dad, Sarah, David, and the kids all standing together as I run toward them with my arms wide open.'

'I've thought about this day, too. I worried it might never come.'

'But it did,' Anna said, smiling at me.

The sky lightened, and I gazed out the window at the frozen Midwestern fields. When we descended for our landing in Chicago, Anna pointed and said, 'Look T.J., snow.'

We touched down at O'Hare a little before 6:00 a.m. Anna unbuckled her seat belt and stood up before the plane came to a full stop.

We grabbed our plastic bags from the overhead compartment and hurried down the aisle to the front of the plane. The pilot and co-pilot came out.

'It's been a pleasure bringing you home,' the pilot said. 'Good luck to both of you.'

We turned to Susan.

'Thanks for everything,' Anna said.

'You're welcome,' she said, giving us a hug.

Someone swung the door of the plane open.

'This is it, T.J.,' Anna said. 'Let's go.'

Chapter 43
Anna

T.J. and I ran through the jet bridge holding hands. When we came out on the other side, the crowd roared. The flash of hundreds of cameras blinded me, and I blinked, trying to focus. Reporters started yelling questions at us immediately. Sarah rushed forward in a blur and gathered me into her arms, crying.

Jane Callahan was nearly hysterical as she engulfed T.J. Tom Callahan and two girls – T.J.'s sisters I assumed – joined in the family hug. David stood beside Sarah, and he reached out to embrace me. I squeezed him tight and then pulled away, scanning the crowd for my parents.

John was standing there.

He hurried forward and I hugged him automatically. I stepped back, wanting him to get out of my way. Confused, my heart began to pound. My eyes darted over the rest of the people standing inside the roped off area, but I didn't see my mom.

Or my dad.

I searched again, frantically, and then I understood why their phone had been disconnected. My knees buckled. Sarah and David caught me.

'Both of them?'

Sarah nodded, tears running down her face.

'No,' I screamed. 'Why didn't you tell me?'

'I'm sorry,' she said. 'Your call caught me off guard, and you sounded so happy. I just couldn't do it, Anna.'

They led me to a chair. Before I could sit down all the way, T.J. appeared beside me.

He sat and pulled me into his arms, rocking me gently while I sobbed. I lifted my head off his chest.

'They're both dead.'

'I know. My mom just told me.'

He kissed my forehead and wiped away my tears as the cameras captured it all. I didn't know it then, but less than twenty-four hours later, the pictures of T.J. holding and kissing me would appear on the front pages of newspapers across the country.

I rested my head on his chest and closed my eyes. Sarah rubbed my back. Finally, I took a deep breath and sat up.

'I'm so sorry,' T.J. said, smoothing my hair back from my forehead.

I nodded. 'I know.'

It was silent except for the clicking and flashing of the cameras. I turned to Sarah and said, 'I want to go home.'

Sarah wrote down her cell phone number so I could give it to T.J. I handed it to him and he shoved it in the pocket of his shorts.

'I'll call you in a little while.' He wrapped his arms around me and whispered in my ear. 'I love you.'

'I love you, too,' I whispered back.

We stood up as Tom and Jane Callahan walked toward us, T.J.'s sisters trailing behind. 'I'm so sorry, Anna,' Jane said. 'Sarah told us about your parents. I felt horrible knowing the news you were coming home to.' She hugged me and when she pulled away she held my hands for a minute. 'We'll call you in a few days. We have some things to discuss.' She smiled and gave me a quick kiss on the cheek.

Tom Callahan smiled and squeezed my shoulder.

'Thank you for chartering the plane,' I said.

'You're welcome, Anna.'

Sarah sent David over to tell the media I wouldn't be giving a statement. John came and stood beside me. He started to reach for my hand and then changed his mind.

'I'm sorry about your parents, Anna.'

'Thank you.'

We stood there awkwardly, like strangers, and he finally said, 'I was so happy when Sarah called. I couldn't believe what she was telling me.'

I took a deep breath and said, 'John –'

'Don't say anything. Just take some time and when you're ready we'll talk. I know you probably want to get out of here.' He glanced over at T.J. who stood nearby with his family. 'I gave all your things to Sarah about a year ago. I hadn't been able to do it until then.' His eyes locked on mine. 'I'm really glad you made it home, Anna.'

He hugged me and walked away and then Sarah and David led me from the gate.

Chapter 44
T.J.

My family surrounded me. Alexis and Grace each held one of my hands and my mom couldn't decide whether she wanted to laugh or cry so she did both.

'I can't believe how tall you are,' my dad said.

Everyone freaked out about my ponytail.

'No scissors,' I explained.

I noticed a tall, blond guy out of the corner of my eye. He walked up to Anna.

Don't talk to her. She doesn't love you anymore.

I watched them until my mom tugged on my arm.

'Let's get you home, T.J.'

I glanced over at Anna one more time. John hugged her and then walked away. I exhaled and said, 'I'm ready, Mom.'

Before we got outside, my mom handed me a coat and some socks and tennis shoes. I shoved the flip-flops in the plastic bag with the rest of my stuff and followed my family to the car.

When we got home, I took a shower, wrapped a towel around my waist, and walked into my old bedroom. It looked exactly the same. My double bed still had the same navy blue bedspread on it and my stereo and CD collection sat in the corner next to my desk. A stack of clothes lay folded on the dresser. My mom did a good job guessing my size considering how much I'd grown.

When I came out of my room, my mom was in the kitchen making breakfast. She gave me a plate of pancakes and bacon and when I finished eating, I sat in the living room talking to my family. Grace, now fourteen, wanted to sit next to me. Alexis, who had just turned twelve, sat at my feet.

I told them everything – Mick, the crash, the contaminated water, the thirst, and hunger, the shark, getting sick, and the tsunami – and I answered all their questions. My mom started crying again when she heard how sick I'd been.

Later that night my sisters went to bed and it was just my parents and me.

'You can't imagine what it's like, T.J.,' my mom said. 'To think your son is dead and then he calls you on the phone. If that's not a miracle I don't know what is.'

'Me, neither,' I agreed. 'Anna dreamed about the day we'd get to make those calls. She couldn't wait for everyone to find out we were alive.'

Silence filled the room for the first time since we'd started talking.

My mom cleared her throat. 'What kind of relationship did you and Anna have?' she asked.

'Exactly the kind you think we did.'

'How old were you?'

'Almost nineteen,' I said. 'And Mom?'

'Yes?'

'It was definitely my idea.'

Chapter 45
Anna

We stopped at the restroom because I desperately needed to blow my nose and wipe my eyes. Sarah handed me some Kleenex.

'I should have known something was wrong when their phone number didn't work. You said they sold the house.'

'I said the house was sold. David and I put it on the market as soon as their estate cleared probate.'

I leaned forward, bracing myself on the bathroom counter. 'What happened to them?'

'Dad had another heart attack.'

'When?'

She hesitated. 'Two weeks after your plane went down.'

I started crying again. 'What about Mom?'

'Ovarian cancer. She died a year ago.'

David yelled into the bathroom. Sarah popped her head out for a second then came back in and said, 'The reporters are headed this way. Let's get out of here, unless you want to talk to them.'

I shook my head. Sarah had brought me a coat and fleece-lined boots. I slipped them on and we walked to the parking garage, the media trailing not far behind. I breathed in the smell of snow and exhaust.

'Where are the kids?' I asked when we arrived at Sarah and David's apartment. I really wanted to hold Joe and Chloe in my arms.

'We took them to David's parents. I'll pick them up tomorrow. They're so excited to see you.'

'What do you want to eat?' David asked.

My stomach churned. I had looked forward to ordering a feast but now I didn't think I could eat.

David must have sensed it because he said, 'How about if I run out for some bagels and you can eat when you're ready?'

'That sounds great, David. Thanks.'

I took off my coat and boots.

'Your clothes are all here,' Sarah said. 'I put them in the spare bedroom closet after John brought them over. Your jewelry and shoes and some other things are in there, too. I've never been able to get rid of any of it.'

I followed Sarah down the hall to the spare bedroom. She opened the closet and I stared at my clothes. Most of them were on hangers and the rest were stacked neatly on the top shelf. A light blue cashmere sweater caught my eye, and I reached out and touched the sleeve, amazed at how soft it felt under my fingers.

'Do you want to take a shower first?' Sarah asked.

'Yes,' I said, grabbing a pair of gray yoga pants and a long-sleeved white T-shirt. I pulled the blue sweater off the shelf, too. A dresser in the corner held my socks, bras, and underwear. I headed into the bathroom and stood under the shower for a long time.

My clothes swam on me, but they were familiar and warm.

'Stefani's on her way over,' Sarah said, handing me a mug of coffee once I settled myself on the couch in the living room.

I smiled at the mention of my best friend.

'I can't wait to see her.' I took a sip of my coffee. Sarah had spiked it. 'Bailey's Irish Cream?'

'I thought you could use a drink.'

'Okay, but only one. I'm a bit of a lightweight these days.' I held the warm mug in my hands. 'How did Mom get along after Dad died?' I asked.

'Okay. She refused to sell the house so David took over the yard work and we hired someone to shovel the driveway and sidewalks when it snowed. We made sure she wasn't lonely.'

'How bad was the cancer?'

'It wasn't good. She fought hard, though, all the way to the end.'

'Did she go to hospice?'

'No. She died at home the way she wanted it.'

We finished our coffee. David came home with the bagels and Sarah urged me to eat.

'You're so thin,' she said, spreading cream cheese on a bagel and handing it to me.

We returned to the couch after finishing our meal. Sarah turned the stereo on and found a classic rock station. She handed me a fresh cup of coffee, no Bailey's this time. David joined us and he and Sarah asked me about the island.

I told them everything. Sarah cried when I told her and David how T.J. and I almost died of dehydration. Hearing that two planes had flown overhead really tore her apart. They were shocked when I told them about the shark and Bones and the tsunami.

'What a horrifying ordeal,' Sarah said.

'Well, we adapted. It was bad near the end, though. I'm not sure how much longer we would have lasted.'

Sarah handed me an afghan and I tucked my legs under it.

'I was surprised to see John at the airport,' I said.

'I called him. He was devastated when your plane went down and he was really happy when I told him you were alive.'

'I thought he would have moved on. Maybe married someone by now.'

'No. He was dating someone for quite a while, but as far as I know he's still single.'

'Oh.'

'What did you decide about him?'

'He's not the one I'm supposed to be with, Sarah. I don't know what would have happened if my plane hadn't gone down, but I had plenty of time to think about what I wanted.' I shook my head. 'It wasn't him.'

'You and T.J. are together, aren't you?' Sarah asked.

'Yes. Are you surprised?'

'Under the circumstances? No. How old is he?'

'Twenty.'

'How old was he when it started?'

'Almost nineteen.'

'Do you love him?'

'Yes.'

'I saw the way he looked at you. How he comforted you at the airport. He loves you, too.' Sarah said.

I put my empty mug on the coffee table and nodded my head. 'Yes. He does.'

The doorbell rang, and Sarah walked across the room. I followed and held my breath as she looked through the peephole and opened the door. Stefani stood there, tears streaming down her face. I pulled her into my arms, no words capable of expressing how it felt to see her again.

'Oh, Anna,' she said, sobbing, squeezing me with the strength of her embrace. 'You came home.'

Chapter 46
T.J.

Later that night I went into my room, stretched out on my bed, and called Anna. 'Hey,' I said when she answered. 'How are you doing?'

'I'm worn out. Too much to process.'

'I wish I could help.'

'It's just going to take time,' she said. 'I'll be okay.'

'I'm lying on my old bed. My mom didn't get rid of anything.'

'Neither did Sarah. I thought people were supposed to give your stuff away when you died.'

'My mom knows about us.'

'Oh, God. What did she say?'

'She asked me how old I was when it started. That's it.'

'She might revisit that later.'

'Maybe. So was that John at the airport?'

'Yes.'

'What did you say to him?'

'Nothing. He cut me off. I'm supposed to call him.'

'Are you going to?'

'Eventually. I can't deal with it right now. A few days ago we were walking on the beach. Now we're home. It's surreal.'

'I know.'

'Are you tired?' she asked.

'Exhausted.'
'Get some sleep.'
'I love you, Anna.'
'I love you, too.'

Chapter 47
Anna

Sarah opened the bedroom door, holding a cup of coffee and the newspaper in her hand.

'Are you awake?'

I sat up and blinked. Daylight filtered in through the sheer curtains. 'What time is it?'

'Almost ten o'clock.' Sarah handed me the coffee and put the newspaper on the nightstand. 'The reporters won't take no for an answer. I had to turn the ringer off.'

I picked up her cell from the nightstand and turned it on. I'd shut it off after I talked to T.J. The screen showed eleven missed calls.

'They're calling your cell, too. I'll get my own phone as soon as I can.'

Sarah waved her hand dismissively. 'No hurry. Maybe we can send David out to pick one up.'

I set the coffee on the nightstand and picked up the newspaper. Pictures of T.J. and I covered the front page. There were the same ones I'd already seen on CNN and several from the airport. The largest one showed T.J. kissing my forehead surrounded by smaller shots of us running hand in hand, embracing, and him wiping my tears away and holding me in his arms. For those who had speculated about the nature of our relationship, one look at the front page probably answered their most burning questions.

I handed the newspaper to Sarah. 'If any reporters get through, tell them I'm not ready to talk, okay?' I picked up my mug and cupped it in my hands. Thoughts of my mom and dad filled my head and I started crying. Sarah climbed in bed and put her arms around me, handing me a box of Kleenex.

'It's okay, Anna. I did that, too, after each of them died. It's going to take a while before it stops hurting so much.'

I nodded my head. 'I know.'

'Are you hungry? David ran out to get breakfast.'

The emotional turmoil ruined my appetite, but my stomach felt empty. 'A little.'

'What do you want to do today?'

'I should probably make some appointments. Doctor, dentist, haircut.'

Sarah left the room and returned with the phone book. 'Tell me who to call.'

Chapter 48
T.J.

Ben burst into my room, holding the newspaper in his hand.

'One question,' he said, walking toward my bed holding his index finger in the air. 'How old were you when you started bangin' her? Because I'm pretty sure from these pictures that you are.'

If he hadn't been looking down at the shot of me kissing Anna, he might have seen my fist coming before it connected with his left eye.

'Jesus Christ! What'd you do that for?' he asked, looking up at me from the floor where he was sprawled, holding his eye.

'*That's* the first thing you say to me after three-and-a-half years?'

He sat up, his right eye already starting to swell.

'Fuck, Callahan. That hurt.'

I got out of bed and held my hand out to him. He grabbed it and I pulled him off the floor. 'Don't ever say something like that about her again.'

'T.J.?' My mom stood in the open doorway. She noticed Ben holding his eye. 'Is everything okay?'

'It's fine, Mom.'

'Yeah we're cool, Jane,' Ben said.

My mom looked at us but didn't ask what had happened. 'What do you want to eat, T.J.?'

'Anything, Mom.'

After my mom left Ben said, 'So are you, like, in love with her or something?'

'Yes.'

'Does she love *you*?'

'She says she does.'

'Does your mom know?'

'Yep.'

'She freak out?'

'Not yet.'

'Well I'm glad you're back, man.' Ben gave me an awkward hug. 'I had a really hard time when they told me you were dead.' He looked down at the floor. 'I spoke at your funeral.'

'You did?'

He nodded.

Ben could hardly stand up in front of everyone in our ninth grade speech class. I couldn't picture him addressing the people at my funeral. Maybe I shouldn't have punched him. 'That was cool of you, Ben.'

'Yeah, well, it made your mom happy. Anyway, you're gonna cut your hair, aren't you? You look like a god-damned girl.'

'Yeah.'

My mom made me a cheeseburger and French fries, and Ben sat with me while I ate. My parents both hugged me a couple times and my mom kissed me. Ben probably wanted to make a smart-ass comment but he held some ice on his eye and kept his mouth shut. Grace and Alexis sat at the table for a while, telling me about school and their friends. I drained the last of my Coke.

'I can't get you in with Dr Sanderson until tomorrow.

I thought maybe they would squeeze you in but apparently they're overbooked.'

'It's okay, Mom. I've waited this long. One more day isn't going to matter.'

She wiped her hands on a towel and smiled at me. 'Do you want anything else to eat?'

'No. I'm full. Thanks.'

'I'm going to make you a haircut and dentist appointment.' My mom turned off the stove and left to make the calls.

'So do you have a job or what?' I asked Ben. 'It's the middle of the day.'

'I'm in college. It's winter break.'

'You went to college? Where?'

'University of Iowa. I'm a sophomore. You gotta come visit me. What about you? What are you gonna do?'

'I promised Anna I'd get my GED. After that I have no idea.'

'You gonna keep seeing her?'

'Yeah. I miss her already. I've been waking up next to her for three-and-a-half years.'

'Dude, if I ask you another question will you please not punch me?'

'Depends what it is.'

'What's it like being with her? Is it true what they say about older chicks?'

'She's not that much older.'

'Uh, okay. So anyway, how is it?'

'It's incredible.'

'What's she do?'

'She does everything, Ben.'

Chapter 49
Anna

My hairdresser, Joanne, walked into Sarah's living room.

'There are reporters downstairs,' she said. 'I think they took my picture.' She shrugged off her coat and hugged me. 'Welcome home, Anna. Stories like yours are why I believe in miracles.'

'Me too, Joanne.'

'Where do you want to cut her hair?' Sarah asked.

I had already taken a shower and my hair was still wet so Joanne had me sit on a stool in Sarah's kitchen.

'What happened here?' she asked, examining the ends of my hair.

'T.J. had to burn it off when it got too long.'

'You're kidding.'

'No. He worried he was going to set my whole head on fire.'

'How much do you want me to cut?'

My hair hung to the middle of my back. 'A few inches. And maybe some long bangs?'

'Sure.'

Joanne asked me questions about the island. I told her and Sarah about the bat that had been stuck in my hair.

'It bit you?' Sarah looked horrified. 'And T.J. stabbed it?'

'Yes. Everything turned out okay, though. It didn't have rabies.'

Joanne dried my hair and smoothed it with a flat iron.

She held up a hand mirror and I checked out my reflection. My hair looked healthy now, with smooth ends.

'Wow. That's a big improvement.'

Sarah tried to pay, but Joanne wouldn't accept any money. I thanked her for coming to the apartment.

'It's the least I could do, Anna.' She hugged and kissed me. After she left I said to Sarah, 'If we can get out the door without being mobbed, there's someplace I really want to go.'

'Sure,' Sarah said. 'I'll call a cab.'

The reporters screamed my name as soon as Sarah and I opened the door. They were waiting on the steps and we pushed past them and slid into the waiting cab.

'I wish your building had a back door,' I said.

'They'd probably be out there, too. Fucking vultures,' Sarah muttered.

Sarah gave the driver an address and soon we drove through the entrance of Graceland Cemetery.

'Can you please wait?' Sarah asked the cabdriver.

A few snowflakes swirled in the gray sky. I shivered but Sarah seemed oblivious to the cold, not even bothering to button her coat. She led me to the grave where our parents, Josephine and George Emerson, lay side-by-side.

I knelt in front of the headstone and traced their names with my finger. 'I made it back,' I whispered. Sarah handed me a tissue, and I wiped the tears pouring from my eyes.

I pictured my dad in his silly bucket hat covered with fishing lures, teaching me how to clean fish. I remembered how he loved to fill his hummingbird feeder and watch the tiny creatures zoom in for a drink, hovering in mid-air.

I thought of my mom, and how much she loved her garden and her home and her grandchildren. Sharing my adventures in the classroom with her over Sunday morning brunch wouldn't happen now. She would never be able to give me advice, and I'd never hear either of my parents' voices again. I bawled, letting it all out. Sarah waited patiently, giving me time for the catharsis I desperately needed. My tears finally tapered off, and I stood up.

'We can go now.'

Sarah put her arm around me and we got back in the cab. She gave the driver another address and we went to David's parents' house to pick up the kids.

Joe and Chloe stopped playing when we walked into the room. I probably seemed like a ghost to them. Sarah had kept my memory alive but the aunt they thought was dead was now standing in the living room. I knelt down next to them and said softly, 'Boy did I miss you guys.'

Joe came over first. I hugged him tight. 'Let me look at you,' I said, holding him at arm's length.

'I'm losing all my teeth,' he said. He opened his mouth and showed me the gaps.

'You must be keeping the tooth fairy pretty busy.'

Chloe, slowly warming to her long-lost aunt, ventured a little closer and whispered, 'I've lost some, too.' She opened her mouth wide so I could see *her* gaps.

'Geez, your mom must have to put all your food through a blender. You guys are toothless.'

'Aunt Anna, are you gonna live at our house now?' Chloe asked.

'For a while.'

'Will you tuck me into bed tonight?' she asked.

'No, I want her to tuck me into bed tonight,' Joe argued.

'How about I tuck you both into bed tonight?' I hugged them to my chest, fighting the tears.

'Are you guys ready to go home?' Sarah asked.

'Yeah!'

'Then kiss grandma and let's go.'

Later that night, after I put both kids to bed, Sarah poured us a glass of red wine. Her cell phone rang and she handed it to me.

'Hey. How are you?' T.J. asked.

'I'm okay. Sarah and I went to the cemetery today.'

'Was it hard?'

'Yes. I really wanted to go, though. I feel a little better now, after visiting their graves. I'll go back again. What did you do today?'

'I got a haircut. You might not recognize me.'

'I'm going to miss that ponytail.'

T.J. laughed. 'I'm not.'

'I just put the kids to bed. It took two hours because I read them every book they own. Sarah just poured us some wine and Stefani's coming over. What about you? Any plans?'

'I'm going out with Ben if we can shake the reporters.'

'How is Ben?'

'Still running his mouth.'

'Have you been to the doctor yet?'

'I go tomorrow.'

'I hope the appointment goes okay.'

'It'll be fine. Have you gone yet?'

'Tomorrow. Then the dentist in the afternoon.'
'Me too. Remember when I took my braces off?'
'I forgot about that.'
'I'll see you on New Year's Eve, Anna. I love you.'
'I love you, too. Have fun tonight.'

Chapter 50
T.J.

I opened the door when Ben knocked. His eye had swollen shut and turned purple and blue.

'Shit. Sorry about that,' I said.

'Eh, no biggie. You're lucky I'm so easy-going,' he said.

'Frankly, that's your best quality.'

'A bunch of guys from school are home for Christmas break. You up for a party?'

'Sure. Where?'

'Coop's. His parents left for the Bahamas this morning.'

I grabbed my coat. 'Let's go.'

At least twenty of my former classmates were standing shoulder-to-shoulder in Nate Cooper's living room when we showed up. Rock music blasted from the stereo. Everyone cheered when we walked in the door and a bunch of guys shook my hand and slapped me on the back. I hadn't seen some of them since before I'd started treatment for Hodgkin's because I missed so much school that year. It was weird when I realized everyone had graduated but me.

Someone threw me a beer. They wanted to hear about the island, and I answered all of their questions. Ben must have told them how he got his black eye, though, because no one asked about Anna.

I was on my second beer when a girl sat down on the couch next to me. She had long blonde hair and wore a ton of makeup.

'Do you remember me?' she asked.

'Kind of,' I said. 'I'm sorry. I forgot your name.'

'Alex.'

'You were in my class, right?'

'Yeah.' She took a long drink of her beer. 'You look way different than you did when we were sophomores.'

'Yeah, well, that was four years ago.' I finished my beer and looked around for Ben.

'You look good. I can't believe you actually lived on that island.'

'I didn't really have a choice.' I stood up. 'I'm getting ready to leave. See you around.'

'I hope so.'

I found Ben in the kitchen. 'Hey, I'm taking off.'

'You can't go already, man. It's only midnight.'

'I'm tired. I'm going to bed.'

'That's lame dude but okay, I understand.' Ben high-fived me, and I walked out the door.

On the way to the train I thought about Anna, and I smiled all the way home.

Chapter 51
Anna

I woke Joe and Chloe up so we could have breakfast together. We were finishing our toaster waffles and juice when Sarah walked into the kitchen.

'Good morning,' she said. 'Thanks for getting the kids breakfast.'

'Aunt Anna makes the best waffles,' Chloe said.

'Aunt Anna's boyfriend is coming over tomorrow night,' Joe announced.

'How did you know about that?' Sarah asked.

'I heard you and Aunt Anna talking about it.'

'Yes, Aunt Anna's boyfriend is coming over to celebrate New Year's Eve. I expect you two to use your manners and not act like complete hooligans.'

'Aunt Anna needs to get in the shower,' I said to the kids. 'She has a busy day ahead of her.'

'Doctor?' Sarah asked.

'And dentist. That'll be a fun appointment.'

I read a magazine while I waited for them to call my name at the doctor's office. When the nurse asked me to step on the scale, I was shocked when it registered one hundred and two pounds, especially since I'd already had a few days of solid eating. At five foot six, I should have weighed fifteen to twenty pounds more. I probably wasn't even in triple digits on the island.

I sat on the exam table dressed in a paper gown. When my doctor walked in, she hugged me and said, 'Welcome back. I'm sure you've heard this a lot, Anna, but I can't believe you're alive.'

'It's something I don't mind hearing.'

She flipped open my chart. 'You're underweight, but I'm sure you know that. How are you feeling overall? Is there anything specific you're worried about?'

'I feel better already, now that I'm eating more. I haven't had my period in a long time, though. I'm worried about that.'

'Well let's take a look,' she said as she guided my feet into the stirrups. 'Given your low weight, I'd be surprised if you were having periods. Any other problems?

'No.'

'Almost done,' she said. 'I'll run the usual labs but your menstrual cycle should resume normally as soon as you put on some weight. You're obviously malnourished but that's relatively easy to reverse. Make sure to eat a balanced diet. I want you to start taking a multivitamin every day.'

'Will not having a period for so long make it hard to get pregnant someday?'

'No. Once your period comes back, you should be able to get pregnant.' She stripped off her gloves and dropped them in the trash. 'You can get dressed now.'

I sat up on the table. She paused at the door and said, 'I'll write you a new prescription for your birth control pills.'

'Okay.'

I thought it would be easier to accept the prescription instead of explaining that I didn't need birth control pills because my twenty-year-old boyfriend was sterile.

I visited the dentist next and sat uncomfortably in the chair for over an hour while the hygienist took x-rays and scraped and polished my teeth. When she announced I didn't have any cavities, I considered myself lucky.

Sarah had loaned me some cash. After my dentist appointment I took a cab to the nail salon. When Lucy saw my face, she jumped out of her chair and barreled toward me.

'Oh, honey,' she said, wrapping me in a hug. When she pulled away, she had tears in her eyes.

'Don't cry, Lucy. You'll make me cry, too.'

'Anna home,' she said, smiling up at me.

'Yes, I'm home.'

She gave me a manicure and pedicure and spoke so excitedly I caught even less of what she said than I usually did. She mentioned John a couple times but I pretended I didn't understand. When she finished she gave me another hug.

'Thanks, Lucy. I'll be back soon,' I promised.

I left the nail salon and glanced down at my hands. They were freezing without gloves but I didn't want to smudge the polish. My teeth felt clean and smooth when I ran my tongue over them. The smell of hot dogs from a street vendor filled the air as I window-shopped, peering through the glass at the latest styles. I decided to come back the next day and buy clothes that fit.

Unrecognizable, I hoped, in the sunglasses and wool hat I borrowed from Sarah, I strode down the sidewalk with a smile on my face, feeling like there were springs in the bottom of my shoes. I hailed a cab at the corner and gave the driver Sarah's address.

Even the reporters that swarmed me when I arrived at Sarah's apartment couldn't dampen the joy I felt. I pushed my way through them, unlocked the door, and shut it quickly behind me.

T.J. called later that night.

'How did it go at the oncologist?' I asked.

'They won't have my scans and blood work back for a few days. He said he was optimistic though since I haven't had any symptoms. I went to my regular doctor, too.'

'How did that go?'

'I need to gain weight, but otherwise I'm fine. I told him about getting sick on the island. He's pretty sure he knows what I had. You were right. It *was* viral.'

'What was it?'

'Dengue hemorrhagic fever. Transmitted by mosquitoes.'

'You always were covered in bites. So it's like malaria?'

'I guess. They call it "breakbone fever." They're right.'

'How serious is it?'

'It has about a fifty percent death rate. The doctor said I was lucky I didn't go into shock or bleed to death.'

'I can't believe the things you've survived, T.J.'

'Me neither. How was your doctor appointment? Is everything okay?'

'I'll be fine as soon as I gain some weight. My doctor said the malnutrition wouldn't be difficult to reverse. I'm supposed to take a vitamin every day.'

'I can't wait to see you tomorrow night, Anna.'

'I can't wait to see you, too.'

On New Year's Eve, I took a shower, styled my hair, and put on the makeup I bought when I went shopping. My new lip stain wouldn't come off when I kissed T.J., which I planned to do a lot. I snipped the tags off a new pair of jeans and a navy blue v-neck sweater, then pulled them on over a black push-up bra and lacy underwear.

When T.J. knocked, I ran to the door and opened it.

'Your hair!' I said. Cropped brown hair framed his face and I ran my fingers through it. Clean-shaven, he wore jeans and a gray sweater. I inhaled his cologne. 'You smell good.'

'You look beautiful,' he said, bending down to kiss my lips. He had briefly met Sarah and David at the airport, but I introduced them again. The kids stole looks at T.J., peeking out from behind Sarah.

'You must be Joe and Chloe. I've heard a lot about you,' T.J. said.

'Hi,' Joe said.

'Hi,' Chloe echoed. She hid behind Sarah again, sneaking another look at T.J. a few seconds later.

'We better hurry, David, if we want to make those reservations,' Sarah said.

'You're leaving?' I asked.

'For a couple hours. We thought we'd get the kids out of the house for a little while.' She grabbed her coat and smiled at me. I smiled back.

'Okay. See you later.'

I jumped into T.J.'s arms as soon as the door closed, wrapping my legs around his waist. He carried me down the hallway while I kissed his neck.

'Where?' he asked.

I grabbed the doorway when we reached the spare bedroom. 'Here.'

T.J. kicked the door closed with his foot and deposited me on the bed.

'God, I've missed you.' He kissed me, slid his hands under my sweater, and whispered, 'Let's see what you've got on under here.'

We barely made it back out to the couch by the time Sarah, David and the kids came home two hours later.

'Are you having fun with your boyfriend, Aunt Anna?' Chloe asked.

Sarah and I looked at each other and she raised her eyebrows at me before disappearing into the kitchen.

'Yes, I'm having a lot of fun with him. Did you have a good dinner?'

'Uh huh. I had chicken nuggets and French fries and Mommy let me have orange soda!'

Joe came over and sat next to T.J.

'What about you?' T.J. asked him. 'What did you have?'

'I had a steak,' he said. 'I don't order off the baby menu.'

'Wow, a steak,' T.J. said. 'I'm impressed.'

'Yeah.'

Sarah came back into the room with a glass of wine for me and a beer for T.J. 'We brought you dinner. It's on the counter.'

We thanked her and went into the kitchen to warm up our food. Steak, baked potatoes, and broccoli with cheese sauce.

T.J. ate a piece of steak. 'Your sister is awesome.'

Sarah put the kids to bed at 8:30 and the four of us sat around talking, the stereo on low.

'So you're saying you had a pet chicken named Chicken?' David asked.

'It used to sit in Anna's lap,' T.J. said.

'Amazing,' David said.

Later, when I went into the kitchen to refill our drinks, Sarah followed me.

'Is T.J. staying over?'

'I don't know. Can he?'

'I don't care. But you get to answer Miss Chloe's questions in the morning because I guarantee you, she'll have some.'

'Okay. Thanks, Sarah.'

We walked back into the living room, and T.J. pulled me onto his lap. David turned on the T.V. The ball was about to drop in Times Square and we counted backward from ten and yelled 'Happy New Year.'

T.J. kissed me, and I thought I could never be happier than I was at that moment.

Chapter 52
T.J.

My mom was sitting in the living room drinking coffee when I walked in the door at 9:00 a.m. on New Year's Day.

'Hey Mom. Happy New Year.' I hugged her and sat down. 'I stayed at Anna's last night.'

'I thought you might.'

'Should I have called?' Other than going out with Ben, or to the appointments my mom had scheduled, I'd spent every minute since I got home with my family. I knew they'd understand my wanting to see Anna, but it hadn't occurred to me to let anyone know I was going to be out all night.

'It would be nice if you did. Then I wouldn't worry.'

Shit. I wondered how many sleepless nights she'd had in the last three-and-a-half years, and I felt like an even bigger asshole for not calling. 'I'm sorry Mom. I wasn't thinking. I'll call next time.'

'Do you want some coffee? I can make you breakfast.'

'No thanks. I ate at Anna's.' We sat in silence for a minute. 'You haven't said anything about me and Anna, Mom. How you feel about it?'

My mom shook her head. 'It's not what I would have chosen, T.J. No mother would. But I understand what it must have been like for the two of you on the island. It would be hard *not* to form a bond with someone under those circumstances.'

'She's a great girl.'

'I know she is. We wouldn't have hired her if we didn't think so.' My mom set her coffee cup down on the table. 'When your plane went down, part of me died, T.J. I felt like it was my fault. I knew how angry you were about spending the summer away from home, and I didn't care. I told your dad we needed to vacation somewhere far away so you'd concentrate on your schoolwork, without any distraction. That was partly true. But mostly it was because I knew when we got home I'd lose you to your friends. You were finally healthy and you wanted nothing more than to go back to the way things were before you got sick. I was selfish, though. I just wanted to spend the summer with my son.' My mom's eyes filled with tears. 'You're an adult now, T.J. You've been through more in your first twenty years than most people endure in a lifetime. Your relationship with Anna is not something I'm going to fight. Now that I have you back I just want you to be happy.'

I noticed for the first time how worn out my mom looked. She was forty-five but a stranger would probably guess her age as ten years older. 'Thanks for being cool about it, Mom. She's important to me.'

'I know she is. But you and Anna are at very different stages in your lives. I don't want to see you get hurt.'

'I won't.' I kissed my mom on the cheek and went to my room. I stretched out on my bed and thought about Anna, pushing everything my mom said about different stages right out of my head.

Chapter 53
Anna

T.J. and I rode the elevator to his parents' apartment on the twelfth floor. 'Do not touch me. Do not even *look* at me inappropriately,' I warned him.

'Can I think super dirty thoughts about you?'

I shook my head. 'That's not helping. Oh, I feel sick.'

'My mom's cool. I told you what she said about us. Just relax.'

Tom Callahan had called Sarah's cell phone on New Year's Day. When the name showed up on the caller ID, I thought it was T.J., but when I said hello, Tom greeted me and asked if I'd like to come over for dinner the next night.

'Jane and I have a few things to discuss with you.'

Please don't let one of them be that I slept with your son.

'Sure, Tom. What time?'

'T.J. said he'd pick you up at 6:00.'

'Okay. I'll see you tomorrow night.'

I spent the twenty-four hours since Tom's call feeling like I was about to throw up. I couldn't decide whether to bring Jane flowers or a candle, so I brought both. Now, in the elevator, my nervousness threatened to overtake me. I handed the gift bag and bouquet to T.J. and wiped my damp palms on my skirt.

The elevator doors opened. T.J. kissed me and said, 'It'll be fine.'

I took a deep breath and followed him.

The Callahan's Lake Shore Drive apartment was taste-fully decorated in shades of beige and cream. A baby grand piano sat at an angle in a corner of the vast living room and Impressionist paintings hung on the walls. The plush couch, loveseat, and matching chairs – piled high with tasseled pillows – surrounded a large, ornate coffee table.

Tom poured pre-dinner drinks in the library. I sat in a leather club chair holding a glass of red wine. T.J. sat in the chair next to me. Tom and Jane were across from us on a loveseat, Jane sipping a glass of white wine and Tom drinking something that looked like scotch.

'Thank you for inviting me here,' I said. 'Your home is beautiful.'

'Thank you for coming, Anna,' Jane said.

Everyone took a drink. Silence filled the room.

T.J. – the only relaxed person there – took a swig from the beer he'd helped himself to and draped an arm over the back of my chair.

'The media have asked if you and T.J. would be willing to hold a press conference,' Tom said. 'In exchange, they'll stop bothering you.'

'What do you think, Anna?' T.J. asked.

The idea filled me with dread but I was tired of fighting my way past the reporters. Maybe if we answered their questions, they'd leave us alone.

'Would it be televised?' I asked.

'No. I've already told them it would have to be a closed press conference. They'll hold it at the news station, but they won't broadcast it.'

'If the reporters agree to back off, I'll do it.'

'So will I,' T.J. said.

'I'll set it up,' Tom said. 'There's something else, Anna. T.J. already knows this but I've been on the phone with the attorney for the seaplane charter. Because the death of the pilot caused the crash but the supplier of the life raft didn't provide the Coast Guard-mandated emergency beacon, there's comparative fault. Both parties are considered negligent. Aviation litigation is very complex and the courts will have to determine the percentage of liability. These cases can drag on for years. However, the seaplane charter would like to settle with you both and then subrogate against the other party. In exchange, you'll agree not to file a lawsuit.'

My head spun. I hadn't thought about negligence or lawsuits. 'I don't know what to say. I wouldn't have sued anyway.'

'Then I suggest you settle. There won't be any trial. You may need to give a deposition, but you can do that here in Chicago. Since you were in my employ when the crash occurred, my attorney can handle the negotiations for you.'

'Yes. That would be fine.'

'It will probably take several months, or more, before it's finalized.'

'Okay, Tom.'

Alexis and Grace joined us for dinner. Everyone had relaxed considerably by the time we sat down at the dining room table, helped in part by the second round of drinks we all said we didn't want but drank anyway.

Jane served beef tenderloin, roasted vegetables, and au gratin potatoes. Alexis and Grace snuck looks at me and smiled. I helped Jane clear the table and serve a warm apple tart and ice cream for dessert.

When we got ready to leave, Tom handed me an envelope. 'What's this?'

'It's a check. We still owe you for the tutoring.'

'You don't owe me anything. I didn't do my job.' I tried to give the envelope back to him.

Gently, he pushed my hand away. 'Jane and I insist.'

'Tom, please.'

'Just take it, Anna. It will make us happy.'

'Okay.' I slid the envelope into my purse.

'Thank you for everything,' I said to Jane.

I looked her in the eye and she met my gaze. Not many mothers would welcome their son's much older girlfriend into their home so graciously and we both knew it.

'You're welcome, Anna. Come again sometime.'

T.J. took me in his arms as soon as the elevator doors closed. I exhaled and rested my head on his chest. 'Your parents are wonderful.'

'I told you they were cool.'

They were also generous. Because later that night, when I opened the envelope they'd given me, I pulled out a check for twenty-five thousand dollars.

The press conference was scheduled to begin at two o'clock. Tom and Jane Callahan stood off to the side, Tom holding a small video camera in his hand, the only one allowed to tape anything.

'I know what they're going to ask,' I said.

'You don't have to answer anything you don't want to,' T.J. reminded me.

We sat at a long table facing a sea of reporters. I tapped my right foot up and down and T.J. leaned over and pressed down gently on my thigh. He knew better than to leave his hand there for very long.

Someone had taped a large map on the wall showing an aerial view of the twenty-six atolls of the Maldives. A public relations representative for the news channel, assigned to moderate the press conference, began by explaining to the reporters that the island T.J. and I lived on was uninhabited and likely sustained significant damage due to the tsunami She used a laser pointer and identified the island of Malé as our starting point. 'This was their destination,' she said, pointing to another island. 'Because the pilot suffered a heart attack, the plane crash-landed somewhere in between.'

The first question came from a reporter standing in the back row. He had to shout so we could hear him.

'What went through your minds when you realized the pilot was having a heart attack?'

I leaned forward and spoke into the microphone. 'We were scared he would die and worried that he wouldn't be able to land the plane.'

'Did you try to help him?' another reporter asked.

'Anna did,' T.J. said. 'The pilot asked us to put on life jackets and go back to our seats and buckle in. When he slumped over, Anna unbuckled and went forward to start CPR.'

'How long were you in the ocean before you made it to the island?'

T.J. answered that question. 'I'm not sure. The sun set about an hour after we crashed and it came up after we made it to shore.'

We answered questions for the next hour. They asked us about everything from how we fed ourselves to what kind of shelter we built. We told them about T.J.'s broken collarbone and the illness that almost killed him. We described the storms and explained how the dolphins saved T.J. from the shark. We talked about the tsunami and our reunion at the hospital. They seemed genuinely in awe of the hardships we faced, and I relaxed a little.

Then a reporter in the front row, a middle-aged woman with a scowl on her face asked, 'What kind of physical relationship did you have on the island?'

'That's irrelevant,' I answered.

'Are you aware of the age of consent in the state of Illinois?' she asked.

I didn't point out that the island wasn't in Illinois. 'Of course I am.' In case not everyone knew, she decided to enlighten them.

'The age of consent in Illinois is seventeen, unless the relationship involves a person of authority such as a teacher. Then the age is raised to eighteen.'

'No laws were broken,' T.J. said.

'Sometimes victims are coerced into lying,' the reporter countered. 'Especially if the abuse occurred early on.'

'There was no abuse,' T.J. said.

She addressed me directly with her next question.

'How do you think Chicago taxpayers will feel about paying the salary of a teacher suspected of sexual misconduct toward a student?'

'There wasn't any sexual misconduct,' T.J. yelled. 'What part of this are you not getting?'

Though I knew they would ask about our relationship,

I never considered the possibility that they'd accuse us of lying about it, or think I somehow forced myself on T.J. The seed of doubt the reporter planted would undoubtedly multiply, fed by rumors and speculation. Everyone that read our story would question my actions and my integrity. At the very least, it might be difficult to find a school district willing to take a chance on me, effectively ending my career as a teacher.

When my brain finished processing what her questioning had done, I barely had enough time to scrape my chair back and run for the women's restroom. I flung open the door of a stall and leaned over the toilet. I'd been unable to eat before the press conference and my empty stomach dry-heaved but nothing came up. Someone opened the door.

'I'm okay, T.J. I'll be out in minute.'

'It's me, Anna,' a female voice said.

I came out of the stall. Jane Callahan was standing there. She opened her arms to me and it was so like something my own mom would have done that I threw myself into them and burst into tears. When I stopped crying, Jane handed me a tissue and said, 'The media sensationalizes everything. I think some of the general public will see through it.'

I wiped my eyes. 'I hope so.'

T.J. and Tom were waiting for us when we walked out of the restroom. T.J. led me to a chair and sat down beside me.

'Are you okay?' He put his arm around me, and I rested my head on his shoulder.

'I'm better now.'

'It'll all work out, Anna.'

'Maybe,' I said. *Or maybe not.*

The next morning, I read the newspaper coverage of the press conference. It wasn't as bad as I'd expected, but it wasn't good either. The article didn't question my teaching ability, but it echoed some of the points the reporter made about the likelihood of a school district agreeing to hire me. I handed it to Sarah when she walked into the room. She read it and made a disgusted noise.

'What are you going to do?' Sarah asked.

'I'm going to talk to Ken.'

Ken Tomlinson had been my principal for six years. A thirty-year veteran of the Illinois public school system, his dedication to the students and his support of the teachers made him one of the most respected men in the district. He didn't spend a lot of time worrying about things that didn't matter, and he told the best off-color jokes I'd ever heard.

I stuck my head into his office a little after 7:00 a.m. a few days after the press conference. He pushed his chair back and met me at the door.

'Kiddo, you don't know how happy I am to see you.' He hugged me. 'Welcome home.'

'I got your message on Sarah's answering machine. Thanks for calling.'

'I wanted you to know we were all thinking about you. I figured it might be a little while before you could make it in.' He sat down behind his desk and I sat in a chair across from him. 'I think I know why you're here now.'

'Have you had any calls?'

He nodded. 'A few. Some parents wanted to know if

you'd be returning to the school. I wanted to tell them what I really thought about their supposed concerns, but I couldn't.'

'I know, Ken.'

'I'd love to give you your old job back, but I hired someone two months after your plane went down, when we'd all lost hope of you ever being found.'

'I understand. I'm not ready to go back to work yet anyway.'

Ken leaned forward in his chair and rested his elbows on the desk. 'People want to make things into something they're not. It's human nature. Lay low for a while. Let it blow over.'

'I would never do anything to harm a student, Ken.'

'I know that, Anna. I never doubted you for a minute.' He came out from behind the desk and said, 'You're a good teacher. Don't let anyone tell you you're not.'

The halls would fill with teachers and students soon, and I wanted to slip out unnoticed. I stood up and said, 'Thanks, Ken. That means a lot to me.'

'Come back again, Anna. We'd all like to spend some time with you.'

'I'll do that.'

The details of the press conference spread like wildfire and it didn't take long for our story to reach a worldwide audience. Unfortunately, most of the information was incorrect, embellished, and not even close to the truth.

Everyone had an opinion about my actions, and they discussed and debated my relationship with T.J. in chat rooms and on message boards. I provided many late night talk show hosts with monologue material, and I was the punch line of so many jokes that I stopped watching television altogether, preferring the solitude and comfort of the music and books I missed so much on the island.

T.J. took his share of ridicule, too. They laughed about his tenth grade education but said that maybe it didn't matter considering the other things he must surely have learned from me.

I didn't want to go out in public, worried that people would stare. 'Did you know you can buy almost everything you need on the Internet?' I was sitting on the couch next to T.J., typing on Sarah's laptop. 'They'll ship it right to your doorstep. I may never leave the house again.'

'You can't hide forever, Anna,' T.J. said.

I typed 'bedroom furniture' into the Google search box and hit enter. 'Wanna bet?'

The insomnia started a few weeks later. First, I had trouble falling asleep. With Sarah's blessing, T.J. spent the night often, and I'd listen to his soft breathing, but I couldn't relax. Then, even if I managed to fall asleep, I'd wake up at two or three in the morning and lay there until the sun came up. I had frequent nightmares, usually about drowning, and I'd wake up drenched in sweat. T.J. said I often cried out in the middle of the night.

'Maybe you should go back to the doctor, Anna.'

Exhausted and fraying, I agreed.

'Acute stress disorder,' my doctor said a few days later. 'This is actually very common, Anna, especially in women. Traumatic events often trigger delayed onset insomnia and anxiety.'

'How is it treated?'

'Usually with a combination of cognitive behavioral therapy and drugs. Some patients get relief from a low dose antidepressant. I could prescribe something to help you sleep.'

I had friends who had taken antidepressants and sleeping pills and they'd complained about side effects. 'I'd rather not take anything if I can help it.'

'Would you consider seeing a therapist?'

I was ready to try anything if it meant getting a full night's sleep. 'Why not?'

I made an appointment with a therapist I found in the yellow pages. Her office was in an old brick building with a crumbling front step. I checked in with the receptionist, and the therapist opened the door to the waiting room and called my name five minutes later. She had a warm smile and a firm handshake. I guessed her to be in her late forties.

'I'm Rosemary Miller.'

'Anna Emerson. Nice to meet you.'

'Please have a seat.' She pointed at a couch and sat in a chair across from me, handing me one of her business cards. A lamp burned brightly on a low table next to the couch. A potted ficus tree stood near the window. Boxes of Kleenex were scattered on every available surface.

'I've followed your story in the news. I'm not surprised to see you here.'

'I've been suffering from insomnia and anxiety. My doctor suggested I try therapy.'

'What you're experiencing is very common, given the trauma you suffered. Have you ever seen a therapist before?'

'No.'

'I'd like to start by taking a full patient history.'

'Okay.'

She droned on for forty-five minutes, asking me questions about my parents and Sarah and my relationships with them. She asked about my prior relationships with men and when I told her the bare minimum about John, she probed further, asking me to go into more detail. I fidgeted uncomfortably, wondering when we were going to get to the part where she fixed my insomnia.

'I may want to revisit some of your patient history in the coming weeks. Now I'd like to discuss your sleep habits.'

Finally.

'I can't fall asleep or stay asleep. I'm having nightmares.'

'What are the nightmares about?'

'Drowning. Sharks. Sometimes the tsunami. Usually there's water.'

Someone knocked on the door and she glanced at her watch.

'I'm sorry. We're out of time.'

You have got to be kidding me.

'Next week we can start some cognitive therapy exercises.'

At the rate we were going, I might not get a good night's sleep for months. She shook my hand and walked me to the lobby. Once outside, I dropped her business card in a garbage can.

T.J. and Sarah were sitting in the living room when I got home. I plopped down on T.J.'s lap.

'How did it go?' T.J. asked

'I don't think I'm a therapy person.'

'Sometimes it takes a while to find a good one,' Sarah said.

'I don't think she's a bad therapist. There's just something else I want to try. If it doesn't work, I'll go back.'

I left the room and returned a few minutes later, dressed in running tights and a long sleeved T-shirt layered under a sweatshirt and nylon windbreaker. I pulled on a hat and sat down on the couch to lace up my Nikes.

'What are you doing?' T.J. asked.

'I'm going for a run.'

Chapter 54
T.J.

I carried the last box up the stairs to Anna's new place, a small one-bedroom apartment fifteen minutes from Sarah and David.

'Where do you want this one?' I asked when I walked through the door, shaking the rain from my hair.

'Just set it down anywhere.' She handed me a towel and I stripped off my wet T-shirt and dried myself off.

'I'm trying to find the sheets,' Anna said. 'They delivered the bed while you were gone.' We searched until we found them, and I helped her put them on.

'I'll be right back,' she said. She returned with a small object and set it on the nightstand, plugging it into a nearby outlet.

'What's that?' I asked, lying down on the bed.

She pushed a button and the sound of ocean waves filled the room, almost drowning out the rain that beat against the window.

'It's a sound machine. I ordered it from Bed, Bath, and Beyond.'

She stretched out beside me. I reached for her hand and kissed the back of it, then pulled her toward me. She relaxed, her body melting into mine.

'I'm happy. Are you happy, Anna?'

'Yes,' she whispered.

I held her in my arms. Listening to the rain and the

crash of the waves, I could almost pretend we were still on the island and nothing had changed.

She didn't ask me to move in; I just never left. I spent a few nights at home, because it made my parents happy, and Anna and I stopped by a lot to hang out or have dinner. Anna took Grace and Alexis shopping a couple of times, which thrilled them both.

She wouldn't take any money for rent so I paid for everything else, which she barely allowed. I had a trust fund my parents set up when I was younger. I would have had access to it when I turned eighteen and the money was mine now. The balance in the account would easily cover living expenses, a car, and the cost of my college education. My parents wanted to know — and they asked me all the time — what my plans were, but I wasn't sure what I wanted to do. Anna hadn't said anything, but I knew she wanted me to start working on my GED.

People sometimes recognized us, especially when we were together, but Anna slowly became more comfortable being out in public. We always went outside, to the park and on long walks, even though spring was still weeks away. We went to the movies and sometimes out for lunch or dinner, but Anna liked eating at home. She cooked me anything I wanted, and I slowly gained weight. She did, too. When I ran my hands over her body, I didn't feel bones anymore. I felt soft curves.

At night, Anna laced up her running shoes and ran almost to exhaustion. She returned to the apartment, stripped off her sweaty clothes, and took a long, hot shower, joining me in bed afterward. She had just enough energy to make love and then she crashed, sleeping soundly. She still had the occasional nightmare or trouble falling asleep but nothing like before.

I liked our routine. I had no desire to change it.

'Ben invited me to spend the weekend with him,' I told Anna over breakfast a few weeks later.

'He's at the University of Iowa, right?'

'Yeah.'

'I love that campus. You'll have a great time.'

'I'm leaving Friday. I'm catching a ride with a friend of his.'

'Check out the school, not just the bars. You might want to consider going there after you finish your GED.'

I didn't tell Anna I had no interest in a college that was in another state, away from her. Or any interest in college at all, actually.

A wobbly six-foot-high beer can pyramid stood in the corner of Ben's dorm room. I stepped over empty pizza boxes and piles of dirty laundry. Textbooks, tennis shoes, and empty Mountain Dew bottles covered every inch of the floor.

'Jesus, how can you stand this?' I asked. 'And did someone take a piss in your elevator?'

'Probably,' Ben replied. 'Here's your ID.'

I squinted at the driver's license. 'Since when am I five-eight, blond, and twenty-seven?'

'Since now. Are you ready to go to the bar?'

'Sure. Where do you want me to put my stuff?'

'Who cares, dude.' Ben's roommate had gone home for

the weekend so I threw my duffel bag on his bed and followed Ben out the door.

'Let's take the stairs,' I said.

We had a good buzz going by nine o'clock. I checked my cell but there were no messages from Anna. I thought about calling her, but I knew Ben would give me shit about it so I put my phone back in my pocket.

He invited some people over to our table to do shots. No one recognized me. I blended into the crowd like any other college student, which was exactly the way I wanted it.

I sat between two very drunk girls. One of them downed a shot of vodka while the other paused, holding the glass to her lips. She leaned toward me, her eyes glassy, and said, 'You're really hot.' Then she set the shot down and puked all over the table. I jumped up and pushed my chair back.

Ben motioned for me to follow him and we walked out of the bar. I took deep breaths of the cold air to clear the smell out of my nose.

'You want to get something to eat?' he asked me.

'Always.'

'Pizza?'

'Sure.'

We sat at a table in the back. 'Anna told me to check out the campus. She said I should think about coming here after I get my GED.'

'Dude, that'd be awesome. We could get our own place. Are you gonna?'

'No.'

'Why not?'

I was drunk enough to be honest with Ben. 'I just want to be with her.'

'Anna?'

'Yes, dumbass. Who else?'

'What's she want?'

The waitress came to our table and set a large pepperoni and sausage pizza down in front of us. I put two pieces on my plate and said, 'I'm not sure.'

'Are you talking, like, get married and have a kid with her?'

'I'd marry her tomorrow.' I took a bite of my pizza. 'Maybe we could wait a little while for the kid.'

'Will she wait?'

'I don't know.'

Chapter 55
Anna

Stefani and I ordered a glass of wine at the bar while we waited for a table.

'So T.J. went to visit his friend this weekend?' Stefani asked.

'Yes.' I glanced at my watch. 8:03. 'My guess is they're heading full speed toward wasted right now. At least I hope so.'

'You don't care if he gets trashed?'

'Do you remember what we did in college?'

Stefani smiled. 'How is it that we never got arrested?'

'Short skirts and dumb luck.' I took a sip of my wine. 'I want T.J. to have those experiences. I don't want him to feel like he's missed out.'

'Are you trying to convince yourself, or me?'

'I'm not trying to convince anyone. I just don't want to hold him back.'

'Rob and I want to meet him. If he's important to you we'd like to get to know him.'

'Thanks. That's really nice of you, Stef.'

'The bartender put two more glasses of wine in front of us. 'These are from the guys sitting over in the corner.'

Stefani waited a minute and then grabbed her purse hanging on the back of her chair. She rummaged around inside and pulled out a mirror and lipstick, turning back around.

'Well?'

'They're good-looking.'

'You're married!'

'I'm not gonna go home with one of them. Besides, Rob knew I was a flirt when he married me.' She applied her lipstick and used a cocktail napkin to blot. 'And no one has sent me a drink since the mid-nineties so shut up.'

'Do we have to go over and say thank you or can we just ignore them?' I asked.

'You don't want to talk to them?'

'No.'

'Too late. Here they come.'

I looked over my shoulder as they approached.

'Hi,' one of them said.

'Hi. Thank you for the wine.'

His friend chatted with Stefani. I rolled my eyes when she flipped her hair and giggled.

'I'm Drew.' He had brown hair and he was wearing a suit and tie. He looked like he was in his mid to late thirties. Attractive, if you liked the banker type.

'Anna.' We shook hands.

'I recognized you from your picture in the paper. That was quite an ordeal. I assume you're tired of talking about it.'

'I am.'

The conversation stalled so I took a sip of my wine.

'Are you waiting for a table?' he asked.

'Yes. It should be ready soon.'

'Maybe we can join you?'

'I'm sorry, not tonight. I just want to spend time with my friend.'

'Sure. I understand. Maybe I could get your phone number.'

'I don't think so.'

'Oh come on,' he said, smiling and turning on the charm. 'I'm a nice guy.'

'I'm seeing someone.'

'That was fast.' He looked at me strangely. 'Wait, you don't mean that kid, do you?'

'He's not a kid.'

'Yes he is.'

Stefani tapped me on the shoulder. 'Our table is ready.'

'Thanks again for the wine. Excuse me.' I grabbed my purse and coat, slid off the bar stool, and followed Stefani.

'What did he say to you?' Stefani asked when we sat down at the table. 'You didn't look thrilled with him.'

'He discovered I wasn't single. Then he called T.J. a kid.'

'His ego is probably a bit bruised.'

'T.J. *is* young, Stefani. When people look at him, they don't see what I see. They see a kid.'

'What do you see?' Stefani asked.

'I just see T.J.'

He came home Sunday night, tired and hung over. He set his bag down on the floor and pulled me into his arms. I gave him a long kiss.

'Wow,' he said. He cupped my face in his hands and kissed me back.

'I missed you.'

'I missed you, too.'

'How was it?'

'His dorm room is a pit, a girl almost puked on me, and somebody peed in the elevator.'

I wrinkled my nose. 'Really?'

'I gotta tell you. I wasn't super impressed.'

'You'd probably feel differently if you'd gone to college right after high school.'

'But I didn't, Anna. And I'm still behind.'

Chapter 56
T.J.

'I don't have to wear a tie, do I?'

I had on a pair of khakis and a white button down dress shirt. A navy blue sport coat lay across the bed. We were meeting Stefani and her husband Rob for dinner, and I was already more dressed up than I wanted to be.

'You probably should,' Anna said, walking into the bedroom.

'Do I have a tie?'

'I bought you one when Stefani told me where they wanted to go for dinner.' She reached into her closet and pulled it out, threading it through the collar of my shirt and tying it for me.

'I can't remember the last time I wore one of these,' I said, pulling on the knot to loosen it a little. I had met Stefani and Rob the week before, when they invited us over to their place. I liked them. They were easy to talk to, so when Anna said they wanted us to go out to dinner with them, I said sure.

'I'll be ready in a minute. I just have to decide what to wear.'

She stood in front of her closet in her bra and underwear so I sprawled out on the bed and enjoyed the view.

'I thought you said thongs were uncomfortable.'

'They are. But I'm afraid it's a necessary evil tonight.' Anna pulled a dress out of her closet. 'This one?' she asked, holding a long, sleeveless black dress against her chest.

'That one's nice.'

'What about this one?' The other dress was dark blue, short, with long sleeves and a low-cut front.

'That's hot.'

'I think we have a winner then,' she said, putting it on. It clung to her. She stepped into a pair of high-heeled shoes.

I'd never seen her so dressed up before. She usually wore jeans – mostly Levi's – and a T-shirt or sweater. Sometimes she wore skirts but nothing like this. Her boobs had gotten bigger now that she was closer to her normal weight, and the bra she wore pushed them up. What I could see between the deep v-neck of her dress made me want to see more.

Twisting her hair, she gathered it into a knot at the back of her neck and put on earrings, the same dangly kind I'd used for fishhooks on the island. She wore red lipstick. I stared at her mouth and wanted to kiss her.

'You look incredible.'

She smiled. 'You think so?'

'Yes.' She looked classy. Beautiful. Like a woman who had her shit together.

'Let's go,' she said.

I was younger than everyone in the restaurant by ten to twenty years. We were a few minutes early, so Anna and I followed Stefani and Rob into the dimly lit bar to wait for our table. More than one head turned when Anna walked by.

Stefani started talking to some guy. Rob and I were

debating fighting our way through the crowd to get some drinks when a woman holding a stack of menus approached us.

'Your table is ready,' she said.

Stefani turned back to the guy she'd been talking to. He wore a suit, but he'd loosened his tie and unbuttoned the top two buttons of his shirt. He held a glass of something that looked like whiskey. He was there alone, and I wondered if he had come in after work.

'Why don't you join us for dinner,' Stefani said to him, 'Do you mind?' she asked us.

'That's fine,' Anna said.

I shrugged my shoulders. 'Sure.'

When we sat down, Stefani introduced him, 'This is Spence. We worked on the same account last year.' She and Rob sat beside him while Anna and I sat across from them. I shook his hand, noticed his bloodshot eyes, and realized he was wasted.

Rob ordered two bottles of wine and the server poured everyone a glass after she made him go through the whole cork-sniffing, wine-swirling bullshit routine.

I took a drink of mine. It was red and so dry I struggled not to make a face.

Spence zeroed in on Anna right away. He watched her take a sip of her wine. His eyes drifted from her eyes to her mouth then down to her chest.

'You look familiar,' he said.

She shook her head. 'We've never met.'

This was what Anna hated about meeting new people. They would try to place her and eventually they'd re-member her face from all the media coverage. Then the questions would start, first about the island and then about us.

Fortunately, he was drunk enough not to make the connection and Anna seemed to relax. He might not have recognized her, but he wasn't done with her either.

'Maybe we went out once.'

Anna lifted her glass and took another drink. 'No.'

'Maybe we can go out sometime?'

'Hey,' I said sharply. 'I'm sitting right here.'

Anna put her hand on my leg and pressed down. 'It's okay,' she whispered.

'Wait. She's with you?' Spence asked. 'I thought you were her younger brother or something.' He started laughing. 'You've got to be kidding me.' Realization dawned on his face as he glanced from me to Anna. 'Now I know who you are. I saw your pictures in the paper.' He snorted. 'Well that explains how you got her but not why she's still with you.'

Rob glanced at Stefani and then said to Spence, 'Knock it off.'

'Yes. I'm with him.' The way Anna said it, so confident, and the way she looked at him like he was a total dumbass made me feel better than the actual words.

Our server walked over. 'I'm sorry,' she said to me. 'I need to see your ID.'

I shrugged. 'I'm underage. I don't like the wine anyway. Go ahead and take it.'

She smiled, said sorry, and took my glass away. Spence couldn't handle it.

'You're not even twenty-one?' His barely contained laughter broke the silence at the table as everyone tried to act like what happened wasn't totally humiliating for me.

We looked down at our menus. Anna and I still had trouble choosing something to eat in a restaurant. Too many choices.

'What are you getting?' I asked her.

'Steak. What about you?' She grabbed my hand, lacing her fingers through mine.

'I don't know. Maybe pasta. You like ravioli, don't you?'

'Yes.'

'Okay. I'll get that and we can share.'

Stefani tried to keep the conversation going. Our server came back and took our order. Spence stared at Anna's chest and smirked, not even trying to hide it. I knew what he was thinking when he looked at her like that, and it took everything I had not to punch him.

When Spence got up to go to the bathroom Stefani said, 'I'm sorry. I heard his wife left him, and I thought asking him to join us would be a nice thing to do.'

'It's okay. Just ignore him,' Anna said. 'I am.'

No one refilled Spence's wine glass and by the time we finished eating, he seemed a little more sober.

Our server offered dessert but no one wanted any. She told us she'd be back with the check.

'Stefani and I are going to the restroom,' Anna said. 'We'll wait for you by the door.'

Rob and I both tried to pick up the check and finally agreed to split it, each of us pulling out cash. Spence threw a handful of bills on the table. I shoved my wallet in my pocket and stood up.

Rob pushed his chair back, said goodbye to Spence without shaking his hand, and headed for the front of the restaurant.

Spence didn't get up. 'I'm sorry you aren't old enough to drink with the grownups,' he said, slouching in his chair.

'I'm sorry you can't touch my hot girlfriend. And I don't really like wine anyway.'

I laughed at his expression and joined Anna, Stefani, and Rob by the front door.

'What'd you say to him?' Anna asked.

'I told him it was nice to meet him.'

'I'm sorry about tonight,' Anna said, when we got into the cab.

'It wasn't your fault.' I put my arm around her.

Not being able to drink at the restaurant hadn't bothered me but the way Spence looked at Anna had. I knew she wasn't interested in him, but I worried about the next guy. The one who wasn't a drunk asshole. The one who had a college degree, liked wine, and didn't mind wearing a tie. I worried that someday, maybe soon, it would matter to her that I wasn't interested in any of those things.

And when I thought about her being with another guy, I couldn't stand it.

I kissed her as soon as we were inside her apartment, and I wasn't gentle about it, holding her face firmly in my hands and pressing my lips hard against hers. She wasn't anyone's to own – I knew that – but right then she was mine. When we reached the bedroom, I pulled the dress over her head. Her bra came off next and then I pushed her underwear down off her hips until they dropped on the floor. I yanked off my tie and got out of the rest of my clothes. Laying her down on the bed, I bent my head to the place Spence had stared at all night, sucking and leaving a mark that would take days to fade. I touched and kissed her until she was ready, and once I was inside her, I made myself go slow, the way she liked it. When she came she said my name, and I thought, *I'm the one that does that to her. I'm the one that makes her feel that way.*

Afterward, I went into the kitchen and grabbed a beer from the fridge. I took it back into the bedroom and clicked on the T.V., keeping the volume low. Anna slept, the sheets tangled around her waist. Pulling the covers up, I tucked them gently around her shoulders with one hand and cracked my beer open with the other.

Chapter 57
Anna

In April, the spring rains stalled over Chicago for two days, keeping us inside.

T.J. flipped aimlessly through the channels. I lay on the couch with my feet in his lap, reading a book.

'Do you want to go to a movie?' he asked, turning off the T.V.

'Sure,' I said. 'What do you want to see?'

'I don't know. Let's just walk to the theater and choose one.'

I put on a jacket and we left the apartment, walking through the pouring rain while T.J. held an umbrella over our heads. He took my hand. I squeezed it and smiled when he squeezed it back.

T.J. wanted to see *Batman Begins*. We were standing in line to buy popcorn when someone tapped him on the shoulder.

We turned around. A tall guy in a baseball cap stood next to a petite girl wearing a pink hoodie, her hair up in a ponytail.

T.J. smiled. 'Hey, Coop. What's going on?'

'Just trying to find something to do until it stops raining.'

'Tell me about it. This is Anna,' T.J. said, draping an arm over my shoulders.

'Hi,' Coop said. 'This is my girlfriend, Brooke.'

'Nice to meet you both,' I said.

'I keep forgetting you're in town,' T.J. said.

'I'll be stuck at community college forever if I don't get my grades up.'

'Let's hang out sometime,' T.J. said.

'My parents are going out of town next month. I'll have a party. You guys should come.' Coop smiled at me, and I sensed the invitation was genuine.

'Yeah, that'd be cool,' T.J. said.

I glanced at Brooke while T.J. and Coop talked. She was staring at me, her mouth hanging open. To her, I probably seemed ancient.

Her unlined face and rosy skin looked radiant. She had no idea, the way I hadn't when I was twenty, how beautiful young skin was. Though I had often worn T.J.'s baseball cap and my sunglasses on the island, there were times when I hadn't. I thought of the years the sun had beat down on me, and I expected to wake up some morning and discover that my face had turned into leather while I slept. I spent more time than I was comfortable admitting trying to reverse the skin damage the island sun had inflicted, the counter of my bathroom crowded with all the lotions and creams the dermatologist had recommended. My skin appeared healthy, but there was no comparison between twenty and thirty-three. T.J. thought I was beautiful; he told me so. But what about five years from now? Ten?

We walked into the theater and found seats. T.J. put his popcorn between his legs and rested his hand on my thigh. I couldn't concentrate on the movie. Images of T.J. and me drinking keg beer out of plastic cups in Coop's living room while everyone gawked at me crowded my thoughts.

T.J. had done a great job fitting in with my friends. He'd endured Spence's obnoxious behavior and being ID'd for wine he had no desire to drink in the first place. Wearing a tie wasn't his thing, but he did it anyway. He'd carried on a conversation with Rob and Stefani, and he made it look effortless.

It was easier to age up, if you wanted to, by wearing nice clothes and emulating the behavior of people who were older. If I tried to fit in with T.J.'s twenty-something friends by dressing and acting like them, I'd look ridiculous.

The rain had ended by the time we left the theater. We followed the crowd and started walking. I stopped on the sidewalk.

'What's wrong?' T.J. asked.

'I won't always look like this.'

'What do you mean?'

'I'm thirteen years older than you, and I'm getting older every day. I won't always look like this.'

T.J. put his arms around my waist and pulled me close.

'I know that, Anna. But if you think I only care about what you look like then you don't know me as well as I thought you did.'

I walked alone down the aisle at Trader Joe's carrying a basket full of whatever caught my eye, which so far had been two bottles of cabernet, some organic pasta, a jar of marinara and some romaine lettuce, carrots, and bell peppers for a salad.

T.J. was out getting a haircut. We usually shopped for

food together, partly because he insisted on paying for it, and partly because we were still in awe of grocery stores. The first time we went grocery shopping, after I moved into my apartment, we stood frozen in the middle of the store staring at all the food.

I went down another aisle and grabbed some beer for T.J., then found the ingredients to make him a chocolate pie. I was trying to decide what kind of bread to serve with dinner when I felt a tug on my jeans.

A little girl about four years old stood there with huge silent tears running down her face.

'Are you a mommy?' she asked.

I crouched down until I was at her eye level. 'Well, no. Where's your mommy?'

She held tight to a raggedy, pink blanket. 'I don't know. I can't find her, and my mommy said if I ever got lost I should try to find another mommy, and she would help me.'

'Don't worry. I can still help you. What's your name?'

'Claire.'

'Okay, Claire.' I said. 'Let's go ask someone to make an announcement on the loudspeaker so your mom knows you're safe.' She looked at me with tears swimming in her big brown eyes and slipped her tiny hand into mine.

We were walking toward the front of the store when a woman came running around the corner shouting Claire's name. She held a basket in her hand. An infant slept in a carrier strapped to her chest.

'Claire! Oh God, there you are.' The woman ran toward us, dropped her basket, and scooped Claire up in her arms awkwardly, trying not to jostle the infant. The fear on her face dissolved as she squeezed Claire tight.

'Thank you for finding her,' she said. 'I dropped her hand for a minute to reach for something and when I looked down, she was gone. I'm just so tired, because of the baby, and I'm not moving very fast right now.'

She was probably close to my age, give or take a year, and she did look tired, with faint circles under her eyes. I picked up her basket. 'Are you ready to check out? Can I carry this for you?'

'Thank you. I would really appreciate that. I need more than two hands right now. You know how it is.'

I really didn't.

We walked to the checkout and unloaded our baskets.

'Do you live around here?' she asked.

'Yes,' I said.

'Kids?'

'No. Not yet.'

'Thank you so much for your help.'

'You're welcome.' I bent down. 'Bye, Claire.'

'Bye.'

When I got home I put the groceries away, sat down on the couch, and had a good cry.

Chapter 58
T.J.

Anna stood at the kitchen counter making me a chocolate pie. I kissed her and gave her the pink roses I'd bought on the way back from my haircut.

'They're beautiful. Thank you,' she said, smiling up at me. She grabbed a vase from under the sink and filled it with water. She wore her hair in a ponytail, and I put my arms around her from behind and kissed the back of her neck.

'Do you need any help?' I asked.

'No, I'm almost done.'

'Are you okay?'

'Yes, I'm fine.'

She wasn't fine, and I knew she'd been crying the minute I walked in the door because her eyes were puffy and streaked with red. But I didn't know how to fix it if she wouldn't tell me what was bothering her, and part of me wondered if it was better I didn't know in case it had something to do with me.

She turned around and smiled a little too brightly.

'Do you want to go to the park as soon as I finish this?' she asked.

A loose strand of hair had escaped from her ponytail and I tucked it behind her ear. 'Sure. I'll grab a blanket for us to sit on. I bet it's close to seventy degrees.' I kissed her forehead. 'I like being outside with you.'

'I like being outside with you, too.'

When we arrived at the park we spread the blanket out and sat down. Anna kicked off her shoes.

'Someone has a birthday coming up,' I said. 'What do you want to do to celebrate?'

'I don't know. I'll have to think about it.'

'I know what I'm getting you, but I haven't found it yet. I've been looking for a while.'

'I'm intrigued.'

'It's something you said you wanted once.'

'Besides books and music?'

'Yep.' I'd already bought her an iPod and downloaded all her favorite songs because she liked to listen to music when she ran. A couple times a week she went to the library and returned with stacks of books. She read faster than anyone I knew.

'You still have a couple weeks. You'll find it.' She smiled and kissed me, and she seemed so happy I thought that maybe everything was okay after all.

Chapter 59
Anna

I sent out hundreds of resumes. Finding a position so late in the year would be nearly impossible, but I still hoped to find something for fall, even if it was only substitute teaching.

Sarah gave me half the money she received from our parents' estate and I still had quite a bit left from the amount the Callahan's had paid me. The airline settlement would add to the balance. Maybe I didn't have to work, but I wanted to. I missed earning my own money, but mostly I missed teaching.

Sarah and I met for lunch a week before my birthday. The buds on the trees had grown into green leaves and the planters lining the sidewalks held spring flowers. So far, May had been unseasonably warm. We sat on the patio of the restaurant and ordered iced tea.

'What are you doing for your birthday?' Sarah asked, opening her menu.

'I don't know. T.J. asked me the same thing. I'm happy staying in.' I told her how T.J. and I had celebrated my last birthday on the island. How he'd pretended to give me books and music. 'This time, he's getting me something I mentioned I wanted. I have no idea what it could be.'

The waitress refilled our iced tea and took our order.

'How's the job search going?' Sarah asked.

'Not good. Either there really aren't any openings, or they just don't want to hire me.'

'Try not to let it get you down, Anna.'

'I wish it was that easy.' I took a drink of my iced tea. 'You know, when I got on that plane almost four years ago, I had a relationship that was going nowhere and an even slimmer chance of starting a family of my own, but at least I had a job I loved.'

'Someone will hire you eventually.'

'Maybe.'

Sarah peered at me across the table. 'Is that all that's bothering you?'

'No.' I told her about what happened at Trader Joe's. 'I still want the same things, Sarah.'

'What does T.J. want?'

'I'm not sure he knows. When we left Chicago, he just wanted to hang out with his friends and get back to the life he had before the cancer. His friends have moved on without him, though, and I don't think he's figured out what to do next.' I told Sarah about T.J.'s trust fund and she raised an eyebrow.

'In his defense, he's not spoiled by it. But he's not motivated, either.'

'I see your point,' she said.

'I'm waiting again, Sarah. Different reasons, different guy, but four years later I'm still waiting.'

Chapter 60
T.J.

The dog bounded into Anna's apartment and almost knocked her over. She bent down and it licked her face. I dropped the leash on the coffee table and said, 'Happy birthday. I couldn't get that thing in a box if I tried.'

She stood up and kissed me. 'I forgot I told you I wanted a dog.'

'Golden retriever. Full-grown. From a shelter. I've been looking everywhere. They told me someone found him wandering by the side of the road, no collar, or tags. Skin and bones.' When Anna heard that she dropped to her knees and hugged the dog, petting its soft fur. It licked her again, thumped its tail, and ran around in circles.

'It seems healthy now,' she said.

'You're not gonna name it Dog, are you?' I teased.

'No. That would be silly. I'm going to name it Bo. I've had the name picked out for a long time.'

'Then it's a good thing it's a boy.'

'He's the perfect gift, T.J. Thank you.'

'You're welcome. I'm glad you like him.'

Anna still hadn't found a teaching job by the middle of June. She had an interview that went well, at a high school out in the suburbs. She blew it off when she didn't get the job, but she had trouble falling asleep that night, and I found her in the living room reading a book with Bo's head in her lap at three in the morning.

'Come back to bed.'

'I'll be there in a minute,' she said. But when I woke up the next morning her side of the bed was still empty.

She filled her days babysitting Joe and Chloe, reading, and going for long runs. We spent hours outside, either on her small terrace or at the dog park with Bo. We watched the Cubs play at Wrigley Field, and we went to concerts in the park.

She seemed restless, though, no matter how busy we kept ourselves. She stared off into space sometimes, lost in thought, but I never quite had the balls to ask her what she was thinking about.

Chapter 61
Anna

'Look what came in the mail,' I said when I walked in the door, dropping my keys on the table.

T.J. sat on the couch watching T.V. Bo slept beside him. 'What is it?'

'It's the registration form for the GED preparation class. I called the other day and asked them to send information. I thought you could sign up, and I could start helping you study.'

'I can start in the fall.'

'They have summer sessions, though, and if you start now, you can finish by the end of August and then maybe enroll at a community college in September. If I manage to find a teaching job, we can both be at school all day.'

T.J. clicked off the television. I sat down beside him, scratching Bo behind the ears. Neither one of us said anything for a minute.

'At least one of us should be able to get on with their lives,' I said.

'What's that supposed to mean?' he asked.

'I *can't* find a job. You *can* go to school.'

'I don't want to be cooped up inside all day.'

'You're inside right now.'

'I was just waiting for you to get home so we could take Bo for a walk. What are you really trying to say, Anna?'

My heart started pounding. 'We can't keep trying to re-create the island here in this apartment.'

'This apartment is nothing like the island. We have everything we need.'

'No, you have everything you need. I don't.'

'I love you, Anna. I want to spend the rest of my life with you.' His words carried an unspoken meaning. *I'll marry you. We'll have a family together.*

I shook my head. 'You can't know that, T.J.'

'Of course not,' he said sarcastically. 'How could I possibly know what I want? I'm only twenty.'

'I've never talked down to you because of your age.'

He threw his hands up. 'You just did.'

'There are things you need to finish. And so many things you haven't had a chance to start. I can't take that away from you.'

'What if I don't want those things, Anna? What if I want you instead?'

'For how long, T.J.?'

Realization dawned on his face. 'You're afraid I won't *stay?*'

'Yes,' I whispered. 'That's exactly what I'm afraid of.' What if T.J got tired of playing house, and decided that settling down wasn't what he really wanted?

'After all we've been through together you don't trust me enough to believe I'll stick around?' The hurt in his eyes turned to anger. 'Bullshit, Anna.' He walked over to the window and stared outside. Turning back around he said, 'Why don't you just say what you really mean? That *you* want to look for someone your own age.'

'What?' I had no clue where he'd gotten that idea.

'You'd rather have a guy that's older. Someone people don't treat like a kid.'

'That's not true, T.J.'

'There'll always be some asshole who thinks he can hit on you right in front of me. They don't take me seriously. To them, you're the one killing time. Did you ever think that I might worry about you leaving *me*?'

An emotionally charged silence filled the apartment. The minutes felt like hours as both of us waited for the other to say that our fears weren't justified, but neither of us did.

I thought it would hurt less if I ripped the band-aid off quickly. 'You need to be on your own, T.J., and know what that's like before you can be sure you want to be with someone.'

The look on his face was pure anguish. He crossed the room and hesitated, standing only a few steps away from me, staring into my eyes. Then he turned his back on me and walked out the door, slamming it behind him.

I didn't sleep that night. I sat on the couch in the dark, crying into Bo's fur. The next morning I left the apartment early, having promised Sarah I'd watch the kids while she and David went to Sunday brunch. When I got back I discovered T.J. had ripped off a band-aid of his own because all his things were gone and his key to my apartment was on the kitchen table.

It hurt like hell.

Chapter 62
T.J.

Ben and I rented a two-bedroom apartment for the summer, on the third floor of an old building four blocks from Wrigley Field. His parents moved to Florida after telling him they were tired of the snow and cold. Ben didn't mind since he and his older brother both went to college out of state, but he needed somewhere to live until classes started back up in the fall.

'You wanna get a place with me, Callahan?' he'd asked. 'We can party like nobody's business.'

'Why not,' I'd answered. If Anna was so determined not to have me miss out on anything, sharing an apartment with my best friend was probably a step in the right direction.

Ben was majoring in finance and accounting and he somehow managed to land an internship at a downtown bank. He had to wear a tie every day.

I talked my way into a construction job, and I was out in the suburbs every morning by 7:00 a.m., framing houses. I caught a ride with a guy on the crew, and he taught me everything I needed to know and kept me from looking like a complete dumbass. It wasn't that different from building the house on the island except I used a nail gun and there was a lot more lumber lying around.

Most of the guys weren't real talkative, and I didn't have to carry on a conversation with anyone if I didn't feel like it. Sometimes the only noise was the sound of our tools and the classic rock music coming from the boom box. I never wore a shirt and pretty soon I was almost as tan as I'd been on the island.

At night, Ben and I drank beer. I missed Anna and thought about her constantly. Without her next to me I slept like shit. Ben knew better than to say anything about her, but he seemed worried about me.

Hell, 1 was worried about me.

Chapter 63
Anna

The temperature reached eighty-five degrees by two in the afternoon. The heat rolled off me like the sweat that ran down my face as my feet pounded the pavement.

It didn't bother me. I could handle heat.

All through the end of June and July I ran – six, then eight, then ten miles every day, sometimes more.

I didn't cry when I ran. I didn't think, and I didn't second-guess myself. Breathing deeply in and out, I put one foot in front of the other.

Tom Callahan called in early August. When the name came up on my caller ID my heart leapt, plummeting a second later after I answered and realized it wasn't T.J.

'The seaplane charter settled this morning. T.J.'s already signed the papers. Once you add your signature, it's done.'

'Okay,' I grabbed a pen and scribbled down the address he gave me.

'How are you, Anna?'

'I'm fine. How is T.J.?'

'He's keeping busy.'

I didn't ask him what that meant. 'Thanks for letting me know about the attorney. I'll make sure to sign the papers.' There was silence on the other end for a second and then I said, 'Please say hello to Jane and the girls for me.'

'I will. Take care, Anna.'

That night, I curled up on the couch with Bo to read a book. Two pages in, someone knocked on my door.

Hopeful excitement washed over me, my stomach filling with butterflies. I'd wondered all day, after talking to his dad, if T.J. might reach out to me. Bo went crazy, barking and running around in circles, as if he knew it was him. I ran to the door and flung it open but it wasn't T.J. standing there.

It was John.

He wore a guarded expression. His blond hair was shorter than it used to be, and he had a few lines around his eyes, but otherwise he looked the same. He held a box in his hands. Bo nudged his legs, sniffing and circling.

'Sarah gave me your address. I found some more of your things and thought you might want them back.' He looked over my shoulder, trying to see if I was alone.

'Come in.' I shut the door after he crossed the threshold. 'I'm sorry I never called. That was rude of me.'

'It's okay. Don't worry about it.'

John set the box on the coffee table.

'Would you like something to drink?'

'Sure,' he said.

I went into the kitchen, opened a bottle of wine, and poured us each a glass. My choice of beverage reflected my sudden need for alcohol more than any desire to be hospitable.

'Thanks,' he said when I handed him a glass.

'You're welcome. Sit down.'

He sneezed twice. 'You got a dog. You always wanted one.'

'His name is Bo.'

He sat in the chair across from the couch. I set my glass on the coffee table in front of me and started pulling items out of the box. It was like seeing my clothes hanging in Sarah's spare bedroom closet. Possessions I had almost forgotten but recognized immediately as soon as I saw them again.

I removed the rubber band from a stack of pictures. The one on top showed John and me standing in front of the ferris wheel at Navy Pier, our arms around each other, him kissing my cheek. I leaned across the coffee table and handed him the picture. 'Look how young we were.'

'Twenty-two,' he said.

There were vacation pictures and group shots with our friends. A picture of my mom and John standing in front of the Christmas tree. One of him holding Chloe in the hospital a few hours after Sarah had given birth.

Looking at the pictures reminded me of the history I had with John, and that a lot of that history had been good. We'd started out with so much promise but then our relationship stagnated, crushed under the weight of two people wanting different things. I snapped the rubber band back on the pictures and set them on the table.

I pulled out an old pair of running shoes. 'These have some miles on them.' The next item – a Hootie & the Blowfish CD – made me smile.

'You played that *constantly*,' John said.

'Don't make fun of Hootie.'

There were a couple of paperbacks. A hairbrush and a ponytail holder. A half-empty bottle of Calvin Klein CK One perfume, my signature scent for most of the nineties.

My fingers grazed something near the bottom. A night-gown. I looked at the sheer black fabric and recalled a hazy memory of John taking it off me in the middle of the night, shortly before I left Chicago.

'I found it when I changed the sheets. I never did wash it,' he said softly.

Reaching in one last time, I came up with a blue velvet-covered box. I froze.

'Open it,' John said.

I lifted the lid. The diamond ring sparkled, nestled in satin. Speechless, I took a deep breath.

'After I dropped you off at the airport I drove to the jewelry store. I knew if I didn't marry you I'd lose you, and I didn't want to lose you, Anna. When Sarah called to tell me your plane went down, I held that ring in my hand and prayed they would find you. Then she called and told me you were presumed dead. The news devastated me. But you're alive, Anna, and I still love you. I always have, and I always will.'

I snapped the box shut and hurled it at John's head. With surprisingly fast reflexes, he deflected my throw and the box bounced off his crossed forearms and skittered across the hardwood floor.

'I loved you! I waited eight years for you and you strung me along until my only option was to break my own heart!'

John stood up from his chair. 'Jesus, Anna. I thought a ring was what you wanted.'

'It's never been about a ring.'

He crossed the room and paused at the door.

'So it's because of the kid, then?'

I winced at the mention of T.J. Standing up, I marched

over, scooped the ring off the floor, and handed it to him. 'No. It's because I would never marry a man who only asked me because he felt he had to.'

The next morning I went to the attorney's office, signed the papers promising I wouldn't sue the seaplane charter, and collected a check. I deposited it at the bank on the way home. Sarah called my cell phone an hour later.

'Did you sign the papers?' she asked.

'Yes. It's too much money, Sarah.'

'If you want my opinion, one point five million wasn't nearly enough.'

Chapter 64
T.J.

I dragged my ass up the stairs at 9:30 on Saturday night and as soon as I walked in the door, I figured out that the party had started without me. There were at least fifteen people drinking beer and taking shots in our kitchen and living room.

The guys on the crew and I were trying to finish framing a rush job in Schaumburg and we'd been putting in fourteen hour days, six days a week, for the last month, working until it got dark. I wanted everyone in our apartment to disappear.

Ben came out of his bedroom, a girl trailing behind.

'Hey man, grab a shower and get back out here.'

'Maybe. I'm tired.'

'Don't be a pussy. We're heading to the bar soon. Party until then and if you're still tired, you can crash when we clear out.'

'Okay.'

I took a shower and pulled on a pair of jeans and a T-shirt, leaving my feet bare. Weaving through the people partying in my kitchen, I said hi to the ones I knew and wondered where the hell the rest came from. I grabbed a Coke and a pizza box out of the refrigerator, then leaned against the counter eating the slices cold.

'Hi, T.J.,' a girl said, coming over to lean against the counter next to me.

'Hey.' She looked familiar, but I couldn't think of her name.

'Alex,' she said.

'That's right. Now I remember.' She was the girl that sat down next to me on the couch at Coop's party when I first got back from the island. The one with long blond hair and too much makeup. I kept eating my pizza.

She leaned around me to the refrigerator and opened it. When she bent over to grab a beer, her boobs almost fell out of her tank top.

'Do you want one,' she said, holding up a can.

I drained the last of my Coke. 'Sure.'

She grabbed another beer and handed it to me. When I finished eating I opened it, took a long drink, and set it back down on the counter.

Ben walked in and handed me a lit joint. I took it and inhaled, holding the smoke deep in my lungs. After exhaling, I asked Alex, 'You want a hit?'

She nodded, took a long drag, and handed it back to me. We killed it off, taking turns back and forth. Maybe if I got high enough I'd actually sleep through the night instead of waking up every hour.

Alex handed me another beer. When I went into the living room to sit on the couch, she followed me. She never left my side after that.

We drank beer and took hits until I couldn't see straight. People cleared out to go to the bar with Ben, and then it was just Alex and me. I was about to tell her to catch up with the others because I wanted to crash, but before I could say anything, she stood up, swaying, and pulled me toward my bedroom. When she put her hand between my legs, I stopped thinking with my brain and let another part of my body take over.

My pounding head woke me the next morning. Alex lay beside me, naked, with makeup smeared across her face.

I threw back the covers and headed for the door, grabbing some clothes on my way out. There was something stuck to the bottom of my foot, and I bent down and removed the condom wrapper I had stepped on.

Thank God.

I tossed it into the garbage can when I got to the bathroom. The hot water filled the room with steam and I took a shower, washing all traces of Alex away. I dressed and brushed my teeth, then went into the kitchen and drank three glasses of ice water.

I was watching T.V. when she walked into the living room a half hour later. She found her purse and jacket, and I met her at the door. 'Take a cab,' I said, pushing a crumpled ten into her hand.

'Call me,' she said. 'Ben has my number.'

'I'm sorry. I'm not going to.'

She nodded and avoided my eyes. 'Well at least you're honest.'

Ben staggered out of his room at noon.

'Holy fuckballs, Callahan. My hangover is epic.' He scratched himself and flopped down on the couch next to me. 'There's some chick in my bed, but she's not the one I brought home last night. The girl I brought home was much hotter than that.'

'I think she's one and the same, Ben.'

'Yeah, probably. How'd it go with what's her name? You score?'

'Yeah.'

'Callahan's *back in the game*,' he said, raising his hand to high-five me.

'I don't want to be in the game.'

Ben lowered his hand, a puzzled expression on his face. 'What, she wasn't any good? I thought she had a hot body.'

'Yeah, and any guy last night could have had her if he wanted.'

'Well I don't know what to tell you, man. I know you're bummed that things with Anna didn't work out, but I don't know what you're looking for.'

I do.

I started working on my GED in July. After spending all day framing houses, I went home, took a fast shower, and joined all the other dropouts at a community center downtown for two hours every night. By the end of August, I had earned my GED and enrolled at a community college for the fall semester, quitting my construction job when classes started. I didn't have any idea what I wanted to study, and I couldn't see wasting the next two years inside a classroom, but I didn't know what else to do.

Ben moved back to Iowa City and I moved home, which made my parents happy, especially my mom. I was so used to working all day and then going to the GED class at night that I felt restless in the afternoon. Most of my friends went to college out of state or far enough from the city to make hanging out difficult during the week.

I came home one day in October. The falling temperature and changing leaves reminded me of Anna, and how much she liked fall. I wondered if she found a teaching job. I wondered if she found someone else.

'Hey, Mom,' I said, throwing my backpack on the counter.

'How was school?' she asked.

'Okay.' I hated being the oldest freshman in every class, and most of the time I was bored out of my mind. 'There's something I want to do,' I said, grabbing a Coke out of the fridge. 'Will you help me?'

She smiled and said, 'Sure, T.J.'

I had been too sick to take driver's ed when I was sixteen so for the next month, as soon as I got home from class, my mom taught me how to drive. She had a Volvo SUV and we went out to the suburbs and found empty parking lots and quiet streets. We drove for hours together. She seemed really happy spending time with me, and I felt like an asshole for not being around more.

One day, when I was behind the wheel, I said, 'Did you know Anna would break up with me?'

My mom hesitated for a second. 'Yes.'

'How?' *And why didn't I?*

She turned the radio down. 'Because I had you when I was twenty-five years old, T.J., and I wanted you so badly. Then it took five more years before I got pregnant with Grace. I felt anxious, then worried, and then almost frantic when it didn't happen right away. Then two years after Grace, Alexis came along, and I finally felt like my family was complete. Anna's probably ready for a family of her own, T.J.'

'I would have given it to her.'

'She might have felt it would be unwise to accept.'

I kept my eyes on the car in front of me. 'I told her I wanted to spend the rest of my life with her. She told me I had things to finish. Things I still needed to experience.'

'She was right. It says a lot about her that she didn't want to take that away from you.'

'It's my decision, Mom.'

'But you're not the only one affected by it.'

I came to a sudden realization, and I pulled over, clenching my teeth so hard they hurt.

'Is that why you were so cool about her?' My face burned. 'Let's all be nice to T.J.'s girlfriend while we wait for her to dump him?' I pounded the steering wheel with my fists.

My mom flinched and then rested her hand on my arm. 'No. I like Anna. I like her even more now that I've gotten to know her. She's a nice girl, T.J. But I tried to tell you she was at a different stage in her life and you didn't want to listen.'

I stared out the window until I calmed down, then pulled away from the curb. 'I still love her.'

'I know you do.'

I got my driver's license and bought a black Chevy Tahoe SUV.

After class ended for the day, I went driving, first in the suburbs and then out in the country, listening to the classic rock station.

I passed a property with a For Sale sign stuck in the ground at the end of the driveway, and I drove up to a small, light blue house and parked. No one answered my knock so I walked around to the back yard. There was land as far as I could see. I grabbed a fact sheet from the plastic tube attached to the For Sale sign. It listed the phone number of a realtor. I folded it up, stuck it in my pocket, and drove away.

Chapter 65
Anna

Bo and I walked the city streets for hours. His leash came unhooked one warm day in September, and I spent a frantic ten minutes trying to catch up with him as he galloped down the sidewalk, weaving through the crowd. I finally got close enough to grab his collar, and I snapped the leash back on, relieved. A little boy stood a few steps away, watching from an open doorway that faced the street. The sign above his head read Family Shelter.

'Is that your dog?' he asked. He wore a striped T-shirt and needed a haircut. Freckles dotted his nose and cheeks.

I stood up and led Bo over to him. 'Yes. His name is Bo. Do you like dogs?'

'Yeah. "Specially yellow ones."'

'He's a golden retriever. He's five years old.'

'I'm five years old!' he said, his face lighting up.

'What's your name?'

'Leo.'

'Well, Leo, you can pet Bo if you want to. You have to be gentle with animals, though, okay?'

'Okay.' He stroked Bo's fur carefully, looking at me out of the corner of his eye to see if I noticed how gentle he was being. 'I better go. Henry said not to leave the doorway. Thanks for letting me pet your dog.' He hugged Bo and before I could say goodbye, he darted back inside. Bo strained at his leash, wanting to follow him.

'Come on, Bo,' I said, pulling firmly. Leading him from the doorway, we walked back home.

I went back the next day, alone. Two women, one with a baby on her hip, lingered near the entrance.

'Hey, white girl, Bloomie's is *that* way.' She pointed while her friend laughed.

I ignored her and walked through the doorway. Once inside, I scanned the room for Leo. It was Monday, and there weren't any kids around. Under federal law, all children were guaranteed an education whether they had a permanent residence or not. Thankfully, the parents at the shelter appeared to be taking advantage of that right.

A man walked up to me, wiping his hands on a dish-towel. Mid fifties, I guessed. He wore jeans, a faded, nondescript polo shirt, and tennis shoes.

'Can I help you?' he asked.

'My name is Anna Emerson.'

'Henry Elings,' he said, shaking my outstretched hand.

'There was a little boy yesterday. I met him when he was standing in the doorway. He liked my dog.' Henry smiled and waited patiently for me to get to the point. 'I was wondering if you needed any volunteers.'

'We need a lot of things here. Volunteers are definitely one of them.' His eyes were kind and his tone was mild but he'd probably heard this kind of thing before. House-wives and junior leaguers from the suburbs, swooping in intermittently so they could brag to their book clubs about how they were making a difference.

'Our residents' needs are very basic,' he continued. 'Food and shelter. They don't always smell the best. A bath can be a low priority compared to a hot meal and a bed.'

I wondered if he recognized my name, or my face from the pictures in the newspaper. If he did, he didn't mention it. 'I've been dirty, and I don't really care how anyone smells. I know what it's like to be hungry and thirsty, and without shelter. I have plenty of time and I'd like to spend some of it here.'

Henry smiled. 'Thank you. We'd like that.'

I started arriving at the shelter around 10:00 a.m. every day, joining the other volunteers in preparing and serving lunch. Henry encouraged me to bring Bo.

'Most of the kids here love animals. Not many of them have ever had a pet.'

The younger children who weren't in school yet spent hours playing with Bo. He never growled when they stroked his fur a little too rough or tried to ride him like a pony. After lunch, I read to the kids. Their exhausted and stressed-out mothers warmed to me as I held their toddlers and babies on my lap. In the late afternoon, the school-aged kids returned, and I helped them with their homework, insisting they complete it before we played any of the board games I bought at Target.

Leo could usually be found at my side, eager to share everything that happened at school. His enthusiasm for kindergarten didn't surprise me; most kids loved a secure classroom environment, the homeless even more so. Many of them didn't own books or art supplies and they loved learning songs in music class and running around on the playground at recess.

'I'm learning how to read, Miss Anna!'

'I'm so happy that you're excited about reading, Leo.' I hugged him. 'That's wonderful.'

He smiled so brightly I thought he would burst, but then his expression turned serious.

'I'm gonna learn real good, Miss Anna. Then I'm gonna teach my dad.'

Dean Lewis, Leo's dad, was twenty-eight, had been out of work for almost a year, and was one of only two single dads living at the shelter. I sat down next to him after dinner. He eyed me warily. 'Hi, Dean.'

He nodded. 'Miss Anna.'

'How's the job search going?'

'I haven't found one yet.'

'What kind of work did you do before?'

'Line cook. I was at the same restaurant for seven years. Started out washin' dishes and worked my way up.'

'What happened?'

'Owner fell on hard times. Had to sell. The new boss fired us all.'

We watched Leo play a spirited game of tag with two other children. 'Dean?'

'Yeah.'

'I think I might be able to help you.'

It turned out that Dean could read a little bit. He'd memorized common words – and the entire menu at the diner where he worked – but he struggled to fill out job applications and he'd never filed for unemployment after losing his job because he couldn't decipher the forms. A friend had helped him fill out an application at an Italian restaurant, but they fired him after three days because he couldn't read the orders.

'Are you dyslexic?' I asked him.

'What's that mean?'

'The letters don't seem like they're in the right order.'

'No. They're fine. I just can't read 'em.'

'Did you graduate high school?'

He shook his head. 'Ninth grade.'

'Where's Leo's mom?'

'No clue. She was twenty when he was born, and when he turned one, she said she couldn't handle being a mom any-more, not that she ever acted like one. We couldn't afford cable, but we had an old T.V. and VCR and she'd watch movies all day long. I'd come home from the restaurant and Leo would be screaming and crying, his diaper soakin' wet, or worse. She took off one day and never came back. I had to find daycare and we already lived paycheck to paycheck. Once I lost my job, it didn't take long to fall behind on the rent.' Dean looked down at his feet. 'Leo deserves better.'

'I think Leo's pretty lucky,' I said.

'How can you say that?'

'Because at least one of his parents cares. That's more than some kids get.'

For the next two months, I worked with Dean every day, from the time lunch ended, until the time Leo and the other kids came home from school. Using phonics workbooks, I taught him the various combinations of letters, and soon I had him reading *Goodnight Moon* and *Brown Bear, Brown Bear, What do You See?* to the toddlers. He was often frus-trated, but I pushed him hard, building his confidence by praising him whenever he mastered a challenging lesson.

When I returned home from the shelter after serving dinner, I went for a long run. September turned to October, and I added more layers and kept going. One day in November, Bo and I stopped to get the mail. I pulled out a few bills and a magazine and there it was. A regular sized envelope with T.J.'s name and address handwritten in the upper left-hand corner.

I hurried upstairs and unlocked the door to my apartment, unclipping Bo from his leash. When I opened it and read what was inside, I started crying.

'Open the goddamned door, Anna. I know you're in there,' Sarah yelled.

I was lying on the couch staring at the ceiling. The last twenty-four hours worth of Sarah's voice mails and texts had gone unanswered, and it was only a matter of time before she showed up at my apartment.

I opened the door. Sarah charged into the apartment, but I sidestepped her and went back to the couch.

'Well at least I know you're alive,' she said, standing over me. She took in my appearance, her eyes flicking from my messy hair down to my wrinkled pajamas. 'You look like hell. Have you even showered today? Or yesterday?'

'Oh, Sarah, I can go *a lot* longer than that without a shower.' I pulled a fleece blanket over my legs and Bo rested his head on my lap.

'When's the last time you went to the shelter?'

'A few days ago,' I mumbled. 'I told Henry I was sick.'

Sarah sat down on the couch. 'Anna, talk to me. What happened?'

I went into the kitchen and returned with an envelope. Handing it to Sarah I said, 'I got this in the mail the other day. It's from T.J.'

She opened it and pulled out a business card from a sperm bank. Under the phone number it said, *I made arrangements.*

'I don't understand,' Sarah said.

'Look on the back.'

She flipped it over. On the back, he'd scrawled *in case you never find him.*

'Oh Anna,' Sarah said. She pulled me into her arms and held me while I cried.

Sarah convinced me to take a shower while she took care of dinner. I padded back into the living room with my wet hair combed back, wearing a clean pair of flannel pajama pants and a sweatshirt.

'Don't you feel better now?' Sarah asked.

'Yes.' I sat down on the couch and pulled on thick socks. Sarah handed me a glass of red wine.

'I ordered Chinese,' she said. 'It should be here any minute.'

'Okay. Thanks.' I took a sip of wine and set my glass on the table.

She sat down beside me. 'That was quite an offer T.J. made.'

'Yes.' Tears welled up in my eyes again and spilled onto my cheeks. I wiped them away with the back of my hand. 'But there's no way I could ever hold a baby in my arms that had his eyes, or his smile, if I couldn't have him, too.' I picked up my glass and took another drink of my wine. 'John would never have done something so selfless.'

Sarah wiped a tear I'd missed. 'That's because John was kind of an asshole.'

'I'll go back to the shelter in the morning. I just had a rough patch.'

'It's okay. It happens.'

'I never loved John the way I loved T.J.'

'I know.'

I dragged a Christmas tree up the stairs and shoved it through the doorway of my apartment. When I finished decorating it, my first tree in four years sparkled under twinkling lights and shiny ornaments. Bo and I spent hours lying in front of it, listening to Christmas music.

I helped Henry decorate the tree at the shelter, too. The kids pitched in, hanging the snowflake ornaments we made out of construction paper and glitter.

Dean received an early Christmas gift. He'd filled out an application at a nearby restaurant and they'd hired him two weeks ago. Reading the orders the waitresses thrust at him wasn't a problem anymore, and he turned the food around fast, quickly earning himself a reputation as a hard worker. He used his first paycheck to put down a deposit on a furnished apartment. I co-signed the lease, paying the first year's rent up front. He didn't want to accept it, but I convinced him to, for Leo's sake. 'Pay it forward someday, Dean.'

'I will,' he promised, hugging me. 'Thank you, Anna.'

I spent Christmas Eve with David, Sarah, and the kids. We watched Joe and Chloe open their gifts, wrapping paper flying, and spent the next hour assembling toys and installing batteries. David played so many video games on the PlayStation I bought for Joe that Sarah threatened to unplug it.

'What is it about video games that turn men back into boys?' she asked.

'I don't know, but they all love 'em, don't they?'

Chloe strummed her Barbie guitar, loudly, and after an hour of listening to it, I made a mental note not to buy her any more instruments. I wandered into the kitchen where it was quiet and uncorked a bottle of cabernet.

Sarah joined me a minute later. She opened the oven and checked the turkey. I poured her some wine, and we clinked our glasses together.

'To having you home to celebrate with,' Sarah said. 'I remember last Christmas, how hard it was without you, and Mom and Dad. Even with David and the kids I still felt a little bit alone. Then two days later you called. Sometimes I still can't believe it, Anna.' She set her wine down and hugged me.

I hugged her back. 'Merry Christmas, Sarah.'

'Merry Christmas.'

I went to the shelter at noon on Christmas Day, bearing gifts for the kids: hand-held video games for the boys, lip gloss and costume jewelry for the girls, and stuffed animals and books for the younger kids. The babies received soft fleece blankets, diapers, and formula. Henry dressed up like Santa Claus to pass everything out. I fastened reindeer antlers to Bo's head and tied jingle bells to his collar. He barely tolerated it.

I was reading *Frosty the Snowman* to a lapful of kids when Henry walked over holding an envelope. When I finished the book, I sent the kids off to play.

'Someone made an anonymous donation a couple days ago,' Henry said. He opened the envelope and showed me a cashier's check made out for a substantial amount. 'I wonder why someone would do that and not give me the opportunity to thank them,' he said.

I shrugged and handed the check back to him. 'I don't know. Maybe they didn't want anyone to make a big deal out of it.'

That's why.

Bo and I walked home after I helped serve Christmas dinner. A light snow was falling and the streets were empty. Without warning he bolted, yanking the leash out of my hand. I sprinted after him, stopping short a few seconds later.

T.J. stood on the sidewalk in front of my apartment. When Bo reached him, he bent down and scratched him behind the ears, looping his hand through the end of the leash. I approached, holding my breath, propelled forward by sheer longing.

He stood up and met me halfway.

'I've thought about you all day,' he said. 'On the island, I promised that if you just held on we would spend this Christmas together, in Chicago. I will always keep my promises to you, Anna.'

I looked into his eyes and burst into tears. He opened his arms and I fell into them, crying so hard I couldn't speak.

'Shhh, it's okay,' he said. I buried my face in his chest, breathing in the smell of snow, of wool, of him, as he held me tight. A few minutes later, he put his hand under my chin and lifted it. He wiped my tears, as he had so many times before.

'You were right. I did need to be on my own. But some

of the things you wanted me to experience already passed me by, and I can't go back. I know what I want and it's you, Anna. I love you, and I miss you. So much.'

'I don't fit in your world.'

'Neither do I,' he said, his expression tender yet resolute. 'So let's make our own. We've done it before.'

I heard my mom's voice in my head, almost as if she was standing beside me whispering in my ear. The same question she told me to ask myself about John.

Is your life better with him, Anna, or without him?

I decided, right then, standing on that sidewalk, to stop worrying about things that might never go wrong.

'I love you, T.J. I want you to come back.'

He held me tight and my tears flowed until his sweater was wet. I lifted my head off his chest. 'I must cry more than anyone you know,' I said.

He brushed the hair back from my face and smiled. 'You puke a lot, too.'

I laughed through my tears. His lips brushed mine and we stood on the sidewalk kissing, covered in snowflakes, while Bo waited patiently at our feet.

We went inside and talked for hours, lying on a blanket in front of the Christmas tree.

'I never wanted anyone else, T.J. I just wanted what was best for you.'

'*You* are what's best for me,' he said, cradling my head in his arms, his legs intertwined with mine. 'I'm not going anywhere, Anna. This is right where I want to be.'

Chapter 66
T.J.

I glanced at the clock one morning two weeks later. I was still on winter break from school and Anna and I were having a late breakfast.

'I have to go out for a while and then there's something I want to show you,' I said. 'What time will you be home from the shelter?'

'I should be back by three o'clock. What is it?' she asked, setting down the newspaper.

I put on my coat and grabbed my gloves. 'You'll see.'

Later that afternoon, I parked in front of Anna's building and opened the car door for her. Having her in the passenger seat was something I had been looking forward to.

'Are you a good driver?' she asked, when I slid behind the wheel.

I laughed. 'I'm an excellent driver.'

We headed out of the city, Anna growing more curious. Ninety minutes later I said, 'We're almost there.'

I made a left off the highway and drove along the gravel road. I turned again, glad I had four-wheel drive because five inches of snow covered the driveway. Pulling up in front of a small, light blue house, I parked in front of the garage and turned off the engine.

'Come on,' I said.

'Who lives here?'

I didn't answer her. When we got to the front door, I pulled a key out of my pocket and unlocked it.

'This is yours?' Anna asked.

'I bought it two months ago and closed on it today.' She walked in and I followed her, switching on lights. 'The previous owners built it new in the eighties. I don't think they ever changed a thing,' I said, laughing. 'This blue carpeting blows.'

Anna toured every room, opening closets and commenting on the things she liked.

'It's perfect, T.J. All it needs is a little updating.'

'Then I hope you won't be too disappointed when I tear it down.'

'What? Why would you tear it down?'

'Come here,' I said, leading her to a window in the kitchen that looked out into the back yard. 'What do you see out there?'

'Land,' she said.

'When I would take long drives, I'd pass this place and one day I pulled in and looked around. I knew right then I wanted to buy it, to have land of my own. I want to build a new house here, Anna. For us. What do you think about that?'

She turned around and smiled. 'I'd love to live in a house you built T.J. Bo would love it out here, too. It's beautiful. Peaceful.'

'That's because we're out in the sticks. It'll be a long commute into the city, to the shelter.'

'That's okay.'

I exhaled, relieved. Reaching for her hand, I wondered

332

if she noticed mine was shaking a little. She looked shocked when I pulled the ring out of my pocket.

'I want you to be my wife. There's no one else I want to spend the rest of my life with. We can live out here, you, me, our kids, and Bo. But I get it now, Anna. My decisions affect you, too. So now you have one of your own to make. Will you marry me?'

I held my breath, waiting to slide the ring on her finger. Her blue eyes lit up and a smile spread across her face.

She said yes.

Chapter 67
Anna

Ben and Sarah met us at the Cook County Courthouse in March. A spring snowstorm was bearing down on the Chicago area and T.J. and I – wearing jeans, sweaters and boots – had chosen warmth over fashion.

Getting married in front of a judge might not have been the most romantic choice, but I'd vetoed a church wedding. I couldn't imagine walking down the aisle if it wasn't on my dad's arm. David had offered, but it wouldn't have been the same. A destination wedding, somewhere tropical – an island perhaps – wasn't an option either.

'Your mom is not going to be happy about missing this,' I said. Jane Callahan had been surprisingly accepting of our engagement; maybe she decided that opposing it would do no good. She already had two daughters, but she'd done a wonderful job welcoming a third, and I had no desire to upset her.

'She has Alexis and Grace,' T.J. said, waving his hand dismissively. 'She can go to their weddings.'

While we waited for them to call our names a man, probably wearing every item of clothing he owned, circulated through the waiting couples trying to sell wilted bouquets of flowers, his boots held together by duct tape. Many shunned him, wrinkling their noses at his long, unwashed beard and straggly hair. T.J. bought every flower he had and took a picture of me holding them in my arms.

When it was our turn, Ben and Sarah stood up with us while we spoke our vows. The brief ceremony took less than five minutes; Sarah dissolved into a puddle of tears anyway. Ben was speechless and, according to T.J., that didn't happen very often.

T.J. dug our wedding bands out of the front pocket of his Levi's. He slid the ring on my finger and held out his left hand. When the gold band was in place, I smiled.

The judge said, 'By the power vested in me in Cook County, I hereby pronounce Thomas James Callahan and Anna Lynn Emerson legally wed. Congratulations.'

'Is this the part where I kiss her?' T.J. asked.

'Go ahead,' the judge said, scrawling his signature on the marriage license.

T.J. leaned in, and it was a good kiss.

'I love you, Mrs. Callahan.'

'I love you, too.'

T.J. held my hand when we left the courthouse. Big, lazy snowflakes fell from the sky as the four of us piled into a cab, heading to a celebratory lunch at the restaurant where Dean Lewis worked. Ten minutes later, I asked the cab driver to pull over. 'It's just a quick stop. Can you wait?' He agreed, parking in front of a nail salon. 'We'll be right back,' I told Ben and Sarah.

'You want to get your nails done now?' T.J. asked, following me out of the cab.

'No,' I said, pushing open the door. 'But there's someone I want you to meet.

When Lucy saw us she rushed over and hugged me.

'How you doing honey?'

'I'm fine, Lucy. How are you?'

'Oh fine, fine.'

I put my hand on T.J.'s arm and said, 'Lucy, I want you to meet my husband.'

'This John?' she asked.

'No, I didn't marry John. I married T.J.'

'Anna married?' At first she looked confused, but then her face lit up and she threw herself at T.J. and hugged him. 'Anna married!'

'Yep,' I said. 'Anna is married.'

Chapter 68
T.J.

Anna and I climbed into my Tahoe three months later, on a warm day in June. She wore sunglasses and my Chicago Cubs baseball cap. Bo sat in the back seat, his head hanging out the open window. On the radio, the Eagles were singing 'Take it Easy' and Anna kicked off her shoes, turned up the volume, and sang along as we drove out of the city.

They'd recently poured the foundation for our new house. Anna and I had pressed our hands into the wet concrete and she'd written our names and the date next to them with her finger. I hired a crew and we'd started framing; the house was already taking shape. If everything went according to schedule, we'd be able to move in by Halloween.

When we arrived, I parked and grabbed the nail gun out of the back. Anna laughed and plunked a cowboy hat down on my head. Though I should have been wearing safety goggles, I wore aviator shades instead. We walked over to a pile of cut lumber, and I grabbed a couple 2X6's.

'Pretty fancy lookin' tool you've got there,' Anna teased. 'I thought maybe you'd want to do this old school. With a *hammer*.'

'Hell, no,' I said, laughing and holding up the nail gun. 'I love this thing.'

What we were about to do now was Anna's idea. She

wanted to hold a few boards for me, just like she did when I built our house on the island.

'Indulge me please,' she'd said. 'For old time's sake.'

Like I'd ever say no to her.

'You ready?' I asked, positioning the 2X6 into place.

Anna held the board steady 'Bring it, T.J.'

I took aim and pulled the trigger.

Bam.

Epilogue

Anna

Three years later

The house is a sage-green Craftsman-style ranch with cream-colored trim, surrounded by trees. Its three-car garage houses T.J.'s Tahoe, his work pickup truck, and my white Nissan Pathfinder, nearly impossible to keep clean when you live on a gravel road.

There's a den with French doors near the large kitchen, and one wall is nothing but floor to ceiling bookshelves. I can often be found there, curled up in the overstuffed chair, my feet on the ottoman.

There are two porches, one in front, and one in back. The one in the back is screened-in, and T.J. and I spend a lot of time there, not worrying about bugs, especially mosquitoes. Bo has the run of the yard and when he isn't chasing rabbits, he's content to nap at our feet.

Our four-bedroom home has every modern convenience you could ever want. We don't have any fireplaces, though. We don't own a grill, either.

We have a houseful tonight. Everyone has gathered to celebrate my thirty-eighth birthday. They're all welcome here anytime.

In the kitchen, my mother-in-law and sister sit at the island, trading recipes and sipping wine. No one will let me cook on my birthday so Tom is bringing dinner from the city. He'll be here soon so there's not much to do but relax.

T.J's sisters, Alexis and Grace, now seventeen and nineteen, are sitting on the front porch with Joe and Chloe. Thirteen-year-old Joe wishes there was at least one boy around, but he has such a crush on Alexis he doesn't really mind hanging with the girls.

I grab two beers from the fridge and wander into the family room. T.J. lounges on the couch watching T.V. I bend over and kiss him, then open the beer and place it on a nearby table.

'How's the birthday girl'? He speaks softly because our daughter is asleep on his chest, her thumb in her mouth. We both know that if Josephine Jane 'Josie' Callahan wakes up before she has enough sleep there will be hell to pay.

'I can put her down in her crib,' I whisper.

He shakes his head. 'She's fine.' That little girl has T.J. wrapped around her finger.

I hand the second beer to Ben. He's sitting in the chair next to the couch looking remarkably comfortable with Thomas James Callahan III asleep on his lap. Surprising, because when Ben came to the hospital after we had the twins, he told me he'd never held a baby before.

'What are you gonna call him,' he asked, after T.J. got him settled in a chair and carefully handed him our son. 'If there are two T.J's, I'll get confused.'

'We're going to call him Mick,' T.J. said.

'You're naming your kid after Mick Jagger? That's so cool!'

T.J. and I laughed and smiled at each other.

'Different Mick,' T.J. said.

We didn't try to have a baby right away. I was adamant about not rushing anything, and if it turned out we waited too long, well, there were lots of ways to have a family. It ultimately took six months of trying and a boost from a fertility drug, the conception taking place in a doctor's office, the way we always knew it would, using sperm T.J. banked when he was fifteen years old.

I like to think things happen for a reason, and I believe the twins arrived exactly when we were ready for them. 'Two will be hard,' everyone said, but T.J. and I know what hard is and being blessed with two healthy babies isn't it. I'm not saying it's easy, though. We have our days.

The twins are already eleven months old and it's true what they say, time does speed up when you have kids. It seems like just yesterday I was waddling around with my hand on my lower back, wondering how much longer I would be carrying them and now here they are, crawling everywhere and getting close to taking their first steps.

I leave T.J. and Ben and head back into the kitchen. David has joined Jane and Sarah, and he gives me a kiss on the cheek.

'Happy birthday,' he says, handing me a bouquet of flowers. I trim the stems under running water, then place them in a vase and set them on the counter next to the pink roses T.J. gave me this morning.

'Wine?' I ask him.

'I'll get it. You sit down and relax.'

I join Sarah and Jane. Stefani is here, too. Rob and the kids have the stomach flu so she has come alone, not wanting to risk getting anyone sick. At moments like this, when everyone I love and care about is under one roof, I feel complete. I only wish my parents were here, too. To know my husband. To hold their grandchildren.

I still went to the shelter three days a week until just recently, but the commute into the city finally took its toll. Jane watched the twins on the days I volunteered, but it was time to do something different. I set up a charitable foundation to assist homeless families, and I run it out of our home office, the twins playing at my feet. It makes me happy. Henry's shelter gets a large donation every year and always will.

I also tacked up a flyer at the local high school and I've picked up a few students to tutor. They come to our house in the evening and we sit at the kitchen table crossing off completed assignments one by one. Sometimes I miss standing in front of a classroom, but I think this is enough, for now.

T.J. runs a small construction company. He builds homes, one or two a year, framing them alongside the men he employs. He never went back to school after completing his first semester at community college, but I don't care. It's not my choice to make. Outside is where T.J. is happy.

He also gives his time, and money, to Habitat for Humanity. Dean Lewis volunteers there, too; the sixth house he helped build was his own. He married Julie, a girl he met at the restaurant, and Leo loves being a big brother to the baby girl his parents named Annie.

I brought lunch to T.J. at his construction site a few months ago. Watching him do what he loves makes me happy, too. A new subcontractor, there to work on the plumbing, whistled and yelled out 'Hey, baby,' when I walked up, not knowing who I was. T.J. set him straight immediately. I know I'm supposed to be offended, to view the catcall as an affront to women and all that. I'm okay with it, though.

T.J. and I found out something interesting a couple of years ago. A police officer from Malé called us with a few questions, hoping to close out the case of a missing person. The family of a man who disappeared in May of 1999 recently discovered a journal in his belongings. In it, Owen Sparks, a dot-com millionaire from California, wrote in meticulous detail about a plan to trade his high-pressure lifestyle for the peace and solitude of island-living in the Maldives. They followed his trail to Malé, but that's where it ended. The officer wanted to know more about the skeleton T.J. and I discovered. There's no way to know for sure if it was him, but it seems likely. I wonder if Owen would have made it if he'd had someone to lean on, the way T.J. and I did. I guess we'll never know.

I carry a pitcher of lemonade out to the front porch and refill drinks, inhaling the smell of fresh-cut grass and spring flowers. Tom pulls into the driveway. We decided that a feast from Perry's Deli is perfect for this warm May evening and David comes out of the house to help Tom carry it all in. Stefani and I set it out on the kitchen island

343

and I am just about to call everyone in to make a plate when Ben walks up to me, holding Mick out in front of him. The smell of the dirty diaper is hard to miss.

'I think something came out of Mick's butt,' he says.

'There are diapers and wipes by the changing table in the nursery and can you make sure to use plenty of diaper cream because Mick has a little bit of a rash.'

Ben stands, frozen, wondering how he's going to get out of it when T.J., who has been watching the whole thing, starts laughing.

'Dude, she's messing with you.'

Ben looks at me and I shrug, smiling. 'It's just so easy.'

The relief on his face is so profound it's almost comical.

T.J. holds out his arms for Mick. 'Josie's got a load, too. I might as well change them both.'

'You're a good man,' I say. And he is.

Ben hands the baby over.

'Pussy,' T.J. says to him as he walks out of the room, his arms full of his children. I smile because I know T.J. is teasing, but also because I know he's happy to have his best friend involved in our lives. At twenty-four, Ben could just as easily be at the bars instead of here, holding a baby. He has a serious girlfriend named Stacy, and T.J. says she's the one responsible for turning Ben into a mature adult. He's not quite there yet.

Everyone fills a plate and finds somewhere to sit. Some choose the front steps, some the screened-in porch, and others, like T.J. and me, remain in the kitchen.

We strap the twins into their high chairs and give them small pieces of bread and deli meat. I spoon potato salad into their mouths and take bites of my sandwich and sips of my iced tea. T.J. sits beside me, retrieving the sippy cup Josie insists on flinging to the ground, just to see if he'll pick it up for her. He always does.

When everyone finishes eating, they sing happy birthday to me. I blow out all thirty-eight candles Chloe insisted on putting on the cake. It's an absolute inferno, but all I can do is laugh. From now until September twentieth, when T.J. turns twenty-five, I'm technically fourteen years older than him, not thirteen, but there's nothing I can do about that either.

They all toast me with their drinks. I'm so happy I feel like crying.

Later, when everyone has gone and we've put the twins to bed, T.J. joins me on the screened-in porch. He brings two glasses of ice water and hands one to me. 'Thanks,' I say. The novelty of cold water in a glass has not worn off for either of us. I take a long drink and set it on the table beside me.

He sits down on the rattan love seat and pulls me onto his lap.

'You might not be able to do that much longer,' I say, kissing his neck, which I do for two reasons: T.J. likes it, and it's how I check for lumps. Thank God I've never found one.

'Sure I will,' he says, smiling and rubbing my belly.

We decided to try for one more child. It happened the first month, surprising us both. There's only one baby this time and we don't know if it's a boy or a girl. We don't care, as long as it's healthy. I'm due in four months so the twins will only be fifteen months old when I give birth, but that just means that sometimes we get what we wish for.

I often think about the island. When the kids are older, we'll have quite a story to tell them.

We'll edit, of course.

We'll also tell them that this house, and the property that surrounds it, is our island.

And that T.J. and I are finally home.

Acknowledgements

Without the contributions, assistance, and support of the following individuals, *On the Island* would still be a file taking up space on my hard drive. Words cannot express how truly thankful I am to have such wonderful and enthusiastic people in my life.

I owe a huge debt of gratitude to author Meira Pentermann. Meira believed in me long before I did and her valuable guidance helped make *On the Island* the book it is today. She is the ultimate critique partner, beta reader, and cyber-sister.

My twin sister Trish who will always be the first person I show my words to.

My husband David because his encouragement means more to me than he'll ever know.

My children Matthew and Lauren. Thank you for being patient while mom spent all that time with her laptop. I love you both.

Elisa Abner-Taschwer, for being the best de facto publicist and all-around cheerleader a writer could ever hope for.

I'd like to give special thanks to my beta readers and those who received advance reader copies of *On the Island*. You made me smile with your kind words, and you built my confidence more than you'll ever know. Penne Heede Pojar, Beth Knipper, Elisa Abner-Taschwer, Lisa Green, Brooke Achenbach, Julie Gieseman, Trish Garvis, Trish

Kallemeier, Noelle Zmolek, Stacy Alvarez, Stefani Blubaugh, Mindy Farrington, Taylor Kalander, David Green, Tami Cavanaugh, Amy Gulbranson, Stefanie Martin, Shellie Mollenhauer, Christy Cornwell, Missy Pomerantz, and Jill LaBarre.

I was also fortunate to work with the following talented people who were instrumental in making sure *On the Island* was the book I hoped it would be. I look forward to partnering with them again.

Developmental editing by Alison Dasho.

Copyediting by Anne Victory at Victory Editing.

Digital formatting by Guido Henkel.

Original cover image by Getty Images.

Original cover design by Penne Heede-Pojar.